LEAVE WELL ALONE

LEAVE WELL ALONE

AJ Campbell

2020
Code Grey Publishing

LEAVE WELL ALONE
By AJ Campbell

Copyright © AJ Campbell 2020

Produced and published in 2020
by Code Grey Publishing

ISBN 978-1-8381091-0-3

Cover Design © Tim Barber, Dissect Designs 2020

Typeset in Minion Pro 11.5pt / 15.4pt by Blot Publishing
www.blot.co.uk

For Andy, Billy, Edward, Josh and Max.
My everything.

All actions have consequences –
some more far-reaching than others.

Prologue

It only takes a single blow.
Fury powers me beyond my perceived competence.
I strike her face. She stumbles and trips,
smacking her forehead on the worktop.

Bone smashing onto stone.

A sound that will stay with me forever.

Nothing registers at first.
Paralysed, I glare at her motionless body.

He thrusts his fist at me. 'What have you done?'

PART 1

Chapter 1

EVA

London
December 2010

That bone-chilling winter's day when my brother returned home for good was when I first contemplated murdering my mother.

Disturbing? Worse, though, was how, as time passed, the fleeting thoughts of watching her die at my hands became more gratifying.

These thoughts scared me. A mature student, I was the type of person who had piles of *The Big Issue* under the bed and volunteered weekly with my boyfriend at the local homeless shelter. I rescued wallflowers at parties, was an organ donor and wheeled the neighbour's bins out every Thursday morning. Not some psychopath who contemplated topping people.

I sat in the lounge waiting for Ben to arrive. Flames danced in the open grate, casting much-needed heat into the room. I'd just finished putting up a tree. Nothing big, only a mini artificial I'd found at Borough Market that morning. The lights flashed intermittently, as though the batteries were on their last legs. 'Tenner to you, Blondie,' the stallholder had offered with a toothless grin and hopeful expression. I'd have preferred the real deal, one of the Nordic firs stacked up next to the boxed imitations, but student loans didn't stretch to much more.

I picked up my book, *Law of Contract*, and glanced at my watch. Ben was due in twenty minutes, and to stand half a chance of handing in my essay by the end of term, I needed to finish reading the first section at least. My phone beeped. A text from Jim. I shivered as I tapped a reply that dinner at our favourite restaurant next Friday sounded perfect. If he could get a table. It was usually fully booked at weekends. But knowing him, he'd find a way.

My stomach yo-yoed at the sound of the doorbell. He was here. Ben was at my front door. I threw my book aside and ran to greet him like a child dashing to see what Santa had delivered. It was hard to believe he'd been away for almost a decade. And I'd only seen him in the flesh once in those ten years when I'd visited him for a holiday in Barcelona. How time flies, even though most of it hadn't been fun for me. He'd left the summer after our disastrous trip to Hamburg, with a hug and a fake smile. 'You'll understand when you're older, Sis,' he'd said. And that was that. That was all I got as he boarded a National Express on the Bethnal Green Road with untied shoelaces and a half-packed holdall.

He was back now, though, in time for Christmas. My brother was back.

Opening the door, I noticed it before anything else. There it was. The jagged scar on the right side of his neck. It had faded over the years, but there was no mistaking it. A streak of pale pink shouting out, 'Here I am, don't you remember?'

I didn't need any reminders.

4

He flung his arms wide. 'Sis, I've missed you.'

'Me too,' I said, returning his heartfelt hug.

His arm around me, we giggled our way down the hallway like the inseparable kids we once were. Reaching the kitchen at the back of the house, I switched on the lights, and a cosy halogen glow illuminated the room against the winter afternoon shadows.

He skimmed his fingers along the chrome handle of one of the centre island drawers. 'Nice kitchen.'

'Not bad, eh?' I pointed to the unit attached to the double-door fridge. 'Especially the built-in coffee machine.'

He moved over to a section of worktop that housed a pop-up knife block. 'I'm more impressed with this.'

I filled the kettle. 'How was Peru?' I asked.

'There's a lot to tell you about.'

'You're not going back to Spain, then?' I asked.

'Nope. I gave up my flatshare before I went to Peru. I'm going to try and make a go of things here.'

I took a step back. 'You think you can settle now?'

'I think I can.'

Honestly, Ben? Why now? I knew him too well. 'What's different?'

'This and that,' he said with a shy smile.

I searched the cupboards for the packet of Hobnobs I'd added to the week's shopping list. When we were little, we'd always joked that Hobnobs paved the way to his heart. His dark eyes glinted when I offered him one. I kept peeking over at him while I prepared our drinks. I couldn't help myself. Thanks to modern technology, we'd Skyped at least monthly in the last few years, but nothing compared to having him next to me, in the flesh. His mass of fearless curls now dangled

5

way past his collarbones, and he still looked as if he didn't eat enough. He slipped off his jacket, a burgundy canvas more suited to an autumn breeze than the bitter cold of winter.

'You need something warmer. We wear winter coats here, you know,' I said with a laugh.

'I'm waiting for some cash from someone who owes me. I'll get myself one then.'

'Legitimate cash, I hope?'

He stuck his tongue out at me. 'Not my game anymore.' He chucked his jacket across the breakfast bar. 'This is going to be the coldest December since Met Office records began in 1910.'

'How do you know?'

He shrugged. 'Heard it on the radio.'

I smiled. His ability to relay random facts and figures was the fallout from our dysfunctional childhood, whereas counting things calmed me. Not that I'd needed to for a long time. I picked up the tray. 'Come on, let's go next door. I've lit a fire.'

'Blimey, haven't you got all grown up?' he chuckled.

Warmth welcomed us as we entered the lounge. I stoked the fire and threw on another log. Falling into the deep sofa, I beckoned him over.

His eyes scanned the room. 'You've done well for yourself.'

'None of it belongs to me. It's Jim's house, not mine.'

'You know what I mean.' He glanced around the room. It wasn't big, but it was light and airy. Painted powder blue, it had a host of period features including ornate cornices and a two-hundred-year-old marble fireplace. Jim told me he had sweated blood, every evening until midnight for weeks, to restore it.

'Jim's always been the same. A man destined to be rich

and successful.' He examined the photographic prints lining the walls, pointing to a picture of a group of Thai women wearing straw hats, coasting along the canals of Thailand selling their mangoes and dragon fruit, coconuts, flowers and vegetables. 'The Damnoen Saduak floating market near Bangkok.'

'How do you know?'

'If you were on Facebook, you'd know I've been there. Who's the artist?' he asked.

'Dan, Jim's friend.'

'Oh right, Dan's work, is it? How's he doing these days? I've not seen him for yonks.'

'How do you know him?'

'From when I sometimes hung out with Jim when we were younger. Who would've thought, after all these years, you and Jim an item? Why did you keep that quiet?'

I shrugged. 'I didn't know if it would last.' That was the truth. I had never thought Jim would be so interested in me.

'How long have you been together?'

'Soon after I started renting a room here, September time.' I tried to remember the exact date. It was after Jim's birthday because Jess had still been on the scene. He'd thrown a cocktail party for his friends who had packed the whole of the downstairs. I would never forget that night. Seeing Jim and her together for the first – and last – time. I felt as though I'd been in a theatre watching a play – a spectator of the suit-and-little-black-dress-show. They'd acted the perfect couple amongst their family of friends, the supreme performance.

'Wouldn't have put you two together.'

'And why not?'

He thought for a moment, sipping his tea. 'The age gap, and where you've both come from, I suppose. You're such different people.'

'What does that matter? Why should my past define my future? Anyway, he's only ten years older than me. That's nothing.'

He nudged my shoulder. 'I always knew you'd make it big time. Always the grounded one, weren't you, Miss Eva Mitchell?'

'I had little choice. Not sure I'd call this big time, though.'

We chatted for a while longer before he slurped the last of his drink and placed his mug on the coffee table. 'Come on. Let's go.'

'Where're we going?'

His fists sank into the sofa and he pushed himself up, his eyes bright. Reaching out, he tugged me up. 'There's someone I want you to meet.'

*

We linked arms as we journeyed into town. 'I can't stay too long. I've got a shift at work tonight,' I said.

'Where're you working?'

'Didn't I tell you? I've got a part-time job in a bar and bistro about a five-minute walk from home. Marco's. Helps keep the student debt under control.'

He nodded. 'You did mention it. I remember now. So, is it serious? You and Jim.'

I nodded. 'Pretty full on.'

'He's a decent guy. He'll look after you.'

'I don't need looking after, thanks. I'm twenty-three now – not a child anymore.'

He ruffled my hair. 'Don't be so touchy.'

'He's taking me to Paris for two days next week – an early Christmas present.'

'See what I mean? He's one of the good guys. Always was. Ever since we were kids. Everyone liked Jim Barnes.'

'I can't remember him from when we were kids.'

'You were too young. He was always good to me.'

'What about you? Tell me about this girl you're so desperate to introduce me to.'

'Her name's Emily. Emmy for short. She's a medical student.' He beamed like a love-struck teenager. 'I'll let you make up your own mind.'

Covent Garden station was heaving, spewing out passengers into the mass of passing shoppers. The crowds shuffled us along the street as snowflakes settled on our hair like confetti. I felt an unusual tug of joy as we walked along. I smiled up at Ben. His dark eyes gleamed. I could see glimpses of the brother I'd once adored. The Ben before. Before he started not only colouring outside the lines, but off the page too – before Hamburg – before he left me.

'I need to find a present for Gill,' I said. Gill was my best friend. She'd just returned from a trip to Nepal in celebration of her sixtieth birthday. I guided him into a stationery shop where I found a handmade notebook with recycled paper. I knew she would adore it. She had a thing about notebooks. I found a few more Christmas gifts for Jim's family while Ben waited outside talking on his phone.

We met Emmy in a lively coffee shop on a side street off the cobbled piazza where 'Last Christmas' was blasting out from a flat screen fixed to the wall. She stood when we entered and waved. Slight and short, with a chic, shoulder-length bob, she was pretty – really pretty. Her flawless skin glowed, and long mascara-thickened lashes bordered her doe-like eyes. Ben introduced us as she slid a laminated menu across the table.

'I hear you're studying medicine,' I said.

She smiled. Her teeth were as straight as her fringe. And movie star white, of course. She spoke softly. 'My fourth year now, but I want to be a psychiatrist, so I'm a way off. And you? Law?'

'First-year mature student.'

'Enjoying it?'

I nodded. 'Lots of work, though.'

She laughed in agreement. 'Tell me about it. I've had a week off, playing catch-up.' She flashed her henna-decorated hands at me. 'Oh, and a family wedding. Back on duty tonight.'

'I'm starving; can we choose?' Ben said.

Tinsel looped the neck of the cheery waitress who pencilled our order on to a notepad. She was high on the spirit of the season, swaying her hips and humming along to the TV now playing 'Rockin' Around the Christmas Tree'.

I smiled, enthused by her festive mood. I fingered a bowl of pot-pourri sitting in the middle of the table, charging the air with wafts of pine and cinnamon, apples and cloves. Warmth radiated through my body. There it was again, that tug of joy. I realised at that moment its message. I'd received the ultimate early Christmas gift – the return of my brother's unbounded enthusiasm for life.

Finally, life was good.

Who was I trying to kid?

The humming waitress delivered our third coffee before Ben broke his news. One moment we were discussing plans for Christmas day. The next he took a deep breath and announced, 'Eva, I need to tell you something.' He snuck a look at Emmy. She gave him a thumbs-up sign.

I grinned, my eyes darting between the two of them. I could sense what was coming. I just knew it. They were getting married, or she was pregnant. I felt a warm glow inside. My family was about to grow bigger than just Ben and me. I was going to gain a sister-in-law, or a niece or nephew.

He fisted his trembling hands and gave it to me like a punch in the face. 'I've found our mum.'

Chapter 2

EVA

A busted lip, a skull ring, a knife in a canal.

A knife in a canal.

'She's living in Dollis Hill,' Ben said.

'How did you find her?' I asked, my voice shaking as much as my hands.

'A private detective.'

'How could you afford that? You're always broke.'

He glanced at Emmy. Concern creased her perfect face, but still she nodded in encouragement. 'One of Emmy's uncles owns an investigations agency.'

I stared at him, unable to find any words, but if looks could've killed, he would've been on his way to a cemetery.

'I'm seeing her tonight.' He hesitated before adding, 'You could come with me.'

I jumped up, sending the metal chair crashing to the floor and coffee sploshing onto the table. The hum of conversation stopped dead as curious eyes turned to us. The waitress spun round from serving a couple at the next table and her hand flew to her open mouth. She gave a muffled gasp. I clasped the edge of the table, surprised and embarrassed by my sudden action.

Ben attempted to stand too, but Emmy tugged his arm. My chest tightened.

'Say something,' Ben said.

What the hell do you want me to say, Ben? Oh, yes, I'd love to. Let's meet up, drink tea, eat cake and play happy families, why don't we? He knew how I felt about our mother. I'd made myself clear on all matters concerning her years before.

'Eva, sit down, let's talk this through.'

Ignoring his pleading expression, and, I thought, Emmy's genuine look of sympathy, I snatched my coat and rucksack from the back of the chair. 'I'm sorry our first meeting has ended this way,' I said to Emmy and, as calmly as I could, headed for the steamed up glass door.

Ben followed me for a while. 'Eva, come back. Please!' he shouted as I charged off, an unleashed fury racing through me like a provoked dog. What? He thought I'd stay for more?

I stomped off through the crowded back streets of Covent Garden, my elbows bashing against strangers. Before he left me, all those years ago, we would have risked everything for each other. I still loved him, but the brother I'd once idolised was no longer my everything. For weeks after he had gone, I used to rush home from school, hoping to find a letter, only to hear my foster mother's voice: 'No, nothing for you today, Eva.' Eventually, the disappointment overrode the hope, and I stopped rushing.

He had left soon after receiving his outstanding GCSE results, which he achieved despite sporadic attendance and minimal effort. He'd had a place waiting for him at sixth form, too. Such a shame. 'This boy has such a gift,' his teachers had told our foster parents. But one he couldn't finish unwrapping – as was typical of Ben. You see, my brother's undoing was his unquenchable desire for more. Forever pursuing something bigger and better to satisfy his hunger, giving up halfway through his own plate, because he wanted what was on someone else's more.

Couples unlinked hands as I barged forwards, ignoring the stares and glares. Constrained by bag-laden shoppers, I tripped and stumbled into the line of a passing Range Rover. It screeched to a halt, horn shrieking. The driver wound down her window, scowling and twirling her index finger against her temple while shouting out obscenities like a fishwife. Full of apologies, I stepped back onto the kerb.

I crouched to retie one of my shoelaces, and it was in that position, bent low, I felt him – a breeze ripping through me, chilling my bones worse than the winter winds. With octopus hands, *he* began touching me, prodding and poking, trying all angles to elicit a reaction. I froze, rigid, waiting for his next move, waiting for his fingers to slide up to my throat. *He* was back. Oh, please, no, no, no. I had to escape. Breathe, Eva. And then, there they were – his fingers circling my neck like a noose.

I shook him off and started to run. Through the streets, discordant voices shouted, 'Watch out!' as the crowds merged into a meaningless haze, pulsing against me in time to my stride. My lungs screamed for air, every breath I took shallow and painful. I shot a look behind me. *He* was still following me, I was sure, burning my tail, pursuing me like a stalker.

It was happening all over again.

Focus, Eva. Get away, I kept telling myself, run into a shop. *You know the game; you learned how to play to win years ago. What was the score last time you tallied it? It has been a while. 40-18? You are well ahead. You have to beat him again.*

I darted into a clothes shop, dazzled and disorientated by the glare of the bright lights. A muscled security guard, muttering into the mouthpiece of his walkie-talkie, raised his eyebrows at me as I browsed the rails, pretending to look interested in the military-style coats, quilted puffas and leather jackets. In, two, three, four. Loud music thumped through me, grating my already frayed nerves. Out, two, three, four.

From the size eight section of the sale rails, I snatched a pair of floral jeans – they would work – and charged towards the changing rooms. The shop assistant – glossy lips, plastic smile – slipped a blue disc onto the hanger of the jeans. 'Number five at the end. Shout if you need any help.' She stifled a yawn and directed me to an empty cubicle. Racing in, I swiped the heavy curtain across the steel pole then slid down the wall, crumpling into myself like a screwed-up piece of paper. The thumping music was piercing my head. No, don't give in, *he*'ll get you. Smack! My fists punched the sockets of my eyes. I started counting the number of flowers in the print of the jeans. One daisy, two daisies, three, daisies, four.

'My mind is strong. I can cope with this,' I repeated until I reached fifty-two on the left leg. 'I never have to see my mum again.' My fingers started tingling, turning numb.

'That's because all your blood is flowing to your vital organs,' Dr Barratta had informed me during one of our sessions all those years ago. An eight-week course of therapy my social worker had enlisted me on to try and get me to mend my unruly teenage ways. 'Part of the fight or flight response, also known as hyperarousal,' Dr Barratta said. 'Just so you're aware, there are physiological responses to your condition.'

'Is that why I see *him* when I'm stressed?'

'Do you know who *he* is?'

'No. I only ever seen *him* when I'm angsty. *He* is no one I know.'

'That's because *he* is only in your imagination, Eva. You must remind yourself of that when this happens. You need to find a coping strategy. Don't play the game. Or if you do, play to win.'

Shooting pains stabbed my chest as my breath quickened. Not enough daisies. I started counting the petals. Did it matter if some were bigger than others? Should the larger ones count as two?

The sales assistant interrupted me. 'All OK in there? Would you like me to fetch you another size?'

I uttered a casual dismissal and carried on, heat rushing through me. One hundred and seventy-two covered the left leg so far. Where was *he*? Focus, Eva, keep counting.

I reached two hundred and twenty before my chest started to ease. I looked up to the panelled ceiling and closed my eyes, chanting, 'I am strong. I can cope with this.' When I opened my eyes, the room was a different place. Air and space filled my head, and my breath returned to calm normality.

He had gone.

I'd done it. 41-18 to me.

I stared in the mirror. My skin was pallid, and dark patches swelled beneath my bloodshot eyes. Sheer exhaustion that was going to take more than a good night's sleep to clear. I had to get out of there. I needed to get home.

Getting from the changing room to the front of the shop was a blur. I thought *he* had started following me until I realised it was just my paranoia playing its crippling game. Outside, I looked up and down the road, then I turned left and strode up Long Acre to the Tube. I passed a doorway, where a homeless man swathed in a dirty quilt was sitting cross-legged. He met my gaze, rattling an old ice cream tub which was empty save for a few pathetic pennies. I delved into my bag and found my purse, emptying all the coins into his tub.

He smiled. 'Thanks, lass. Happy Christmas.'

I found the tenner I kept in the front of my backpack for emergencies and dropped that in his tub too. 'Happy Christmas.'

At the station, I stopped to contemplate a busker under the awning. He was dressed in Christmas clobber, strumming and singing 'Silent Night'. I swallowed hard. *Why this song? Of all the carols he could have chosen at this moment.* The sound sawed through me, cutting my heart, filling me with sadness.

'All is calm. All is bright.' He winked at me through a space between heads in the crowd.

I tried to respond, for the sake of goodwill to all men, but couldn't find it in myself. Nothing was calm, and nothing was bright. *He* was back. My mother had sent him to try and destroy me again.

Unable to face the claustrophobia of the Tube, I decided to walk the two miles home. I raced through the tumult of passers-by, and the squeaky brakes and honking horns of frustrated drivers, down to the Embankment. At Waterloo

Bridge, thick snowflakes drifted down, darkening skies threatening a snowstorm. I looked around for a cab, but despite the stench of exhaust fumes, not one orange light hovered in sight. Then I remembered that I didn't have any money left anyway. Wrapping my hands in my armpits, I soldiered on over the river, incredulous how the day I'd been looking forward to for so long had unfolded.

Along the Kennington Road, my boots crunched past Marco's Bar and Bistro, reminding me I had to be at work there in under an hour. Inside, I could see the staff preparing for the evening shift, laying tables, aligning the bar stools and sweeping the floor. I groaned. *Why have I agreed to overtime again tonight?* The wind picked up as I turned into Walcot Square, past the Georgian terraced houses, homeward bound. I quickened my pace past the small green, which was not square as the name suggested, but triangular, as though pieces had been chopped off over the years to allow for pavements and parking spaces. A mantle of white covered the grass, so serene in contrast to the hustle and bustle of the Lambeth Road a few streets away.

I found Jim sitting in the kitchen, phone pressed to his ear, eyes glued to his laptop. The usual bundles of folders, documents and charts surrounded him. Breathless, I flung my coat over the long kitchen table, clutching my backpack to my chest like a shield.

He typed a couple more words, then glanced up at me and pressed the phone screen against his jumper. 'Hi darling. You OK?'

I perched on one of the wooden benches on either side of the table. 'You're not going to believe this.'

'Believe what?' he asked, glimpsing at the laptop.

'Ben's found my mother.'

His eyes stretched wide and his lips parted. He put the phone back to his ear. 'I'll have to call you back later, Janita, sorry. Send me the update when you're done, please. And thanks for all your help today.' He ended the call. 'What?' he asked as if he'd misheard me the first time. He clicked his computer closed and reached across for my hand.

'Ben's found my mother,' I repeated.

'Where?' His phone rang. He grimaced. 'It's Warren; I have to take it. We've got a problem. I'll be quick, promise.'

I took the stairs two at a time to my room and fell on the bed, cursing my brother, cursing my mother.

Tammy Mitchell was back. And so was *he*.

Ugly thoughts buzzed about my mind like wasps trapped in a jar. *I will kill her if I ever see her again. I will pull the trigger, thrust the knife – whatever it takes.* I winced. That wasn't me. I wouldn't hurt an ant. But I couldn't help it. That was the effect she had on me.

My mobile rang. I sat up and unclipped the flap of my rucksack to fish it out and gasped as a rolled-up pair of daisy-patterned jeans met my eyes. Shaking, I pulled them out and searched for a security tag, finding one secured to the waistband. *Surely, I haven't?* It had been... what, five? six? years since I'd last stolen anything. I emptied the contents of the bag onto the bed: a book – *Cases that Changed Our Lives*, pens, tissues, mascara, tampon, Double Decker wrapper, phone, and an elastic hairband – all mine, all paid for. I ran to the wardrobe and stuffed the jeans behind the tops and jumpers and stacks of books.

My phone beeped – a missed call from Ben. I sat on the bed and stabbed the ignore button. Selecting the contacts screen, I scrolled down to the Bs, searching to see if I still had her number. Yes, there she was, Dr Sophia Barratta. Her profile picture still sending out a wave of comfort.

After ten minutes or so, the scent of expensive aftershave told me Jim was in the room. 'Two sugars, I think you need it.' Budging a wobbling stack of books aside, he placed a hot cup of tea on the bedside cabinet. I tried to stand, but he eased me back and sat beside me, kissing my cheek, holding me tight. 'What exactly has happened?' he asked in that caring way of his which made me feel like I was the only person who really mattered.

'Ben's seeing Tammy tonight.'

He removed his Gucci glasses. His eyes flickered, brimming with concern. 'Where did this come from?'

I shrugged. 'Who knows?'

'How did he find her?'

I wrung my hands together. 'He met a girl in Peru. Emily. Emmy, he calls her. He took me to meet her today.' I kneaded my fists in my palms. My knuckles popped like burst balloons. 'She comes from one of those large families. You know the sort, where they all live together under one happy roof. Great-grandparents included. She's a really nice girl,' I said, before adding, through gritted teeth, 'but she encouraged him to do this, I'm sure.'

His jaw dropped. 'Why? How?'

'I didn't stay to find out.'

He puffed out his cheeks, tightening his grip around me. 'What a shock this must be for you.'

'I still can't believe it.'

He lifted his hand to peep at his watch. 'I'm sorry, I hate to do this, but I need to go. Can we talk later?' He caressed my cheek. 'I'm meant to be picking Dan up from Waterloo in half an hour.'

'Don't worry,' I lied. *Won't do to keep Dan waiting, will it?* 'I must get to work anyway.'

'You sure you're up to it? You look like you've seen a ghost.'

He didn't know the half of it.

'I'm sure,' I lied again. What was wrong with me? No games, no lies, we'd promised each other.

Chapter 3

JIM

The Manhattan Plaza Hotel, New York
Ten months later, October 2011

I can't recall exactly where this hotel is that I checked into four nights ago. All I know is that it's walking distance from Carnegie Hall. Janita never books far from the office. It's a waste of time. All those precious minutes sitting in traffic when you could be at your desk slogging for the cause. Just one of many unspoken rules which shape our department. I'm high up. At a guess, I'd say, around the thirtieth floor – a mere fragment in the enormity of the Big Apple.

I should have worked it out, Eva. For Christ's sake, it was more straightforward than some of the crap Warren has thrown at me the past few years. I didn't get to be Director with a major player in the private equity market without having some intelligence. How could everything have gone so horribly wrong?

*

Early this morning, I leaned against the floor-to-ceiling window, my face pressed to the glass, and scanned the silhouette of skyscrapers across Manhattan's skyline. Dense clouds scattered the skies, fighting the defiant sun doing its best to grace New York with its presence. A fight it wouldn't win. Not today. Another dark day was in store. I stood there for ages, as still as the Statue of Liberty, contemplating the future. And as bitter tears smudged what should have been a breathtaking view, I swallowed the emotional mass in the back of my throat. A time machine, that's what I needed. A magical vehicle to change the past and transport me back to before Christmas last year when ignorance was bliss. If only.

Despair slowed my heavy steps over to the TV remote, and I switched off my sole companion for the past seventy-two hours. I was done listening to Kim Jong-un's plans to expand North Korea's nuclear weapons programme and the multiple casualties from suicide bombings in Afghanistan. Over at the desk, I collapsed into the chair and stared at my laptop, mesmerised by the glare as I willed words to materialise, sentences to form. Anything to add to the few random notes I managed at dawn when words persisted in playing a challenging game of hide and seek. I rubbed my head; it was killing me, throbbing like toothache. Had been since I arrived here. Usually, I'm so quick at getting words down. I can churn them out like James Patterson. Writing's a big chunk of my day job, but I guess this was a different situation. Life can deal some pretty rotten cards, but God had sure handed me a Texas hold'em starting two and seven this time.

'Come on, Jim. Get a grip,' I yelled at the blank screen as my feet alternated kicking the exposed brick wall behind the desk. 'Get a damn grip.'

Am I an idiot, Eva? All this time, I didn't see the hidden truths and spiralling lies. Can we carry on? What about our Joe?

I yanked open the top drawer and reached behind the hotel directory and hairdryer for the bottle of pills I stole from my father before leaving London. I fingered the label.

Diazepam, 15mg, by mouth as directed.

I've read those words so many times over the past four days. How many would it take? All depends if consumed with alcohol, Google had informed me, while I rolled whisky around my mouth, waiting for my flight in the VIP lounge on the way over here. For a man of my size, I reckoned, if washed down with a generous measure of whisky, half the contents should do the job.

It would be so much easier, wouldn't it? End the stress and be done with the shame. Then no one would need to know, Eva.

I always thought I was tougher than this. The chilled one, the one everyone turns to when the heat becomes too much. That's me. I chucked the pills across the room, aiming at the duty-free Jameson I had bought before boarding the plane.

On the flight, as I downed successive glasses of Glenlivet, my mother's advice echoed from my youth. 'Write it all down, James, it always helps. Fetch a clean sheet of paper and a pencil, and scribble away about whatever's bothering you. Put it in a letter, or a story if that helps. No one need see the finished product.'

I wrote for hours when I was young. Have I ever told you that? During my school years, I won a handful of writing competitions. I don't think I've ever told you that, either. "Clearly expresses ideas" and "Intriguing narrative for such a young mind" were amongst the judge's comments.

That's my plan. I'm going to write it all out, Eva. Get it in the right order and straighten it out in my mind. How it has all evolved for me. Then I can work out where we go from here.

Where to start, though? Where to start? The problem is, I guess, despite spending consecutive dark hours thinking about where to kick things off, I still don't know the best starting point. At the logical beginning, you would say in that rich, smoky tone of yours. I can hear it now. 'Jim, start where it makes sense. At the beginning. What're you hanging about for?' Your voice echoes as if you are in the room with me. 'Just take a deep breath and get writing.'

*

So, where did it all begin, Eva?

Should I go back to when I first met Tammy? When I was three years old, and my mother returned to midwifery at Guildford hospital. That was when Tammy turned up to work as our family nanny. I can barely remember those days, but photographs randomly appear in the earlier volumes of my mother's treasured albums which occupy the bottom shelf of the bookcase in my parents' sitting room. Below the numerous awards my father collected throughout his distinguished career. Now and again, when overcome with nostalgia, my mother gets them out. She'll stare at the photos for hours, skimming a finger around the border of each one as if she's capturing a story. 'Tammy was such a kind person,' she always said to me, 'so patient and reliable. Seven years she worked for us. She thought the world of you and your sisters. Even after she stopped working for us, she still used to come and visit now and again.'

Or do I start with when I first met you? I was eleven by then, an innocent boy teetering on the boundary of adolescence – slightly spotty and beginning to reek of hormones and sweaty shoes. Tammy had come to visit. It was in the Easter school holidays. I remember because Tammy had brought my sisters and me Easter eggs, and Vic had a tantrum. A proper fling-herself-on-the-floor-and-beat-the-carpet hissy fit. All because my Walnut Whip egg was bigger than her Jelly Tots one. It's funny the things you can recall from childhood. Tammy watched, stifling a giggle, as she cradled you in her arms. The baby everyone was aching to see. I couldn't make out what all the fuss was about. Why was everyone cooing and clucking at this head sticking out of a bundle of blankets?

Maybe I need to go back to spring last year and start there. Yes, that makes sense. I think you'd agree. When you turned up in my life again. Ben had sent me an email. He often got in touch. Mainly when he had an ulterior motive, I'd noticed over the years, but that was OK. I'd always had a soft spot for him. He'd had a tough ride over the years. 'Eva's made it to uni,' he'd written. I found myself pausing to re-read that sentence. I'd never considered you'd turn out the academic type. 'She needs somewhere to live in the South London area. I wondered if you're still renting out rooms?'

Oh no, I thought, at the time, that's all I need right now. I was due to exchange contracts the following month on a bachelor's pad up in the City and didn't want a tenant until I'd moved out. I didn't need the hassle. It'd been fun once, and the extra cash a godsend in the early days when Dan and I had first bought Walcot Square. Way back, when funds were tighter than my father's wallet. But I didn't need the extra cash anymore, or the inconvenience of another person stealing the last of the milk I'd need for my morning coffee fix. But Dan did need the money, and his work often took him away. Plus, he drank his coffee black.

He'd called me from New York only the previous evening and told me his company was extending his assignment over there. 'It looks like I'll be here for at least another couple of months. I've been thinking. Do you mind if we find a tenant for my room? I could do with the extra income. You'll be moving out soon anyway,' he'd said. 'And book yourself a flight over here as soon as. I've found a great poker bar you'll love. Played a few games there myself at the weekend.' He ended his sentence with a hiccup, then added, 'Oh, and come alone, the women are… how can I put it? Interesting.'

So along you came last summer, Eva, with your youthful charisma and tenacious attitude, and spun my world one-eighty.

The sun had lain directly behind you, enfolding you into its brightness. So surreal, I had to pinch myself. Your presence, along with your just-crawled-out-of-a-bath scent – old-fashioned soap, vibrant and crisp – touched me in more places than my nose. I thought I was in a three-fold utopian dream. One of those you never want to wake up from, and when you do, you snap your eyes shut and beg for sleep to return you to where you'd left off.

As you stepped onto the black and white Victorian tiled floor, my nerves revved up, and embarrassing beads of sweat trickled down my forehead. Heck, what had happened to the chilled and composed guy fazed by nothing? I kept dabbing my forehead, telling myself it was the heat of the evening, or the Thai curry simmering on the hob for Jess and me, but come on, who was I trying to kid?

I showed you around the house like an enthusiastic estate agent. I had to sell it to you. You had to move in. I started with Dan's room, which would become yours. I'd straightened it up before you arrived: made the bed, removed the empty cups and glasses, stuffed the crumpled boxers and scanty knickers littering the floor into a drawer. You seemed impressed, especially when you saw the en suite with the free-standing roll top bath. I'd even put out fresh towels. After the tour, I offered you a drink.

Much to my disappointment, you glanced at your watch and gasped. 'Must go, I've got another place to see in Balham.'

I tried to hide the desperation from my voice. 'You won't get better than this.'

After closing the front door to promises that you would call after your next viewing, I leaned against the wall to steady myself. Jess was due, and I remember thinking please, Jess, for once, put your bloody need for punctuality aside. The coolness against my forehead settled the giddiness overpowering me. I felt hungover, but I'd not touched a drink all week. The attraction was a drug, intoxicating. I needed another dose of you. You not moving in wasn't an option.

You had all the ingredients for perfection, and I grew to adore everything about you. Your passion for cake, any type. The clothes you wear, the books you read. How you can look so goddamn sexy in trackies, make-up-free, messy hair, sitting cross-legged on the sofa engrossed in a Rendell or a Christie. The way your head cocks to one side when you are deep in thought. The delicate way you eat. Your determination and fierce independence coupled with kindness I've never seen in anyone before – not even my mother.

So, just when I thought my life was on track, barrelling along in the fast lane, overtaking anyone getting in my way, you rocked up. You slowed me down a gear and made me realise I'd been on the wrong road completely. With Jess, for one. We'd been together for five years, then along you came, and I knew. You made all my previous relationships seem like practice sessions. They say that, don't they? That when you meet the one, you'll know. What bullshit I'd have said, before you. When it came to girlfriends, the balance of power had always tilted in my favour. Then you turned up, and, wham, did I know. You touched me where no one ever has – deep in my soul. It didn't take you long either, quickly peeling away the layers until you reached my core. It's hard to explain. You made me see things differently. How can I put it? Perspective, that's it, that's the word. You opened my mind, made me question my motives for everything I did. That changed me. You changed me.

So, I think it's fair to say that you became a part of me as soon as I opened my door to you last summer. You didn't call until later on that night. I sweated all evening until I heard you say, 'Is the room still available?' I welled up, and at that moment, I did something I'd never done before. I mapped out my future with you, picturing the altar we'd take our vows at, our four kids, walking along seashores and watching sunsets, holding hands as we greyed.

Pathetic, Dan would have called me, if I had dared to tell him. 'It doesn't happen like that. Get real,' he would have said.

But it did.

Chapter 4

EVA

Jim offered to drop me at work on his way to pick up Dan. Marco's was only around the corner, but the temperature had dropped further. He turned the heater dial up to maximum, blasting hot air into my face. 'You should've called in sick.'

I felt like I looked – drained. My head, spinning with daisies, needed painkillers. It always did after one of those traumatic episodes. 'I can't. It's too busy.' Tormented by how the day had progressed, I could have done with staying at home, but I needed that job. At least three shifts a week, it covered my rent. Plus, the tips were generous at Christmas. Jim had told me a few times that, considering we were a couple, I didn't need to pay him rent anymore, but I refused to cancel my monthly deposit into his bank account.

He turned on the wipers. They swiped on full pelt, collecting clumps of fresh flakes and raking them into blackness. 'This snow is getting heavier. Why doesn't Dan get a cab?' I asked.

'He'd do the same for me.'

'Where's he been today?'

'Guildford. He had to take a lot of his equipment, so I said I'd pick him up from the station.'

'You're always so good to people.' I stared at him as he gripped the wheel. Spiky black hair, and lots of it; dark eyes, olive-toned skin, straight-edged nose: I really fancied him. He went to the gym most mornings before work and knew exactly what belonged in his wardrobe. And not only did he volunteer at the local homeless shelter every Wednesday night, he also arranged a generous weekly Tesco grocery delivery there. Adding fun and loyalty to those qualities, I knew I'd been handed a winning scratch card with the top prize under one of its opaque, silver-coated rectangles.

Ben's earlier words echoed. 'You're such different people.'

'What are Ben's plans, then? Apart from seeing Tammy.' Jim took his hand off the steering wheel and caressed my knee.

'He reckons he's going to settle here. I'm sceptical. He's been away so long.' I sighed. 'He's built up a following on Facebook and plans to start some excursion business for budget travelling in South America. I hope he can do it this time.'

'What do you mean by that?'

I sighed. 'Oh, you know Ben. You've seen some of the adventures he's tried in the past. He starts with so much enthusiasm but never seems able to see anything through.'

He nodded.

'I think Emmy has changed him.'

'I'll have to catch up with him.'

'He said he wants to see you, too.'

'I haven't seen him since before he disappeared to Spain.'

'Ten years, then.'

'I remember when we were kids. When Tammy was our family nanny, she often brought him to work with her.' He smiled. 'I used to love it. It was like I had a little brother for the day. Which was a blessing when you've got two annoying sisters. I don't know why, but there's a part of me that has always felt sorry for him. It'll be good to see him again.' He hesitated before asking, 'Will you go and see Tammy?'

I glared at him. 'No way.' I pointed to a gap between two parked cars. 'Look, over there.'

He skidded into the space, leaned over and kissed me. 'Bye, darling. I'll be in later with Dan.'

Warmth greeted me like a welcoming host as I entered Marco's. A bright and airy bar and bistro, it boasted the best gin-based cocktails in town and dished up freshly cooked Italian cuisine. Most nights punters crammed the bar, and you'd be lucky to get a table if you hadn't made a reservation, so the hours passed quickly. I had started working there only days after I moved into Walcot Square. Jim and Dan agreed that I would have no difficulty picking up work. My face would fit, they'd told me. The male staff were all strapping and the females slim with long, swinging ponytails.

'Evening, Eva,' Jason, the boss, called out above a medley of Christmas tunes blaring out on repeat. He was sitting in his usual spot at the end of the bar, his butt splayed over a wrought-iron stool. His tone was as annoying as his middle finger prodding the face of his watch like the office time-keeper. I ignored him. The constant pain pounding through my head as though someone was beating my skull with a hammer was enough to deal with. After sticking my belongings in the cramped staff cupboard out the back, I slotted into a space behind the bar.

Carrie greeted me. 'Am I glad to see you.' She blew her dark fringe off her face. 'It's madness in this place tonight.'

I first met Carrie Martinez when we'd found ourselves scribbling away at adjacent desks on our second day at uni. Both mature students, we'd built a rapport straight away even though we were out-and-out opposites. A talented national cyclist, she spent hours at the velodrome in Herne Hill and admitted that she would be on her way to London 2012 if only her love of men and clubbing would stop getting in her way. When she'd told me she needed a job that would fit around uni, training and her debauched lifestyle, I introduced her to Jason. Since she was the daughter of a French model and a Costa Rican father with heavily accented English, I knew he wouldn't pass on her.

'Sorry I'm late,' I said, picking up a bar knife and cutting up slices of lemons and limes ready for the evening rush.

'Good day?' she asked.

I shook my head.

'What's up?'

My hand tightened around the wooden handle of the knife. 'Nothing.'

'Doesn't look like nothing to me, my friend.'

I grabbed another lemon and stabbed the blade into its skin. A warped vision of sticking that same knife into my mum tormented my thoughts. I stopped and threw the knife down. *What is wrong with me?*

'You look as miserable as the boss.' She nodded in Jason's direction. 'Want to come partying after we finish tonight?

Three guys arrived at the bar and ordered pints of Peroni. 'No, I've had a day of it. I just want to go home.'

'What's happened?'

'You don't want to know.'

'Did you see your brother?'

I shoved a glass under the Peroni pump, screwing up my lips. 'Oh, yes, I saw my brother.'

'Why the long face?'

Do I wear it that badly? I paused pouring the pint mid-flow and looked at her. 'To be brief, he's found our mum.' I shook my head. 'After nearly eighteen years of silence, he's traced her. And he's seeing her tonight.'

'Wow, drama. I take it you're none too pleased.'

I narrowed my eyes. 'I'd have preferred it if he'd told me she was dead.'

She gasped.

I couldn't blame her. 'You got any painkillers? I've got a splitting headache.' I felt queasy, too.

'There's some Nurofen in my bag.' She stirred the cocktail she was making and garnished it with a twist of lemon.

When I saw Jason talking to a punter, I sneaked out the back and found the plastic strip of tablets in Carrie's bag. I read the instructions. Take two with water. I popped three out of the packet and swallowed them dry. I stared at a poster on the wall detailing health and safety in the workplace as my mind drifted off to Ben and Emmy sitting in that coffee shop earlier. *How could you, Ben?* I started shaking. 'Calm down, or *he*'ll be back,' I said out loud before taking several deep breaths and rejoining Carrie, rescuing her from the row of tenners and twenties waving along the bar.

When the early evening rush settled down, I was restocking the house Chardonnay when Carrie glided past carrying two plates of insalata caprese. 'Oh, my friend, you must introduce me,' she drawled.

I looked up at the two men strolling towards the bar. Jim and Dan. Heads turned – mainly girls, but some guys too –

to follow the sandy blond. With a strong jawline and athletic build, Dan stood well over six feet and wore jeans and a suede bomber jacket. Carrie and the majority of the clientele may have found him appealing, but I failed to share their vision. A gifted and successful photographer, dream job in a London fashion house, lover of snowboarding and women, he was the kind of guy who turned my stomach rather than my head. His grass-green eyes always seemed to hold mine a moment too long, and there was something about his smile that unnerved me. There was something charming about it too, I had to admit. Or perhaps it was just the combination of his eyes and smile which stamped a hallmark of confidence over his boyish face.

'What's it to be?' I asked, faking a grin at Jim.

'Two pints of your finest, please. And whatever you're having.' Dan and Jim both started the request, but Dan's dominant voice finished it, rising above Jim's. The noise level had increased several decibels owing to the entrance of a party of fifteen or so.

I pulled the pints. Froth overflowed as I handed them over. Dan grabbed a tissue from his pocket and mopped up the spilled lager, starting with that on my fingers. I pulled my hand away from his touch and grabbed hold of the bar, stunned by the chill rushing through me as if someone had opened the door and chucked me out into the icy winds. I glanced up at him, and he stared at me for a few seconds before turning to talk to Jim. I felt awkward. As I invariably did in his company. I always had this distinct feeling that our paths had crossed before. And something told me it hadn't been a positive experience.

Chapter 5

EVA

'See you tomorrow evening,' Carrie called out as we parted ways outside Marco's. The wind whistled through her dark hair, sweeping it across her high cheekbones and into the air. 'I wish you were coming with me.'

'Some other time,' I lied. The boozy, coke-fuelled parties she loved were not my thing. Besides, it had been one hell of a day; all I wanted was sleep. The snow had eased, but the biting wind sliced through me, stinging my cheeks with tears. As I turned into Walcot Square, I stopped suddenly. Footsteps were approaching from behind. Was *he* back? No, *he* couldn't be. I'd got rid of him. *He* never returned so soon. I swung around, but emptiness filled the space behind me. I scanned the Square. All I could see was a woman power-walking her husky on the opposite side of the green. Perturbed, I upped my pace home, and, fumbling for the keys, shouldered open the door.

Up in my room, I charged to the wardrobe and pulled out the daisy jeans. My stomach turned as I dumped them in a plastic supermarket carrier. I shoved the carrier in my backpack which I kicked under the bed.

After taking a shower, I got into bed and found my phone to set the alarm. Several texts from Ben dominated the screen. 'Please call me.' I scrolled through the reams of others he'd sent that evening. 'Come on, please listen', 'Eva, hear me out', 'We need to talk'.

I deleted them all.

I slept fitfully, drifting in and out of a mishmash of unwelcome dreams involving Ben, Jim and Dan. In one, Jim was driving, but a nondescript van rather than his black Porsche. He screeched to a stop outside Marco's and tried to pull me in with him. I wanted to get in, but Dan, wearing daisy-covered jeans, crept up and tugged me away with such force, red marks blemished my arm. We fought – all three of us dealing out vicious exchanges of slaps and punches. An apparition of Ben appeared by the snow-covered bonnet. I screamed at him to help me. 'Mum needs me more than you. She needs me more than you,' he'd taunted like an auditory hallucination.

I woke up before the alarm had even thought about it, knowing there was only one way to clear my head. I jumped up and pulled on some winter running tights and my favourite well-worn hoodie. Once I'd dug my backpack out from beneath the bed, I crept downstairs and slipped through the front door.

An orange strip illuminated the base of the dawn sky, the sun bursting its way through the dark rim, promising a brighter day. I'd always loved that time of the morning, at that time of year, since I'd started running. The heavy snowfall from the previous day had mostly melted, and muddy slush covered the footpaths on the jog up to Geraldine Mary Harmsworth Park. The gatekeeper was opening up. 'You're keen, girl,' he said in a strong Jamaican accent.

Acknowledging him with a quick wave, I carried on into the park. The fresh morning air cleared my mind, but I knew it was going to take more than a three-miler to make sense of my thoughts that day. I stopped to stretch at the Tibetan Peace Garden, my favourite place, by one of the meditation seats around the Mandala. It was usually so tranquil there, I thought I'd find some level of calmness, but that wasn't to be. Knowing I had no choice, I dug my mobile from my backpack.

He answered after the second ring. 'Eva. At last.'

'Can I come over?'

He cleared his throat. 'Thank God you've called. I need to talk to you; there's something you should know.'

'What?'

'Just get over here.' He gave me directions.

'See you in about half an hour,' I said, replacing my headphones and starting to run, past the monkey puzzle trees encrusted with a coat of white and on to the eastern gates. Half-way through the park, I stopped at a concrete bin and glanced around, then removed the plastic supermarket carrier from my backpack and dumped it in.

Lengthening my stride, I paced along Kennington Park Road, but despite David Guetta pumping in my ears, fuelling me along, I couldn't seem to gain my normal speed. I passed Oval, Stockwell and Clapham North stations until I reached the rows of shops, restaurants and bars of Clapham High Street. Signs of the Friday night shenanigans were still apparent. The lingering stench from people caught short, and empty cans scattered in the gutter. Fatigue slowed my pace as I approached Ben's road. I walked the rest of the way watching Clapham wake up as light appeared through windows and a few chimneys started to smoke.

The flat where Ben was staying occupied the ground floor of a converted Georgian house in a quiet crescent, off the south side of the Common. It was similar to Walcot Square, but here the houses spiralled a circular grassy area, today rich with evergreens sprinkled with white. Emmy shared the flat with a fellow student, and Ben had taken up residence temporarily. Until he got himself sorted, he'd told me yesterday, which had made me chuckle to myself. When had he ever managed to get himself sorted?

Ever since that night in Hamburg, he'd been the same. Christmas had been approaching then too. Our foster parents at the time, Diane and Peter Monks, had won first prize in some newspaper competition for a "magical minibreak" to the Christmas markets in Hamburg. On the last evening, they'd left us to scour the marketplace for a couple of hours. We paced up and down lines of stallholders selling kitsch gifts, candied almonds, glühwein and stollen before taking a break, sitting astride a wall on the Mönckebergbrunnen – one of the main shopping streets – sipping hot chocolate from paper cups and munching on gingerbread hearts. The smell of burnt almonds and mulled wine hovered overhead, and a violin trio stood playing 'Stille Nacht' as we watched children riding the intricately carved horses of an old-fashioned carousel.

Ben studied the violinists. 'This song was written by a teacher and a priest in Oberndorf bei Salzburg, Austria. In the year...' He paused for a moment, his eyelids twitching as he selected the date, '...1818.'

I stared at him in disbelief. His mind was stacked with information like a shelf of encyclopaedias. 'How come you know that?'

He shrugged. 'I read it somewhere.' He sat silently after sharing that snippet of trivia. Uncommunicative, as he often was in those days, as though turning sixteen had caused paralysis of his tongue. He gazed ahead dreamily, kicking the wall with unnecessary force. I strained my eyes to catch a glimpse of what he could see. I knew for sure it wasn't the felt slippers, knitted hats and candy sticks on the stalls.

It's on that wall that I'd coaxed him to tell me about the day we last saw our mum. We hadn't seen her for over eight years, and we didn't talk about her often. She was the single topic of conversation that had always threatened our special bond as we were tossed from one foster family to another like bags of non-recyclable rubbish.

I started to play our special game. The one I always initiated, and he would join in at some point. Even when he wasn't in the mood. There was no other way I could persuade him to talk about her. I bounced my bottom on the wall, knocking my knuckles on the stone between us. I would get him to talk about her if it killed me. 'When Mummy finally comes to get us, what do you think will be the first thing she'll say?'

His lips remained tight.

'Where do you think she'll take us?' I tapped his leg. 'Come on, Ben.' Ordinarily, he would reply with one of our memorable places back home in London: the boating lake in Victoria Park, the Bethnal Green Museum of Childhood, the sweet shop on the Columbia Road.

Still no response.

'Where do you think we'll live? That flat on the Hackney Road again?'

He shrugged his bony shoulders, which sagged as though he had a lifetime of dilemmas balanced precariously on top of them. Slamming his fist down by my side, and holding my stare with his dark brown eyes, so dark they could be mistaken for black in a different light, he snapped, 'It's about time you found out about Mum abandoning us.'

The pain in his voice, as well as his face, transfixed me. I clutched the wall.

'You've lived in this distorted dream that she'll come back for us for far too long. But you need to understand that she's never going to,' he told me before relaying details of the night she'd dragged him out to buy medicine to treat my raging temperature but bought a packet of fags instead.

My nails dug into the wall, scraping along the brickwork. His voice lowered, a distant echo as if the memories were trying to drag him back to the day it had all happened. 'She paid for her fags, with a mix of coins. But not the bottle of vodka she'd slipped under her jumper, so she was in a hurry to leave the shop. When the storekeeper charged after us, she pulled a knife on him.' Sadness coated his tone. 'There was a kerfuffle. She fell and smashed the bottle. The place was covered in glass and blood. The police turned up and one of them took me home and stayed until the social worker came. Mrs Parker, she was kind, unlike some of them, but she stank of chip fat.' He closed his eyes momentarily before continuing. 'Mum ended up in the nick.' He turned to me, his eyebrows arched. 'And even when she got out, she never came to get us.'

He jumped off the wall. Turning to me, he swallowed hard as though he had a mouthful of food, before adding. 'I still can't stand the smell of chips.' And, off he charged, leaving behind a half-eaten gingerbread heart.

The fags and the booze – her relief, he told me, from the life she'd created, but decided wasn't for her. As though we'd been pets given at Christmas – desperately wanted to begin with, but needing to be rehomed by the time the daffodils arrived.

I'd spent years imagining how she would come back for us, fantasising about being with her every day, but he'd crushed my dreams. He'd always been the one to shelter me from hurt – my Big Ben, my bodyguard, my guardian. But the time had come, when, perched on that wall in Hamburg, intentionally or not – I couldn't say for sure – his need to spill the facts about our mum outweighed his desire to protect his devoted little sister. Until then I'd lived with the hope that she would come to reclaim us, or even just drop in to say hello. But she never did, leaving me hanging like a new millennium Tracy Beaker.

How could she?

How dare she?

Arriving at Ben's, I knocked on the door and stood waiting beside a dirty terracotta pot containing a casualty of neglect. I swayed from side to side, questions itching on the tip of my tongue to which I wasn't even sure I wanted the answers. The door opened as I went to knock again. My arms folded across my middle. 'How'd it go, then?'

'Come in.' He stepped back, and I entered the narrow hallway where a heap of shoes littered the floor beneath an overloaded coat rack. 'Want some coffee?' He closed the door. 'Or you might need something stronger.'

Chapter 6

EVA

He left me sitting on a floral-cushioned sofa while he went to boil the kettle. Rock music was playing on MTV. I stared around, fascinated by the vast chaos of knick-knacks and paraphernalia. Old watches displaying different times, empty vases, sculptures, ornaments and photographs of varying sizes cluttered the room which smelled faintly of the inside of a charity shop.

He wandered back with two large mugs of coffee. I nodded at a packet of Rizlas and small pieces of cardboard on the surface of a closed laptop. 'Didn't take you long to find a supplier.'

'Trust you to notice.' He offered over a plate stacked with Marmite-smothered toast. 'Want some?'

Suddenly ravenous, I took two slices and bit into one. 'Where's Emmy?'

'On nights. Should be home by now, but that's how it is. Did you know doctors are meant to work forty-eight hours per week according to the European Time Directive, but junior doctors work over a hundred?'

'Guess that's the commitment needed in their profession.'

I pointed a Nike in the direction of the laptop. 'Does she join you in all this business?'

'No.' He tut-tutted and folded his arms in an over-exaggerated manner. 'She's helping me cut down, actually.'

Good luck there, Emmy.

'Interesting flat. Who owns it?'

'The parents of one of Emmy's old school friends. They moved to somewhere in the Middle East; Jordan, I think. Angela needed someone to stay with her. She suffers from anxiety. Emmy said she'd help her.'

'That's handy.'

'Tell me about it. Mates' rates. It's going to be tough until I get my act together.'

We chatted as we sipped our coffee and munched our toast, both waiting for the other to acknowledge the elephant in the room. It was enormous enough; one of us had to. I leaned forward and placed my mug on the magazine-topped coffee table, knowing it would have to be me. 'So, how'd it go?' I asked, my voice edged with agitation.

He half-smiled. 'Good. I'm glad I went.'

My body tensed, muscles tightened. 'Did Emmy go too?'

'Nope, I went on my own and stayed about an hour. Thought I'd keep the first visit short. Just in case.'

In case of what? I wanted to ask but struggled to turn my thoughts into words.

'She lives alone.' He was quiet for a while, then thumped the arm of the sofa. 'She's got cancer.'

'Oh.'

'That all you can say?'

I shrugged.

'She wants to see you.'

'Cancer of what?'

'Breast. Diagnosed last month. She's started chemo.'

'Is it terminal?'

'I didn't ask.'

I snorted. 'It doesn't change anything.'

He stared at me, mouth open, head shaking. 'It must do.'

'It doesn't, because I'll never understand why she left us all those years ago.'

He flopped back on the sofa. 'She wants to see you.'

'All these years she's never bothered to try to find us.'

'She thought we were better off without her.'

I scoffed again. 'Did she actually use those words?'

He nodded. 'There's so much to her story. She wants to see us both, together, to explain everything.'

'Why're you defending her?' I tried to remove my hoodie. It was sweaty, but not from the run. My arm got caught in the sleeve and I struggled to set it free, only adding to my irritation. 'Been through so much? Come on, Ben, accept it; she's never given a damn about anything but herself. Turn that music down, can you?'

He reached for the remote. 'She's had it hard too, Eva. I don't deny what she did was wrong, but I think we need to show forgiveness.'

I stared at him in puzzlement. Was it a bloke thing? Why couldn't I see things the way he did? 'I'll never forgive her. I wish I could, but I can't.'

'I thought that too for all these years, but Emmy has taught me so much. We need to forgive. Otherwise, it'll eat away at us.'

I tutted. 'Ah. Emmy, the psychiatrist.'

He took a spliff from the top of the laptop and tossed it from one hand to another. 'She's helped me.'

'And how's that?' I asked. 'By digging up the past and shovelling it around for fun?'

'She says I show signs of depression. She introduced me to a colleague of hers in Peru.'

I rolled my eyes. 'I thought we'd done the therapy thing when we were kids?'

'Hang on. Let me finish. He helped me no end, especially with my anger issues. There's an emptiness in me, Eva. Something's missing. I don't have an identity. I need to know who I am. Who my – our – family is. It'll haunt me for the rest of my life if I don't face it now.'

'That's profound. Very profound.' There had always been something unhinged about him. I blamed our parents.

'Don't you want to know where our dad is? And if we have other family elsewhere? We could have a whole bunch of them out there.'

'Emmy's a big influence on you, isn't she?'

'Now that I've found Mum, I'm going to search for Dad.' His mouth twitched. 'Mum hasn't a clue where he is now. But I'll find him.'

I stuck my index fingers in my ears. 'I don't want to talk about this anymore.'

He got up. 'I'm going for a smoke.'

He left me staring at an oil canvas hanging above the fireplace, painted in pastel hues. It was of an older woman, nude save for a paisley-printed headscarf tied around her forehead. I gazed at her breasts. They were saggy like used teabags. I wondered if she had children and how many. And if she still saw them.

A few minutes later I joined him as he sat on the back doorstep smoking his joint.

Shivering with cold, I perched beside him. 'I need to go.'

'So soon?' He slipped an arm around me.

'Jim's parents are coming for lunch.' I took the joint from him and took a drag, spluttering as the harshness hit my throat. I took another puff and passed it back to him.

'Didn't think you smoked anymore.'

I shrugged. 'Not since I last saw you.' I coughed, nausea swirling my stomach.

'Do you ever think about that night in Hamburg?' he asked.

'Where did that come from?'

We hadn't spoken about Hamburg for years. After he had left me on the wall that night, I'd trailed the endless markets looking for him, everything racing around me as though I was watching life on fast forward. A stocky man, wearing a skull ring on the middle finger of his left hand, approached me speaking words I couldn't understand, then followed me and chased me when I started running. Sidestepping into the gaps between the bedecked huts, I managed to dodge him. Once I'd outmanoeuvred him, I ran back to the wall to wait for Ben. But Skull Ring Man reappeared only minutes later. I launched myself off that wall like a rocket and legged it back to the B&B.

After calming down, I'd knocked on Diane and Peter's door and told them Ben and I were back. Then, for what had seemed like forever, I waited for him. I lay in bed staring at the numerous pictures of historical ships, sailing on choppy waters, that decorated the small, stuffy room like wallpaper, and listening to people, full of pre-Christmas cheer, spilling out of the surrounding bars into the cold night.

'I've been thinking about it a lot lately,' he said, staring out to the garden where a robin was pecking at a fat ball attached to the fence. 'It still haunts me.'

At some point, I'd heard a key turn in the lock. Ben staggered in, a jumble of expletives stumbling out of his mouth like the drunks from the bars below. Splotches of blood surrounded a slash scoring the right side of his neck, and he was holding a bloodstained knife. I dragged him into the bathroom. More drunks rolled in through the front door of the B&B. We listened to them crashing and slurring their way to bed as he scrubbed the knife until it gleamed like a trophy in the dim bathroom light.

He passed the joint back to me. 'Best not think about it then,' I said, taking another drag.
'Don't you ever worry that it'll all come back to haunt us? That one day that knife will be dredged up from the canals?'

I'd snatched my coat and then the knife and slipped out of the B&B like a ninja, heading for the canal. I remember the trees lining the water's edge, and the wind rustling through the leaves as though it were whispering at me, 'Silly girl. Silly girl.' Two women had sauntered past in miniskirts and stilettos, speaking German. I'd glanced behind me, so did one of them, so I'd stepped up my pace until they were out of sight. When I reached a secluded spot along the banks of the canal I sat down, dangling my legs over the side of the concrete, shaking more than the leaves on the trees were. Despite the temperature, the water hadn't frozen over. I sneaked a look around me – then another. Apart from the start-stop sound of the odd passing bus in the distance, and hoots of laughter from nighttime revellers, all was quiet. Thinking I was safely out of view, I removed the knife from my pocket and dropped it into the flowing waterway.

'It was ten years ago, Ben. They couldn't trace it back to us. Not now.'

'What's wrong with you two, today?' Diane had asked at breakfast the following morning. Ben's face was ashen; mine too, probably. His hood was pulled up, covering all evidence of his unfortunate night. At the airport I'd bought the local newspaper, and when we got home we combed through it with the aid of Ben's German dictionary, like a pair of amateur sleuths. We found the article at the bottom of page two. Thank goodness for the armed robbery that had taken place on the opposite side of town. Otherwise, it could well have made the front page.

> A hunt is underway for a knife
> attacker who stabbed a man in
> a grapple in the city centre last
> night. The victim was taken to
> hospital where he underwent
> surgery for his injuries.

I handed the joint back to him. 'You smoke too much of this shit.'

'Maybe,' he said, taking another drag. 'What're you up to for the rest of the day?'

I sighed heavily. 'Jim's parents are going to see some friends in London, so they're dropping in for lunch beforehand. What're they like? Do you remember them? I don't at all.'

He looked to the sky, deep in thought. 'He's a doctor, right?'

I nodded.

'And she's a nurse?'

'A midwife. But they're both retired now.'

'I can't remember much about him, but I vaguely recall her. She was one of those mums who always wore a pinny and did arty crafty things with Jim and his sisters.'

'Before I go, quick question – how well do you know Jim's friend Dan?'

'Dan?' he repeated.

I nodded.

He took a long hard drag of the joint, twitching as the fix hit his lungs. He took another drag as though he needed it to loosen his memory. 'Those two have been mates forever. I've not seen Dan for years, though, but he's a good bloke from what I can remember. Bit of a party animal. Doesn't take life too seriously. Why?'

'I think our paths have crossed before, but I can't remember when.'

'Maybe when we hung out at Jim's place as kids?'

I shrugged. 'Maybe. There's something about him that really creeps me out.' I rested my head on his shoulder. 'I don't want Tammy to come between us.'

He leaned his head on mine. 'Nothing will ever come between us, Sis.'

'I need to go,' I said, sitting up. 'Tell Emmy I'm sorry about yesterday. I'd love to meet her again and get to know her.'

'She understood. My fault, anyway. I should have told you when we were on our own.' He walked me to the front door. 'Eva,' he called after I'd reached the road, 'it's time to build bridges.'

I thought momentarily before looking back and calling out, 'Tell me, how do you build a bridge across the Pacific Ocean?' I repositioned my headphones and started running, my pulse racing through me like the wind in my hair.

I couldn't keep up my normal pace for long. As I crossed the road along Clapham High Street, I thought my legs might let me down. I grabbed the railings and stumbled along to a black bin where I stood for a while, waiting for the nausea to pass. I knew I shouldn't have touched that joint.

As I walked the rest of the way home, I replayed our conversation over and over in my mind. But it failed to sink in.

Cancer.

The sun had come out. It was a crisp winter's day, but a dark cloud hung over me. Cars slushed past, spraying my leggings with wet muck. It was all such a mess. How could he ever think I'd want to see Tammy Mitchell again, let alone begin to forgive her?

She left me.

She left me.

Chapter 7

EVA

Arriving home, I found Jim was in the kitchen, preparing a risotto. The smell turned my stomach. I went straight to the fridge and grabbed a bottle of water, gulping it down in one. 'My parents will be here soon,' he said, grabbing my arm as I passed. 'You look pale,' he said, kissing my cheek.

'I've been to see Ben.'

He raised his eyebrows. 'And?' He pulled me into him while he ladled stock into the rice.

'I'll update you later. I felt queasy on the way home. Probably something to do with the afternoon ahead. Meeting the parents can never be a completely gratifying affair. Even if they did know you as a child.'

'It won't be that bad.'

'How long are they staying? Jason texted me. Two people have called in sick. He wants me in at five.'

'They'll be gone well before then. Does that mean you will finish earlier?' he asked, a glint in his eyes.

'Fat chance. I'll be there until closing.' Suddenly hungry, I helped myself to a slice of buttered French stick. 'What time are they due?'

He glanced at his watch. 'In half an hour.'

'I'd best get in the shower, then.' I tried to free myself from his grip, but he pulled me back.

'You'll be fine. They'll love you as much as I do. Well, my mother will. I've warned you what a cantankerous old git my father can be.' He arched his eyebrows and grinned. 'Don't say I didn't warn you.'

I headed up to the shower, slouching under the powerful spray, trying to wash the fear, anger and pain from my pores.

She left me.

And although I had tried for years not to let it hurt, it still did.

After Hamburg – as Ben ended up in fight after fight – they put us into therapy. The busybodies who meddled in our lives said we needed healing. Family counselling, they called it – a collection of ardent psychologists giving their maximum to help us deal with our dysfunctional childhood.

'Do you know you can colour your emotions, Ben? You too, Eva. Put a colour to how you're feeling and learn the trigger points that the colours represent. You can then learn how best to deal with them,' one psychologist, Dr Sedgwick, told us. A lanky older man, he had school-uniform-grey hair and a wardrobe of clothing to match. His office, or "discussion lounge" as he insisted upon calling it, was as grey as he was. Wallpaper the colour of dolphin skin covered all four walls, and the sofa we wasted numerous frustrated hours upon was ashen like his face.

He cleared his throat as he handed Ben a laminated disc with the colours of the rainbow arranged in seven segments. Within each segment, shades of the colour darkened until they all merged into a black circle in the centre. Each layer of colour owned an emotion. Ben, his eyes red and cheeks gaunt, smirked with contempt before tossing it into my lap.

Each colour of the wheel detailed a feeling and the black centre the extreme states of existence: hysterical, enraged, loathing and bitterness. Each session, when asked to express his feelings in colour, a lethargic and contemptuous Ben would call out colours to shut Dr Sedgwick up.

'Cerise,' Ben shouted for cranky, or 'champagne' for confused, or 'brown' for bored.

He overused brown, much to Dr Sedgwick's annoyance and our amusement. Never did he select the positive colours in the green arena: emerald for exuberant, pine for peacefulness, jade for jovial. And never would he venture anywhere near the cyan section depicting contentment.

During the sixth or seventh session, while we were discussing our parents, Dr Sedgwick fixed his eyes on me. He tapped his silver pen on the palm of his hand. 'What about your mother, Eva? What colours do you wish to express with thoughts of her in mind?'

He shifted in his seat and loosened his tie as I hissed the bitter, enraged, hysterical loathing of the black inner circle.

She left me.

Richard and Sarah arrived as I was coming down the stairs after my shower. Sarah, short and small-boned, with the elegance of a songbird, greeted me like a long lost child. 'Eva, how wonderful to see you again after all these years.' She held out her slender arms and embraced me. 'She hasn't changed, has she, Richard?' She squeezed my hand.

Richard, towering over her, removed his coat and gloves, ignoring her question. He cleared his throat and nodded at me.

'I was thinking on the way over, we last saw you when you were about three. You were such a cute child.' She gave my hand another squeeze. 'Even after twenty years, you're still as beautiful as ever. Isn't she, Richard?'

He was a broad man, and, apart from a forehead frown so deep he had two grooves that looked like the number 11 etched between his bushy eyebrows, Jim certainly got his looks from him. He ignored Sarah's question and extended his arm to Jim. After they shook hands, Richard with seeming reluctance held out his hand to me. It was cold and clammy. A bit like the feeling in the air. *This is going to be a long afternoon.*

We made our way to the kitchen, Sarah chatting away about the drive over and the beastly weather. She talked a lot, I noticed, as the afternoon progressed. In fact, if talking were an Olympic sport, she would be a triple gold medallist. 'Smells wonderful, James. Tarragon?' she asked, hugging her son. 'You know how much I love tarragon. I remember teaching you to cook risotto when you were a teenager. It always was your favourite dish.'

She sure made up for her husband's reluctance to part with words, which I found odd considering Richard was a retired GP. When she excused herself to go to the toilet, and Jim busied himself serving up the risotto, I struggled to get much from Richard. Until, after curt replies to my various questions, bingo, I called the winning subject. 'What do you do in your spare time?' I asked.

I was sure his lips briefly curled upwards as he began to

tell me about the voluntary role he carried out at his local surgery. 'I spend three half-days there per week,' he said. 'Which invariably turn into full days.'

'Do you still see patients?' I couldn't imagine facing him with a medical problem.

'Oh, no. I'm spearheading a mentoring scheme I've devised for GP doctors and nurses.'

'How interesting.'

'It was a success at my current practice, so I rolled it out to six other practices in the surrounding villages. I'm now implementing it in every GP surgery in Surrey. They need all the support they can get in these times of ever-worsening conditions. Plans are afoot to roll it out nationwide after that.' Without pausing for breath, he briefed me on the state of the NHS and the resulting mental health issues affecting practitioners.

'Father's been nominated for an MBE,' Jim called out. 'Tell Eva about it, Father.'

Richard cleared his throat before telling me about his nomination for services to improving the holistic wellbeing of medical staff.

"Always seek the good in people", Gill had taught me. She would award me full marks here.

As Jim served up his perfectly-cooked risotto, Sarah began to pry. 'James told me Ben's been to see your mum. How did it go?'

Inwardly, I sighed. He hadn't wasted much time.

Jim shot me a look of apology.

'So-so. She's not well,' I said.

'James told me.' She reached aside and touched my hand. 'I'm dreadfully sorry to hear that. Is she having treatment?'

'Chemotherapy. They want to shrink the tumour so they can operate and get it all out.'

'Will you go and see her? I understand why you may be hesitant. It's been hard for you, all these years, but I have to say, Tammy was such a pleasing woman when she worked for us. We missed her after she left, didn't we, Richard?' She turned to her husband, but he didn't reply. He studied his food, tapping his fork on the side of the plate as if miles away.

She continued, 'She adored James, Christina and Victoria. Seven or so years she was with us.'

'Jim said she was kind,' I said.

'Very much so.'

She then made a point of recalling when Tammy had made her last biannual trek with Ben and me to see them, some twenty years before. 'Tammy was perturbed, panicked, not her usual self. I did wonder if she was in a spot of bother.'

'What was wrong with her?' I asked, to be polite. I'd have preferred her to change the subject.

She shrugged. 'I commented on something about Ben's shoes. Not sure what exactly. She got upset, and I never did find out why. For months, I called and wrote her letters, but we never saw or heard from her again.'

Why? I wanted to ask, but Jim steered the conversation towards the friends they were going to see that afternoon, and Richard excused himself to go to the toilet.

Sarah reached across the table and patted Jim's hand. 'I want you to have a word with your father, James.'

'What about?' Jim asked, offering up the last of the risotto.

'He's considering taking a part-time position at Surrey University, teaching undergraduate biology. In addition to that private consultation work he's taken on for a lawyer; medical negligence claims.'

'Whatever for?'

'He says we need the money. I want to go on a cruise. It's our ruby wedding anniversary next year which I think calls for celebration. All my life, I've wanted to go on a cruise.'

'I would've thought that a retired doctor's pension would cover all your needs.'

'Pensions aren't what they used to be. Or so he keeps telling me. He deals with all that side of things. You know me. I just spend what he transfers to my bank account each month.'

'Do you need some money?'

'Don't be silly.'

'I'll sort you a cruise. It could be your anniversary present,' Jim suggested.

She shook her head. 'You've given us enough in the past. I won't hear of it. Don't buy us a thing. I just think your father should take it easy now.'

'Getting out of the house more might improve his moods.'

'James, come on.'

'Don't come on me. You know exactly what I mean.'

'Maybe you could have a quiet word with him. Tell him he needs to slow down.'

'Could do. Not sure what good it would do, though.'

The rest of the afternoon dragged worse than the uni lecture on equity and trusts I'd had to endure earlier in the week. I tried to engage Richard in further conversations, but he wasn't interested, making me feel like the new girl at school trying to impress but failing miserably short of her intentions.

'Get Ben to send Tammy my regards, will you?' Sarah said as she was leaving. 'And tell him, please, when he's free to do come and visit us. It'd be such a pleasure to see him after so long. Tammy too.'

Richard managed a nod in my direction as he left, but that was all.

'He sure is hard work,' I said as Jim closed the front door. 'I don't think he likes me.'

'Don't be silly. He's always been that way.'

'Why?'

'When I was a kid, he slipped a disc, and he's suffered acute back pain ever since. Mother said he never fully recovered. You'll get used to him.'

From what I'd observed that afternoon, I wasn't sure I wanted to.

Chapter 8

EVA

The next day, I'd just finished a breakfast shift at Marco's. A new idea of Jason's. 'Breakfast before shopping. Let's give it a go for December,' he'd said, forever seeking ways to make an extra tenner. Usually, I worked the lunchtime shift on Sundays, but he'd asked me to swap to breakfasts for the time being. I was drinking a quick coffee when Jim stopped by to walk me home. The same as he had every Sunday afternoon since I'd started working there. Before we became a couple he used it as an excuse to spend time with me, something I later got him to admit over a bottle of red at a table for two.

Jim planted himself on the stool next to me. 'Guess what?' he said, 'I'm flying to New York this evening.'

My posture stiffened. *What about our trip to Paris?*

'I'll be back Friday. Warren called this morning. There are problems out there that he wants me to go and fix. Issues with clients pulling their accounts.'

'Sounds like just the opportunity you've been waiting for.' I tried to sound enthusiastic, but disappointment coated my tone.

'I'm so sorry, but I must do this. I'll make it up to you. I promise. I'll rearrange Paris. We can go in the summer or spring. Paris is beautiful in the springtime.'

Damn Warren Price. I'd met him a few weeks previously when waiting for Jim in the reception of their Mayfair offices. After about twenty minutes of flicking through *The Economist*, they had both appeared from the lift engrossed in a head-to-head like a couple of conspirators. Jim introduced us, and Warren held out his hand to me. Gold glinted from the cuffs of his crisp white shirt. 'Pleased to meet you,' he said in a grammar school voice, then turned to Jim. 'See you in the morning. I've asked Janita to book the meeting room for seven and get coffee and croissants in. We can prep in my office beforehand. Must dash.' And off he'd strolled to a waiting cab to take him to a client dinner.

'Let me get this right.' I dropped my head to one side, frowning. 'Warren calls you on a Sunday and expects you to drop everything and board a plane. Just like that?'

'Afraid so. Something's going down over there, and it needs sorting.'

'And that's OK? Being a puppet on a string that dances to his tunes?'

He stroked some loose strands of my hair and tucked them behind my ear. 'For now. You'll be the same when you get out there in the big corporate world.'

'I most definitely won't.' I meant it. I didn't like the rules to succeed in his game. You had to dive in perfectly vertical and prepare for the struggle to the surface, aware that not everyone made it. I'd gone into law for two reasons. Justice and security. To empower me to rid the world of evil, and so I'd never be hungry again like I so often was as a child. I saw myself in a courtroom, fighting for justice or nabbing another criminal in the police rather than in the corporate world.

'When will you be back?' I swallowed the lump in the back of my throat threatening to embarrass me. My feelings for him were often overwhelming. I'd never felt this way about anyone before.

'I've asked Janita to book the red-eye for this Friday. I'll still be able to make dinner. I got us a table by the way.'

'When do you go?'

'A car is picking me up in an hour.'

I rolled my eyes, uncurled my legs and slid off the barstool. 'We'd better get home, then,' I said, winking.

Outside, our breath formed small clouds as we slushed our way home through what remained of the snow. Shivering, I buttoned my coat against the wintry chill.

'You still haven't told me fully how it went with Ben yesterday.'

'She's got cancer. She's having chemo. That's all there is to tell.'

'Does it change anything?' he asked.

'What do you mean?'

Fresh snowflakes floated into our faces. He drew me closer. 'She has cancer. I guess that must make you see things differently.'

'No. It changes nothing at all.'

'What if she dies, like, I don't know... next week?'

'So what?'

He jolted away from me. 'Heck, Eva, that's harsh, even for this situation.'

I shoved my hands in my pockets. He was right. 'I can't help how I feel. This has all come out of nowhere. In twenty-four hours, my life has been turned completely upside down, and there's nothing I can do about it. Anyway, don't judge me. You don't know what I went through growing up without parents.'

'I'm not judging you. I can't even begin to imagine.' He linked his arm through mine. 'My parents have always been there for me. Even if my father is a miserable old bugger, he's still always there.' He snorted. 'Although I often wished he wasn't, so I can kinda understand how you feel.'

'Ben's home. My mother has appeared. And now you're going away.'

'I'll be home before you know it. Dan's around. He can look after you.'

'I can look after myself, thank you.'

At home, we passionately kissed our way up the stairs. As soon as the bedroom door banged shut, we ripped each other's clothes off, leaving them puddled on the floor. He laid me gently on the bed and made love to me with the usual uncontrollable emotion I'd grown to find an addiction.

The doorbell rang. 'That'll be my ride.' We untangled ourselves, and he kissed me hard. 'I'm glad I packed earlier.' We quickly pulled on our clothes and headed down the stairs.

'Phone as soon as you get there,' I said, opening the door. That's when, unexpectedly, the realisation hit that I wouldn't see him for five days. Five whole days. Standing at the door, looking at him, I felt a sudden urge to tell him that he couldn't go. He had to call Warren and tell him to stick it. 'Be safe. I love you,' I said, another lump swelling in my throat. What was happening to me? I'd always been so fiercely independent. I had an unfettered spirit, Gill had always told me. I followed him down the steps to a chauffeur-driven car, my heart pulling at the knots in my stomach.

The driver stepped out, took Jim's case and opened the boot. 'Heathrow?'

'That's right.'

I stood waving goodbye long after the car had turned the corner.

An unfamiliar longing stung my eyes. I could remember only feeling like that when forced to say goodbye to Ben.

My weekend had gone from a car crash to a pile-up at a very high speed.

*

Determined to get my assignments finished before Jim returned at the end of the week, I scanned my workload and tried to tackle an essay on consumer law. But the Sale of Goods Act wasn't selling it to me, so I didn't get far before Ben called wanting to speak about Tammy again. 'You need to find forgiveness, Eva.'

'Leave it,' I told him. I'd locked her in a box and I wasn't sure when, or if, I'd ever want to find the key.

Restless, I went to make a cuppa. As I reached the kitchen, a tall, slender woman I'd never seen before startled me. She had a healthy tan and a blonde bob which bounced as she sauntered towards the doorway. A man's pinstriped shirt covered her body, and there was no mistaking that was all she wore. Dan, wearing a pair of boxers and bed head, jigged behind, holding her slender waist like they were dancing the conga. His eyes met mine. 'Eva. This is Lenka.'

'Hi,' I mumbled.

Lenka nodded and flashed a complement of dazzling white teeth, but didn't utter a single word. I leaned against the wall, allowing them to pass, coughing at the whiff of sweat and duvet. Dan released his hands from her waist and stopped in front of me. I could smell the previous night's beer on his breath. 'Are you OK? I heard Jim leave earlier.' He glanced at his watch. 'He should be at the airport now?'

A burning sensation crept from my neck to my jaw. 'That's right.'

'I'm around most evenings this week if you need anything.'

I pressed myself into the wall as though I wanted it to swallow me. *What is it about him?* 'I'll be fine.'

He started to say something, but stopped himself. Instead he smiled, and followed Lenka, glancing back as he trailed her giggles down the hallway.

I went back upstairs and tried to get on with my work. 'Get a grip, Eva,' I mumbled to myself as procrastination took the form of staring at a scribbled attempt of an essay plan on constitutional law, hoping it would go away. It was as though Jim had taken my concentration with him when he'd left for that plane. Impulsively, I threw down my books and found my coat and backpack. I felt a desperate need to see Gill. She'd understand. She always had.

*

At Liverpool Street, I queued for coffee from the kiosk by platform 5, but when I found myself at the front of the line, wafts of cocoa and sticky bakes enticed me to change my order to a cup of hot chocolate and a caramel brownie. A woman and her daughter waited behind me, discussing their day like two best friends. I glanced back at them, pretending to look over their heads at the departures board. Bags of shopping surrounded their feet, and the mum was ruffling her daughter's hair.

The girl was about eight years old, on the cusp of dissolving childhood innocence. 'Mummy, shall we take something home for Daddy and Jack?'

The mum moved her hand to caress her daughter's cheek. 'How kind of you to think of them.'

The girl clutched her mum's elbow as their conversation flowed to hectic plans for the days ahead: present wrapping, cake icing and mince pie making between visits from various friends and family.

I thought about what could have been, and stuffed the brownie into my mouth.

Travellers on their way to Stansted Airport packed the train, and luggage blocked the aisles, so I found myself squashed against the doors with two teenagers smooching next to me. The girl, her hair in plaits and a ring through her button nose, was propped against the door, and the guy kept pulling on her scarf to draw her mouth towards his. I kept glancing at them, thinking of Jim, willing myself to stop counting the minutes until his plane was due to land back at Heathrow.

The train juddered out of the station towards Essex. I wiped away the condensation misting the window, thinking about Gill as I watched graffiti-covered council flats turn to green fields and impressive houses. I met Gill shortly before my sixteenth birthday. If a God does exist, then, that was the day He came into my troubled life. She was the foster parent who treated me like her own. The train chugged along the line, Cambridge-bound. I leaned my forehead against the window and whispered the advice Gill gave to me one night. Words that became my mantra.

'Only you can choose which fork in the road to take. Flourish or fail. Victory or victim. It's up to you.'

I hopped off the train at Stansted airport. The rush swept me into the terminal where I queued for a cab. When it pulled up at Gill's crooked cottage with its leaded window and timber beams that protruded randomly across its exterior, she was standing on the doorstep – same Adidas tracksuit, same unkempt hairstyle, and same stalwart smile. I paid the driver and opened the garden gate with an overwhelming sense of relief. I was home: roaring fires and cocoa in mugs, proper meals and comforting words, love and hope.

Stamping the snow off of my boots, I flung my arms open wide. 'Happy birthday.'

'Oh, thank you, sweet girl. It's so wonderful to see you. I've missed you so much,' she said, slipping the taxi fare into my hand. Releasing her grip, she looked me up and down. 'Something's not right with you. This university life, is it suiting you?'

'Don't ask.' I removed my scarf and coat, joggling off flakes of snow.

She arranged them on the radiator. 'The kettle's boiling.'

I took her gift out of my backpack and followed her into the kitchen. A small room comprising an assortment of freestanding units which didn't match. At its heart stood a pine dresser, painted powder green with a distressed finish, holding her collection of hand-decorated jugs, all standing in order of size. She'd made a cake – lemon drizzle – my favourite.

I swallowed hard. 'You always know what I need.' I took two plates from the dresser.

'How's that lovely man of yours?' she asked.

'He's gone to New York.'

'With work?'

'Yes. He's desperate for his next promotion. I hope you've got lots of photos of your trip?'

She kept steering the conversation in my direction, asking me questions about uni and workload. Reaching for the sugar bowl, she held up a spoon. 'You taking one or two these days?'

My voice cracked. 'Half please.'

She placed the sugar bowl on the table. 'What's wrong, Eva?'

She knew me too well, but then why wouldn't she? I'd lived with her for five years. 'I think I need to go and see Dr Barratta again.'

She slapped her hands against her cheeks. 'Whatever's happened?'

'*He's* back.'

'Eva! Why?'

'Ben came home at the weekend.' I swallowed hard, my hands shaking. 'He's found Tammy, and she's got cancer, and he wants me to go and see her.'

She sighed and nodded towards the lounge. 'Come, let's take our tea to the sofa.'

Chapter 9

EVA

One week turned into more than two, and on the day Jim was due home, adverse weather delayed his flight by over six hours. But that turned out to be an advantage. I still had two assignments to finish, plus I'd booked a GP appointment for the persistent cold and sickness that had refused to budge since he'd gone. The receptionist had granted me a ten-minute slot which lasted no longer than two. After taking my temperature, and poking a wooden stick down my throat, a look of distaste engulfed the doctor's face as if his professionalism had taken a mid-morning coffee break. 'At this time of year, we see various bugs doing the rounds. Take some paracetamol and make sure you rest.'

It wasn't until later, after I'd taken a shower, that it registered. As I tried to pull on the skinny red jeans I'd not worn for a while, the zip wouldn't budge past half-way.

I froze. I couldn't be. After an initial panic, I finished dressing then dashed to the chemist. Little change from a tenner confirmed my fears. *This wasn't meant to happen.*

When Jim arrived home, after making up for lost time in the bedroom, we went to the kitchen. I made us coffee.

'Come on, then. Tell me, what's up?'

He knew me too well.

Placing our drinks on the table, he straddled the bench alongside the kitchen table. He gently pulled me down beside him and fed me a chunk of Toblerone he'd bought from duty-free. An impressive bright red chandelier hung above the table, housing twelve candle bulbs and circled by an array of fake red gems like oversized translucent rubies. I'd always loved the way it bounced light around the room, but that evening it felt like a spotlight on my emotional state. I plonked my elbows on the table and my heavy head in my hands. 'I'm pregnant.'

*

He took the next day off work. We hopped on the Underground to Hatton Gardens and skipped back on with a three carat, brilliant cut solitaire on the third finger of my left hand. The faulty lighting on the Tube caused flashing sparkles to race around the carriage like fireworks as the train rattled along.

'I don't want to wait; let's get married now,' Jim whispered in my ear later that day as we lay wrapped in each other's arms under hot and sweaty sheets.

I propped myself up on one elbow. 'What's the rush?'

He stroked my face. 'I want you to be my wife now. I can't wait. Before our baby's born. What do you think?'

*

On Christmas morning, we drove to Surrey to see his family. As we hit the M3, snow began to fall, which, along with the constant flashing of red ahead, prevented Jim from driving at his usual speed, which wasn't a bad thing. My stomach couldn't have taken it. 'I'll announce it at dinner. Take the ring off until then,' he said as we crossed a bridge over the River Wey and passed through a tunnel of trees.

'My childhood territory,' Jim said as we entered a quintessential English village blessed with patches of green, an abundance of detached, gated houses, and four pubs, but little else.

My mouth shaped into a big O as we passed an illuminated placard displaying the name Elm House and pulled into the circular driveway of his family home.

'You grew up in a mansion,' I said of the double-fronted Victorian house embellished with a curtain of icicle lights.

He switched off the ignition and laughed. 'I wouldn't go that far.' He released the buckle of his seatbelt, reached across and kissed me and then my belly.

'It's even got its own name.' I gazed around in wonder. 'The drive is big enough for a mini car park. And no one would blame you for driving if you needed a favour from the neighbours.'

He kissed me again. 'I love you, Mrs Barnes-to-be. More than you know. Come on, let's go and see how my father reacts to this.'

'What do you mean?' I asked as I slipped off my engagement ring and handed it to him.

'No girl has ever been good enough for me, but now he's got no choice.'

Sarah stood waving on the steps, her svelte frame swaying in time to her slender hand. She wore a sage green pleated dress and her auburn hair was tied in a bun. Escaped wisps edged her delicate face. I climbed out of the car, and she hurried over and embraced me. 'Merry Christmas, Eva. So wonderful to see you again.'

As we entered the bright and spacious hallway, decked with real ivy and sprigs of shiny holly, Richard was messing about with something in the drawer of an antique cabinet. He stopped and held out his liver-spotted hand to greet Jim. 'Happy Christmas,' he muttered to us both, then abruptly turned and wandered off towards the back of the house.

Jim raised his eyebrows and smirked. 'See what I mean?'

Sarah fussed over us. 'Make yourself at home, Eva. Anything you want, help yourself. Now, what can I get you two to drink?' she asked, taking our coats. We settled with a cuppa to start, and with one hand on my back, Jim steered me to the buzz coming from the lounge. We passed Richard in his study. He was sitting at a large oak desk, writing. Books and papers cluttered the desk and skew-whiff piles of files leaned against the side. It was dark in there, a half-drawn blind keeping out the dying daylight. I shivered as Jim pulled me along to where his sister Christina's four boisterous children were bursting with the magic of Christmas. Like an army of reindeer, they all charged over to Jim, chanting, 'Uncle Jim! Uncle Jim! Look what Santa brought us.'

The lounge was beautiful, if old-fashioned, like something out of one of those homes and gardens magazines you see in surgery waiting rooms. Since forever, whenever I'd gone to the doctors, I always sought that type of magazine, wondering who lived in the houses on display. I'd peruse through them in awe, imagining myself living in the rooms splashed across the glossy pages.

Looking through the large French doors fringed by elaborate curtains, the snow-covered fields looked like the setting for a Christmas card. A pine tree stood in the corner of the room, perfectly dressed with a fairy on top. But she didn't look right. Her head and shoulders were squashed up against the ceiling, and her arms were bent back, making her appear disjointed. A bit how I felt in the Barnes' perfect abode.

Christina hugged Jim, and I heard her whisper, 'Thanks for the money. I love you, bruv.' She then turned to me and hugged me tightly, too, which felt a little odd. As far as I was concerned, I'd never met the woman. 'Eva, great to see you again. It's been too long. Do you remember coming here as a child?'

I shook my head. 'Jim tells me stories, but I can't recall any of them.'

'You were too young, I suppose. Vic and I loved it when Tammy brought you and Ben to see us. In the summer we played in the garden. Remember? The swing? You must remember the swing? You insisted on me pushing you for hours and hours. And you loved painting and drawing. Mother would get the craft boxes out, and we'd have a competition to see who made the best picture. You don't remember any of it?'

'Sorry, no.'

'She was too young,' Jim said. 'Of course she can't remember.'

'I'll fill you in. We had such fun together.' She carried on talking like she'd never stop, reminiscing about eventful days of which I had no recollection. Eventually, she turned her attention to Jim, and I stood and listened as they chatted. They shared the same olive skin and snub noses, I noticed, but where his hair was dark, hers was as blonde as mine. And as a total contrast, their sister Vic's was pumpkin orange. Jim had once shown me a picture of the three of them. I remember him pointing to their hair and telling me how friends had often teased his mother about having entertained the milkman during her childbearing years, much to his father's indignation.

Amid the scent of pine and burning logs, Richard appeared tut-tutting and arranged a laptop on the mahogany coffee table. He pinched a pleat of material at the knees of his trousers and sat down on a leather wingback chair, clearing his throat. 'Vic time,' he called out, and everyone gathered around to Skype Vic in Australia. What had started as a gap year for their youngest, labouring her way around the world solo with a modest bank account and over-packed backpack, was cut short by an unplanned kid. Followed a year later by a mortgage and a marriage, and to a man who wasn't even the father, much to Richard's disgust and Sarah's distress.

After the call, Christina's husband, Adam, poured drinks as the family gathered around the piano. Christina pounded out a medley of traditional carols. When Adam passed me a generous glass of wine, I let out such a massive sigh of relief that I waited for everyone to turn and glare. And then I remembered I shouldn't be drinking and sighed again.

'We all need something to get through days at Elm House,' Adam whispered with a sarcastic laugh before moving on to serve drinks to his kids. A clean-shaven, tidy hair, jumper and tie kind of guy, he wasn't as straight as his appearance suggested.

'How long before dinner?' Richard called across to Sarah. He was still sitting in the wing chair, one knee over the other, tapping a folded newspaper on one of the arms.

'I'm almost ready to dish up,' she replied, coming to stand beside me.

'I'm hungry,' Richard said.

'Won't be long now.' Sarah placed a hand on my shoulder. 'Do join in, dear. I'm so delighted you made it today.'

I turned to her warm and gentle smile. 'Me too,' I said. I didn't mean it, but hey, it was Christmas.

She tidied her bun – which didn't need it – as she asked me about Tammy. I politely answered her questions, and then she left me humming along to the piano. Jim came to stand beside me, bouncing one of his nieces on his shoulders, both of them singing along to the carols. He took my hand and whispered, 'I love you,' and I told him, 'You too.'

It was a wholesome family affair, so foreign to me. But before long – I should have known it would come – the opening verse of 'Silent Night' trickled from the ivories.

'Where's the toilet?' I asked, and followed Jim's directions to the downstairs loo, leaving behind haunting echoes of 'Round yon virgin, mother and child.'

Mother and child.

I leaned against the sink, sweating like it was a summer's day. Sarah's voice thumped in my ear: 'Tammy was such a lovely woman', 'We missed her after she left.' My heart was in overdrive, pounding in my ears like a heavy drumbeat. Hands tightened around my neck. It was happening again. *No. No. Breathe, Eva.* I ripped off my cardigan. I only had a short-sleeved dress on underneath – one that Jim had given me gift-wrapped with a bow earlier that morning – but drops of sweat were dripping down my back and between my breasts. I splashed cold water over my face then sat on the toilet to regain control. I glanced around. Pictures of the Barnes family covered the walls. Single shots and collages of family holidays stared back at me. I looked closer. There was one of a group of kids around the kitchen table. Several years ago, by the look of the décor. I took a closer look. It was Jim and his sisters and Dan, I was sure. Ben too? Yes, there was Tammy in the background, behind the kitchen counter busy with an electric mixer.

It took several deep breaths before I could return to everyone gathered around the table. I'd never seen anything like it. Gold serviettes, folded in gilt napkin holders, lay beside each plate, and an elegant vase filled with red roses, poinsettia and evergreen branches formed the centrepiece. The crystal glasses shone as if Sarah had stayed awake all night polishing them, and amongst the crockery, she'd sprinkled golden stars. A table dressed for royalty.

But even royal families have their problems.

I took the seat between Jim and Richard which Jim had saved for me. 'Where've you been?' he asked with a frown, his hand caressing my shoulder.

Sarah appeared, balancing serving plates like an experienced waitress. 'Don't be shy. There's more of everything.' She unloaded various platters of perfection, fussing and clucking like a mother hen. Adam poured the wine.

'Where's the bread sauce?' Richard asked.

'I forgot it,' Sarah said, getting flustered.

'I'll get it,' Jim said.

'No, no, you sit there and enjoy your dinner. I'll fetch it.'

'Mother, I insist.'

We passed dishes around, everyone loading their plates as if they'd not eaten for a week. Jim returned with the bread sauce and handed the jug to Richard. Then, picking up a spoon, Jim tapped it repeatedly on his wine glass like a master of ceremonies. 'Listen up, everyone. I've got something to announce.' The room went silent as he pulled me up to stand beside him. 'I've asked this beautiful woman to be my wife, and we're having a baby.'

Cheers broke out around the table. Jim replaced the ring on my finger. 'What wonderful news,' Sarah said, sliding out of her chair and dashing to hug me. Christina followed suit, and the kids all jumped up and down in excitement. Richard stayed seated, a look of shock engulfing his face, but at least he managed a mumbled congratulations, an extra hand-shake for Jim and a nod for me.

'We need champagne,' Sarah cried. 'I'll get some after everyone has what they need.'

We pulled crackers and shared jokes as everyone donned their paper crowns – everyone except Richard. He un-wrapped his hat but left it on the table. Scowling, he prodded and poked at his food as if annoyed with what Sarah had served.

'Father, this is one for you,' Christina shouted above the kids arguing over a plastic magnifying glass and a miniature pack of playing cards. 'Will you please be quiet,' she said to them, and tossed her cracker joke across the table to me. 'Eva, read this out to Father, will you?'

Richard placed his knife and fork on his plate and started beating his fingers on the table.

'Doctor, doctor I feel like a–'

Not letting me finish, he reached over, whipped the joke from my hand and screwed it up along with his paper hat into the smallest ball he possibly could. A deed which stunned everyone into silence, including me. He then took aim and slung the ball of tissue into a bowl of Brussels sprouts. Collective gasps echoed around the room. Then, without further consideration, he rose to his feet, cleared his throat, and marched from the room, slamming the door behind him.

Chapter 10

EVA

To begin with, I thought it was all part of an act, some kind of Barnes family tradition. Grinning like an idiot, I checked out everyone's reactions, expecting to see laughter. But no, stupid me, the head of the table's peculiar outburst seemed to have dazed everyone. Christina threw her mother a horrified look, but Sarah ignored her as if her daughter were invisible. Picking up the plate of sliced turkey in one hand, and the stuffing in the other, Sarah started talking at a higher octave. 'Seconds, anyone? Do have some extra. James, Eva, fill your plates, please do. There's plenty.'

In an attempt, it seemed, to lighten the mood and dampen the confusion in the air, everyone started talking at once. Everyone seemed to want to ask what was going on but thought better of it. Adam stood to pass around the gravy. Getting to me, he leaned to my ear and whispered, 'You'd better get used to this now that you're planning to hang around.'

'What?' I asked, confused by his statement.

'This is one entertaining family.'

What astounded me more than Richard's untimely and petulant outburst was that after he left the room, everyone carried on as if lobbing things across the table and into the food was tolerable behaviour.

'What's your dad's problem?' I asked Jim later that night when we were in bed.

He scoffed. 'Me.'

'You?'

'That's the conclusion I've come to. He's never quite forgiven me for not following him into the medical profession. All through school, he pushed me to take the sciences. You should've seen how he reacted when I chose English over Physics A level. You'd have thought I'd been expelled for doing drugs.' He moved his hand to my stomach and stroked it. 'He's got worse since he retired. I still can't believe that he served this village as their GP for over thirty years. He's so well respected around here.'

'That's a long time.'

'People still come to him for advice.' He shivered. 'They wouldn't if they'd seen how he's treated his only son all these years. Did you see him hug Christina this morning? With me, it's always been a pat on the back, which at some stage – I can't exactly pinpoint when – turned into a shake of the hand.'

'Where'd he go this evening after the hat in the Brussels incident?'

'Into his study, probably. You'll get used to him.'

'I don't know if I want to.'

He cuddled up to me, and he fell asleep straight away, but I couldn't. I felt sick. One thing I'd learned since becoming pregnant was that morning sickness is not limited to the first part of the day. The heating was on, making me feel hot and sticky, which didn't help. After a while, I switched on the bedside lamp and picked up my current read, *An Introduction to European Union Law*. But after fifteen pages I was no closer to dropping off, so I threw off the covers, opened the sash window, and inhaled some fresh air. I thought I could hear voices arguing, but must have been mistaken. Silence packed the country air – in stark contrast to the night-time rattle and clatter of London life.

I sat on the bed staring around his bedroom, a shrine to his charmed background. Pictures of him with Dan and various friends and his family decorated the walls, displaying all the momentous occasions of his life: school, holidays, sporting achievements on rugby pitches and tennis courts, his eighteenth and twenty-first birthdays. He'd led such a privileged life, which surprisingly filled me with sadness – not for the material things, but for the family unit he'd been fortunate to have.

How different things could have been for Ben and me if Tammy had hung around. I picked up a photo from the bedside table of Jim's graduation day and fingered the glass. His face was bursting with pride, and his mortarboard sat wonky on his head. His whole family were there, smiling. Even his father's lips stretched to a faint grin. I stared closer. Jim didn't look like Sarah at all, but he shared his father's dark eyes and olive skin. I hadn't noticed how much. I placed it back on the bedside table with a heavy heart as I wondered where Ben and I would have ended up living if my parents had cared enough to hang around.

I lay down and closed my eyes, desperately wishing sleep my way, but the icky feeling wouldn't give up. I needed water. Finding an old towelling dressing gown hanging over a pair of checked pyjamas on the back of the door, I crept down to the kitchen. The door sat ajar, spreading a beam of light across the hallway. I could hear talking. It sounded like a radio debate, similar to the programmes Gill used to listen to on Radio 4, but as I tip-toed nearer, I realised it was Richard and Sarah arguing.

I felt cold even though waves of heat kept sweeping through me. I belted the dressing gown around my waist as I heard Richard mention my name. I should've turned and headed back to bed, but I couldn't help but stay and snoop. They were talking about me, after all. I peered through the opening of the door. Sarah and Richard sat at the kitchen table, their backs to me. Richard lifted his cup and took a sip then clinked it back on the saucer. 'It can't happen. We can't go through with this.'

'You're not being rational.' Sarah's tone was calmer, practical, like an adult reasoning with a child.

His voice boomed. 'We must think of a way to put a stop to it. He'll regret it.'

'Calm down, it's not up to you.' She tried to put an arm around him, but he brushed her off.

'It's all wrong. She's too young, and he'll get hurt.'

My heart was thumping. *Why does he think I'm going to hurt his son?* How little faith he had in me. I debated walking in and asking him what his problem was, but my mouth felt so dry, I couldn't be sure if anything would come out. Unfortunately, at the moment I decided the time had come to return to bed, I coughed – not loud, but loud enough. They both turned, startled. My knees buckled. I grabbed hold of the architrave to steady myself.

'Who's that?' Sarah called out.

I pushed the door open, cursing myself for getting caught. The smell of leftover turkey and stuffing, along with the shame of being caught, made me gag.

Sarah jumped up. 'Eva.'

'Sorry to bother you, but could I have some water, please?' I said, trying to hide the anxiety in my voice.

Sarah continued talking thirty to the dozen as she walked over to the fridge and pulled out a bottle of Evian. Then another. 'Here, take two, in case you and Jim get thirsty in the night, you never know. Stupid me, I meant to put some water in your room.' She laughed. Not with humour, but with nerves that seemed as frayed as mine. *What is going on?*

'Thank you.' I glared at Richard, debating what to say; but, unsure I could trust what might pour out of my mouth, I lost my nerve. 'See you in the morning.'

Snuggling back up to Jim, I tried to sleep, but couldn't. Richard's words rung in my head like an unwanted morning alarm I couldn't turn off. I thought about waking Jim to tell him about the conversation I'd overheard, but as I looked at him sleeping so soundly, I decided it could wait until morning. Finally succumbing to my exhaustion, I spent the night in a mix of weird dreams involving Richard and Sarah, Tammy and Ben; and Dan, of all people.

In the morning Jim stirred early, caressing my hips while kissing my neck. Rumblings echoed from around the house: distant voices, the front door slamming, and the drone of the hoover. I considered telling Jim about what I'd overheard the previous night, but I didn't want to start an argument between him and his father so I kept quiet, ignoring the gnawing sense of torment slowly chewing away at me.

Right or wrong, that's what I did.

Richard didn't appear until it was time for us to leave, not even for breakfast. 'Why so soon?' he demanded as we put on our coats. 'What's the rush? You hardly know each other.' He looked between the two of us, wagging his index finger as if he were scolding two rebellious teenagers. Facts and figures, of statistical evidence relating to the rate of failed marriages, started to roll from his tongue as if he'd hidden himself away all morning researching and rehearsing to insert such mathematical probabilities into the parting conversation.

'You're young, Eva. Why don't you leave it until you've finished your degree?'

'I will be carrying on with my degree.'

He turned to Jim. 'And what about your career? You don't want to waste the years you've invested in getting to where you are now.'

Waste? I'm pregnant. I'm having his grandchild.

'He really is a grumpy old man, isn't he?' I said to Jim as I climbed into the car.

He scoffed. 'I did warn you. I still can't believe he's been nominated for an MBE. Services to the local community. What about services to his family?' Jim snorted as he put the key in the ignition. 'My mum and he are chalk and cheese, aren't they? I'm amazed they've stayed together this long.'

'She's very much under his control, isn't she?'

'Unfortunately, yes. She's always tried to keep the peace. It can't be healthy for her,' he said, pulling out of the driveway.

'Is he the reason Vic went to Australia?

'I don't think so. She'd planned her round-the-world trip for years.' He frowned. 'But he could be the reason she never came back.' He glanced in his rear view mirror. 'He's got so much worse the last few years – these last few months, even,' he added as he slammed his foot down and picked up sixty in less than five seconds.

'Why?'

'Who knows? They've taught me one thing for sure.' He slipped his warm hand over my belly and sped off up the country lane. 'I don't want a toxic marriage like theirs.'

Chapter 11

JIM

The Manhattan Plaza Hotel, New York
October 2011

God, where do we go from here, Eva?

Ever since I can remember, living with my father was like an endless walk around war-torn streets dodging landmines. You never knew when he was going to explode. Incessant perfectionism, constant criticism, unpredictable temper. His orders regularly barked their way up to my bedroom. 'James, get down these stairs, right away.' Never was it, 'Christina, here at once,' or 'Victoria, come now.' Oh no, it was always me. I would find him hands on his hips on the bottom stair, snarling like a wild boar, with my mother hovering like a deer somewhere in the background.

What was it with him? I regularly asked myself.

'It's just his way. He means well,' my mother answered when I grew bold enough to pose the same question to her.

Dan used to say I was lucky to have parents who were still married.

'You coming to Susie's party on Saturday?' he asked one day when we were taking the bus home from school. We were sitting at the top on the back seats, and he was eyeing up a couple of girls sitting with Susie three rows down.

'Not allowed.'

'What?'

'My stupid father. I wish he'd just leave. I'd be better off.'

'You're kidding? I'd do anything to have my dad around, however strict and moody.'

Dan didn't understand. He had been born in the house next door to us, living there until around his tenth birthday when his life had drastically changed. His parents divorced, and he moved with his mum and three brothers to a terraced two-up two-down on the outskirts of town. He and his brothers shared a bedroom so cramped they could reach across to one another from opposite sets of bunks. For two years they all saw their dad regularly. Every Wednesday night for fish and chips, and alternate weekends when he would introduce them to his latest conquest. Of the four brothers, Dan suffered the most after their dad arrived to pick them all up one Saturday morning and, without any forewarning, announced his relocation to America the following week to start a new life with his new wife. That was the last any of them saw of him.

At first, Dan's unfortunate change in circumstances never seemed to affect him, but after his dad's desertion, he camped out at ours more and more often. Not that it bothered me at all. He'd always been like a brother to me anyway. He blamed his noisy neighbours, who, soon after his dad had left, announced the arrival of their triplets. 'Those bloody babies crying all the time drives me insane. Can I kip at yours tonight?' he used to ask until it was taken as read that whoever laid the table for dinner laid it for six, and he stopped asking.

He missed his dad more than he cared to admit, but learned to cope exceptionally well with his fate, keeping up at school and supporting his mum in raising his brothers. When I'd least expect it, though, he'd say something that told me he wasn't so cool with it all. We'd be talking about our favourite band, or football, when he'd drop a remark, almost sarcastically. 'You don't know how lucky you are. I wish I still lived next door in a house like this,' or, 'What I'd give to have my dad still around.'

I never told him that nothing would have pleased me more than to have my father vanish one day, the same as his had.

You understand, don't you, Eva?

Chapter 12

EVA

Between Christmas and New Year, Jim arranged my first scan. 'We need to get you in straight away,' he said when he left for work the day after Boxing Day. He called less than an hour later. 'All arranged. Two o'clock tomorrow.'

Full of trepidation, we entered the sterile-smelling, dimly-lit room at a private hospital he'd sourced up town. A nurse directed me to lie on the couch, lift my T-shirt and lower my leggings. She merrily chatted away about Christmas overindulgence as she tucked some blue paper tissue around the waistband of my leggings and applied a layer of gel to my stomach.

'You OK?' Jim kept asking, and squeezing my hand.

The expressionless face of the sonographer disconcerted me. She kept repositioning the ultrasound screen and squinting as she glided her probe across the gelled area. 'By my calculation, you are ten weeks and two days. All looks as it should.' Jim's intense emotions surprised me as we stared gormlessly at the tiny bones of our baby swimming around its cosy home in my expanding belly. His eyes glassed over.

I, on the other hand, didn't feel ready for this.

'How did that slip your notice?' he asked, wiping his thumb across my cheeks.

I didn't know; I was on the pill. I'd missed a period, only one I thought, but my periods had never been regular, and with life so busy I couldn't be sure. The sonographer handed me a scrunched-up paper towel. I wiped up the transparent goo before Jim helped me off the couch.

'Congratulations,' the nurse said as she handed us a black and white image of our precious treasure. 'We'll see you again at twenty weeks. Not long to go.'

Initially I was scared. I'd always wanted a big family – the big family I'd never had – but was I ready for this? What about uni and the legal career I'd slogged so hard to achieve? Jim bought me a pregnancy calendar that afternoon. A forty-week guide to prenatal care and fetal development which we hung on the fridge. I scanned through it the next day after he left for work, and as I looked forward to tracking our baby's developments it became clear that nothing else mattered.

I wanted this baby.

I was going to have a proper family.

*

'Do you have to go in today?' I moaned when Jim brought me a mug of tea early New Year's Eve morning. I was beginning to realise that my fiancé was a terminal workaholic, and there was no cure in sight for his acute disease.

He leaned over and kissed me. 'I'll finish early, I promise.'

'You work far too much.'

He stood and straightened out his suit, telling me that being a slave to the cause was a must in his game. If you didn't work hard, plenty of other eager players were waiting on the sidelines to jump in and take your place.

So I took the Tube alone to see Ben. I'd only seen him once since he'd told me about Tammy's cancer. Jim and I had met him for lunch after the scan. The beam on his face, as broad as Jim's, had shown how elated he was. 'I can't believe it. I'm going to become an uncle,' he'd said. 'I'm going to have a niece or nephew.' He stared at the scan picture. 'Our family is expanding.'

While I was on the Tube, Ben sent me a text with details to meet him on the Common. Emmy had arranged a gathering for her extended family. They had all travelled from various parts of the UK for the quarterly get-together she took charge in organising, and they were taking the kids for a run around to relieve them of their midwinter cabin fever.

The weather was warmer than it had been for weeks, the sun taking centre stage in the midday sky as I strolled along the Pavement. Crossing the road, I headed in the direction of the Cock Pond, passing joggers and families out for a wander. When I spotted a crowd of thirty or so people in the near distance, congregated under a poplar tree, I knew it was Emmy and her family from all the vibrant saris visible beneath many of the coats – a blaze of colour against the winter bleakness of the Common. Initially, I thought they were arguing, until I approached and could hear the carefree voices of several generations. Ten or so children were running around playing tag, chuckling and screaming as they dodged the one who was It. Emmy was joining in, her black hair secured into two ponytails which see-sawed as she darted between them all. I stood for a moment, watching their carefree spirit, trying to recall ever feeling like that as a child. I couldn't.

I saw Ben before he saw me. A group of the smaller children surrounded him. They were attached to him like charms on a bracelet. The adults huddled around talking to him, while he played rock paper scissors with the youngsters. He had a broad smile on his face and was brimming with enthusiasm – a picture of contentment. The Ben before.

'Eva,' Emmy called out waving to me. 'Ben, come and take over. Please.' She bounded over to me breathless. 'Congratulations on all your news. Show me this ring I've heard all about, then I'll introduce you to my family.' I held out my hand. 'That's no diamond. That's a boulder,' she said, her eyes wide.

After an hour on the Common, we strolled back to Ben and Emmy's flat. The women clustered in the kitchen like hens in a cage, and the men in the lounge, everyone indulging in a rich feast of chickpea tikka wraps and paneer grilled sandwiches laced with coriander and green chillies. The afternoon passed hectic with happiness. There was something about them all, and I couldn't help but watch them affectionately sharing stories, telling jokes, teasing and chuckling: a proper family.

A proper family.

I was sitting in the lounge eating a vegetable samosa when Emmy wandered over and sat on one of the arms of the chair.

'Did Ben tell you how sorry I was about our first meeting? Not a good start, eh?' I said.

She held a palm up to me. 'No need to apologise.'

Ben came and sat on the other arm and she changed the subject. 'So, when is the baby due?' she asked.

'End of June,' I said, pulling a face to show my mock fear.

'What about uni?' Ben asked.

'Exams are in May. Motherhood doesn't entitle you to any dispensation. Baby's not going to be here until the end of June, so I'll have plenty of time.'

He laughed. 'You not quitting, then? That's my Eva.' He put an arm around me. 'Did you know that the average age of women giving birth is twenty-nine point four years.'

'I'm six and a bit years under average, then.'

'All the more years to make me an uncle several times.'

Emmy gave him an affectionate smile. So did I.

'I saw Mum the day before yesterday,' he said. My stomach turned, and it wasn't from the life growing inside of me. 'I went with her to the hospital. She's started another round of chemo.'

'That's positive news.'

'I offered to stay with her, but she didn't want me to. She's pretty tough, you know.'

'Who's looking after her?'

'She's got a network of neighbours to call on if she wants. There's a guy, Bob, who lives next door to her who helps her out, but she says that most days she'd rather be alone. She says you can go and see her at any time.'

'Any more food, you two?' Emmy asked, standing up.

'Those samosas are something else,' I said. 'I'll come with you.'

*

As I wished people goodbye, with promises to visit them at Emmy's next get together, I felt an unbearable emptiness; a numbness that something was missing from my life. How could I feel so empty with another life so advanced inside of me? As I walked towards the front door, I silently counted each step I took, and after wishing each group of people a happy New Year, I glanced behind me, appreciating their powerful family unit.

Could Ben, Tammy and I rescue our little family to have the same?

Gill once told me that forgiveness allows for healing. It was shortly after social services secured my foster placement with her. I must have been about sixteen. We'd been drinking cocoa around her fireplace one evening before bed, discussing Tammy. 'Forgiveness is something you do for yourself, not the person who has wronged you. Not for your mother, but for you. It's a means of honouring yourself. Permitting yourself to be happy in yourself and with the world.'

'How do I do that?'

'It's a gradual process. Start by thinking about the positive things her actions have brought to your life.'

'Like what?'

'Her actions have made you the incredible person you are today. You're a survivor.' She got up to tend the fire, throwing a big log onto the dwindling flame. Bright orange sparks flew up. 'Only you have control over what happens to you, Eva.'

Could I find forgiveness in me?

Could I?

PART 2

Chapter 13

EVA

May 2011

The fetal monitor showed a dangerously declining heart rate. 'Fetal distress,' the consultant mumbled to the midwife. He had turned his back to me, but that didn't stop me hearing his crushing words. 'We need to deliver this one now.'

An immediate threat to life of mother or baby. I had seen the section on emergency caesareans in all the maternity literature. An ordeal I thought would never happen, so I'd only skim-read through it. My birthing experience would be straightforward. I'd be in and out of hospital the same day. I had been so sure of it. Nothing could have prepared me for what happened next – all the books, films, Internet searches, YouTube clips – nothing. Events unfolded noisily as panic echoed around me, stressed voices calling out medical terms I didn't understand. They rushed me into a cold theatre. It smelled of fear. Or was that my sweat? Two gowned men wheeled a formidable incubator into the room as the anaesthetist held a mask over my face and told me to count back from one hundred.

*

Jim didn't witness the delivery either. He wasn't allowed,

despite his forceful protests. We both missed one of the most significant events in our lives. The birth of our first child. I woke up in the recovery room, my hand enclosed in Jim's. 'Where am I? What's happened?' I asked, disorientated from the drugs and the shock of an emergency delivery.

'We've got a son,' Jim whispered, his euphoria wrapped in anguish.

I tried to sit up, but the pain shooting across my middle wouldn't allow me. 'Where is he?'

The midwife rested a reassuring hand on my shoulder, guiding me back down. 'Your baby has been born prematurely. He's had to go to the neonatal intensive care unit while we see to you.'

'What's wrong with him?'

'We don't know if anything is wrong with him at the moment. Only that he will need extra support during the coming weeks. Time will tell.'

'Why did he come so early? I had another seven weeks to go.'

'There could be several reasons, which will all be investigated in due course. But it's a question we may not be able to answer. Please don't worry. He will be in good hands in the NICU.'

Don't worry? I couldn't concentrate on anything else she said. The whole experience had robbed my ability to focus. I'd thought I'd have an easy delivery, that we'd be a family of three cuddling on the sofa at home the same day I gave birth. Not my belly ripped open like a Christmas turkey.

I turned to Jim. 'Why are you not with him?'

'Darling, I don't want to leave you.'

'Go! Now! Please don't let our baby die.'

*

Hours later, Jim pushed me in a wheelchair past all the mothers with their healthy babies and down the darkened corridor to where our Joe began his life – a hot and stuffy, brightly lit cave, where a stench of antiseptic, mingled with dismay, crushed the air. Six artificial wombs lined the walls – substantial, enclosed tubs of plastic –with a host of devices and a network of respiratory support miraculously connected to the minuscule babies inside, struggling for their lives. Machines continuously beeped and monitors constantly alarmed. Such a foreign environment, but with a language we were soon to learn.

A fragile bundle of bones, Joseph James Barnes had tipped the scales at scarcely three pounds. He was so small, like a baby bird; I could have held him with one hand if I'd been given a chance. His skin, as translucent as rice paper, had a bluish tinge and was covered in downy hair. I think they mentioned his heart then, something about its irregular beat, but I couldn't be sure. I couldn't think through the fog of the trauma and the high of the painkillers.

Things remained critical as we survived each day praying our Joe would live. He needed help breathing. 'CPAP - continuous positive airway pressure,' the neonatologist explained. 'The constant pressure helps keep the airways open and reminds the baby to breathe. The good thing is that we haven't needed to ventilate him.' They'd placed him on a special therapy blanket and attached lights to his incubator and covered his eyes with miniature black goggles as though he was on a salon sunbed. Added to the numerous monitors, cuffs and probes attached to his tiny body to keep track of his vital signs, and the feeding tube wormed into his nose, little remained to be seen of our baby's face and body. 'Oh, and the lights are to treat his jaundice, caused by the elevated levels of bilirubin in his blood,' the neonatologist continued.

Too many new words threatening my baby's life.

*

Four days into the living nightmare, a staff nurse appeared by Joe's incubator; Scottish, red-headed Mia with a pink complexion scattered with freckles. I'd taken a particular liking to her; she had a no-nonsense approach and wore her sympathetic smile as a permanent feature. Like a swan, she glided effortlessly around solving constant problems when she must have been paddling frantically below the surface to keep pace with the demands of the ward. 'Stay seated,' she told me. She beckoned over another nurse and the two of them opened up the incubator and started unclipping wires. My pulse started racing. 'It's time for you to hold your baby,' Mia said, that smile of hers trying to reassure me. 'Have you heard of kangaroo care? Unbutton your shirt. We're going to lift Joe over to you and place him on your chest.'

'What about all the tubes and his oxygen mask?'

She didn't need to answer that question. They moved with such skill, it was evident they could have done this while looking the other way. 'Skin-to-skin contact. It benefits preemies in all kinds of ways. Controls body temperature, keeps their heartbeat regular, helps them gain weight.'

Joe's wrinkled body wriggled like a fish out of water in Mia's capable arms while the other nurse guided the spaghetti of lines, wires and tubes. Mia carefully placed him on my chest, belly down like a frog, instructing a glassy-eyed Jim to cover Joe with a blanket. Initially I felt anger that our first intimate moments together were so public and sterile, but, as I covered Joe's head with the palm of my hand, and his heart hammered against my skin, I calmed, and the realisation hit me.

I was a mum.

*

In the first few weeks, between the nurses twice-daily change of shift, I remained a constant feature beside Joe's incubator. After recovering from my surgery, I was no longer able to stay at night. Leaving Joe each evening was heart-wrenching, but I had no choice. Jim returned to work after the first week. 'I'll save my paternity leave for when we take him home,' he told me, arriving around six every evening to spend some time with our sick baby and then accompany me home. It made sense, but I knew the real reason. The trauma of seeing his critically ill son was too much for him to bear. Jim was used to fixing everything, but he didn't have the tools to fix his broken son.

His parents came to visit the third weekend; it would have been rude to put them off any longer. Sarah, dying to see her grandson, hadn't stopped calling.

'Congratulations, Father,' Jim said as we approached them sitting on a bench in the hospital gardens sipping from lidded drinks. Richard stood and offered Jim his hand. Sarah patted the bench beside her, her face lined with compassion.

I shot Jim a look, confused. 'Congratulations?'

'Father's MBE was officially announced today,' Jim said. 'Remember me telling you it would be announced on the Queen's official birthday?'

I shrugged. If he had, I hadn't been listening. 'Congratulations, Richard,' I said, shaking his hand. 'When's your investiture?'

'I'm awaiting the date.'

I smiled. It was all the enthusiasm I could muster for his achievement.

Jim told me to relax for five while he took them up to the ward to meet their grandson. Blessed with the best of the British sunshine, I removed my cardigan and dug out my sunnies, watching webs of water spinning out of the curved edges of the garden's fountain. The whirr of people chatting, and small groups of hospital workers eating their lunch on the grass square, provided a welcome relief to the clattering and clanging of the NICU.

I breathed in the summer-infused air, gazing at Big Ben in the distance. Big Ben – my brother's nickname when we were young because he was so much taller than me. 'I'll take you there one day,' Ben had forever promised. Just after Hamburg, he'd kept his promise and taken me on the Tube one Saturday afternoon. As we stood looking up at the imposing structure, he'd said, 'Do you know it's ninety-six metres high?' And I remembered thinking, so are you in my eyes.

I slumped on the bench and tried to relax, my skin soaking up the sun's powerful rays, but it was no good. Maternal instinct kept tugging my thoughts back to my baby's temporary home.

*

After detecting a heart murmur, they carried out various tests I'd never before had cause to encounter: echocardiogram, electrocardiogram, chest X-rays and blood tests. With the results analysed, a group of residents crowded in an office with us, clutching a series of clipboards and charts, and delivered their verdict that our son had a congenital heart problem.

'PDA – patent ductus arteriosus is the medical name,' the lead paediatric cardiologist, Dr Miles, informed us as Jim and I sat zombified, fearing the worst. 'Which in simple terms means a hole in the heart. It's the most common congenital heart defect in newborns, occurring when the normal closure of the ductus arteriosus does not occur. Extra blood goes from the aorta into the lungs and can lead to all kinds of complications.'

He might as well have been speaking in Chinese; his words made no sense. My muscles tightened with panic. *Is my baby going to make it?*

'Small PDAs aren't necessarily cause for concern, and they will close spontaneously. If not, we correct the issue with medication. Unfortunately, in Joe's case, he's showing symptoms otherwise. It's large enough to require surgery, I'm afraid. PDA ligation surgery, we call it.'

'But he's too small. He'll die,' I said, my voice barely a whisper.

'Rest assured, this is not an uncommon condition. Especially amongst the premature population.'

Exhausted and distressed, I thought it was all my fault for one reason or another. I'd drunk in the first trimester, heavily some nights. Oblivious to the seed of life developing into the broken baby we were now discussing. 'Did I do something wrong? Something I drank or ate?'

Dr Miles browsed through his paperwork, flicking pages back and forth. 'You didn't take any anticoagulants or antiepileptic drugs in the first trimester, did you? You're not diabetic?'

'No.' My words were still a whisper as I waited for vindication. The self-blame that had plagued me since Joe's arrival.

Dr Miles spoke with irritating politeness as he removed his Harry Potter-style glasses. 'Then I doubt it was anything you did. Like I said, many babies are born with this condition, and there's nothing anyone can do. You or us.' He took some additional notes, scratching his greying temple, while we sat like mute muppets in his airless room. 'I'll arrange surgery as soon as.'

A golden-framed photo beside his computer of him and, I assumed, his wife and two young children smiling alongside Mickey Mouse, only added to my exasperation. 'Why didn't you detect this before? Isn't this the reason you do scans?'

'Not detectable in every case, I'm afraid.' His reply was short and sharp as if he was saving his words for the next set of parents who might need them more than us, squashing all hopes to shift my guilt onto someone else.

He wrote notes, all about our baby and this wretched disease, as we twiddled our thumbs dumbfounded. Powerless parents trapped in a maze of helplessness.

Chapter 14

EVA

I never let on to Jim about what I truly went through during the weeks of Joe's recovery. He was enduring enough torture of his own. I could tell from the stressed look his face wore every evening when he turned up at Joe's bedside, and the generous measure of whisky he poured when we arrived home from the hospital each night.

Time dragged, hours crawled along slowly, but the days whizzed past. I counted a lot. It kept me balanced. The hours since Joe had arrived. The ventilators pumping another breath into the babies fighting battles to thwart death. How often a medic crossed the threshold of the ward each hour. 'When will we be able to take him home?' I asked Dr Miles when he reported that the surgery had gone well.

'That's a question parents often ask, but, sadly, one I can't answer. Babies develop in different ways, and we don't know what lies ahead. It's often a case of one step forward and two steps back until things improve. Generally, we like to see a steady weight gain and independent feeding. And of course, no breathing problems. He's on the right track, but we never know what's around the corner.'

Ecstatic at becoming an uncle, Ben became my rock during those days – composed, reliable and steady. And Gill, as always, travelling up every week. On her first visit, she brought me a beautiful notebook with tiny rainbows printed on the cover. 'Use this to motivate you through these challenging times. Write each day, even if it's only a few sentences. It will track Joe's progress, and you'll be able to look back and see how far he has come.'

Surprisingly, Dan too became a regular visitor. He often turned up unexpectedly, arriving with a bar of my favourite chocolate or a trashy magazine he'd grabbed in the foyer.

'You can't have too much crappy news in these situations,' he'd laugh, throwing me a scandalous weekly I'd never read. And sometimes, when Jim was working late, Dan would turn up in the early evening and sit with me for ten minutes before telling me we were going out.

'Where to?'

'Anywhere to make you smile.' He'd whisk me straight out like a superhero, making me laugh all the way to the pub for a quick pint. Then he'd escort me home and fry up some concoction which wasn't always edible, so he'd nip out and grab a takeaway. His relaxed take on life was a welcome consolation. Especially after days when I couldn't see an end.

Ben dropped by most afternoons, if only for half an hour. His euphoria at having someone else to add to his slowly expanding family proved infectious and lifted me out of some dark moods, if only temporarily. He used to cradle Joe's head through the portholes in the side of the incubator while chatting away to him like he would a mate. 'Research says babies benefit from being talked to,' he'd repeat as he told his nephew all about his adventures in Peru.

'I want to tell you something,' Ben said one afternoon. It was a Sunday. I knew because Jim was there. Only two visitors per baby were allowed in the NICU at any one time, so Jim and I met Ben in the café at the main entrance to swap over. Ben tapped his fingers on the table. 'But I don't want to upset you.'

I eyed him questioningly.

'I know you don't want to talk about Mum, but I wanted you to know that she and I are going to start family counselling.'

He paused, expecting me to say something.

'Emmy has put us in touch with a really great therapist called Karen. Karen Fleming. We're going for our first session next week.'

I put my hand in my bag and started fiddling with a cuddly toy Dan had bought for Joe. A small giraffe that could stand unaided. It wasn't allowed in the incubator, so I carried it around in my bag. I didn't know why, but I found its coat, as smooth as Joe's skin, a comfort. When I couldn't stroke my baby, I could stroke his cuddly toy.

'I'd love it if you came to a session with us.'

Jim's jaw clenched. 'Leave it, Ben. It's not the time.'

'It's Mum's birthday next week.'

'I said, leave it.' Jim's tone cut the conversation dead.

*

One saving grace was that Emmy was studying in the same hospital, so she often popped up to the sixth floor to see me. Her company proved comforting in all the frustrating uncertainty, and she had a gift for saying the right thing. She provided reassurance from a medical perspective that we would soon be heading home. 'Joe's doing great,' she told me every time she visited.

One afternoon she arrived exactly at the right time. Joe had had a bad couple of days and the medical team had frightened me with the news that he needed a blood transfusion. 'No need to panic. Just a top up to treat anaemia. All in the normal course of recovery,' the neonatologist said.

But I did panic. Every time something new occurred. A different drug Joe needed, another test, a slight temperature he had developed. 'Are you OK?' Emmy asked, peeping at Joe sleeping in his incubator.

I didn't answer. I was struggling to swallow the lump that had been in my throat since hearing the words "blood transfusion" that morning. It was so big it kept getting stuck.

'Let's go for coffee,' she said. She grabbed my hand and pulled me up. 'Cake too.'

I hesitated, glancing from Joe to her.

'He'll be fine,' she said, looping her arm through mine. 'Blood transfusions happen all the time on the NICU. These little ones just need rebalancing sometimes. Think of it like us getting a cold and dosing ourselves with vitamin C.'

Somehow, I couldn't adopt her thought process. I couldn't quite equate a dose of Berocca to a bag of life-saving blood.

As we made our way to the café, she relayed a funny story a nurse had told her that morning. I gave a half-hearted laugh. 'You know what? I think we could both do with some fresh air. Let's make it a takeout and wander over to the park.'

She relayed more funny stories as we waited in the long line of eleven adults and four kids. I kept counting as we inched forward. When we reached the front, she ordered two black coffees to go.

'Regular or large?'

'Large.' Emmy nudged me. 'Chocolate muffin?' She ordered two when I nodded.

As the hospital's automatic doors thumped shut behind us, severing the whiff of antiseptic and ineffable sadness, we simultaneously took a deep breath of fresh air. We looked at each other, and I managed to laugh with her. 'It's tough in there, eh?' she said.

'Some days are better than others. Some hours even. Some minutes.'

I counted the number of people who passed us as we strolled over to Archbishop's Park. A little jewel of green space amid London's madness. Emmy had taken Jim and me there during Joe's surgery. It was a beautiful June day. Cloudless skies accompanied a light wind which brushed away the film of NICU staleness on my ashen cheeks. We passed joggers and mothers with strollers, and a group of lively students kicking a football between makeshift goals. Emmy guided us towards a bench near the children's playground. She unpacked our drinks and snacks as I watched kids jumping and climbing, sliding and swinging, 'I hope that will be Joe one day,' I said, choking on my words.

'Of course it will. Have faith, Eva.'

'I'm so scared he won't make it out alive.'

'Believe me, I've seen many children a lot sicker than Joe head home.'

'I wish I knew what caused it. His heart condition.'

'You may never find out. This happens all the time in preemies. Genetic factors could play a role, but there's no clear explanation.'

My hours of research had reached the same conclusion.

'Seek the positive. He's on the mend.' She steered the conversation to Ben. 'We were choosing images for his new website last night,' she said. 'It's coming along really well. Did you know it's Tammy's birthday tomorrow?' she said, ripping open two sachets of sugar.

'Ben told me.'

'I've got a couple of days off. We're going to take her out for lunch.'

I bit my lip, then surprised myself by saying, 'Ben wants this thing with our mother to work so much, doesn't he?' I remembered back to the emptiness I had felt on New Year's Eve. When I'd visited Emmy and her family on Clapham Common. I felt the same now. 'You know, since meeting your family at New Year, part of me wants to want it as much as he does, but I don't know how to.' I sighed heavily then took a sip of coffee. 'I haven't even told Jim that.'

Gently she touched my arm. 'Ben's needs are greater than yours at the moment, that's all. You never know what might happen.'

'I wish I understood why he wants it so badly.' I pushed my uneaten muffin aside.

She fished a wooden stick out of the bag and stirred her coffee. 'He's hurting, Eva. I know you both suffered horrific childhoods.' She didn't know the half of it. 'But for him, the need to find his family, to know where he came from, is stronger than yours. Have you ever seen the film, *Oranges and Sunshine*?'

I shook my head.

'It explores the importance of family. For numerous years, from the forties to the sixties, thousands of British children, from broken homes and single-parent families, were shipped out to Australia with the promise of better lives but ended up suffering abuse. I watched it for one of my psychology courses last year before I went to Peru. A social worker investigated the lives of these child migrants. It became her life's work.'

'What's this got to do with Ben?'

'Thousands of people came forward and told their story. The film examines how their childhood psychologically damaged the majority of them all their lives. How they felt they never belonged anywhere.' She emptied a capsule of milk into her coffee. 'They were never able to settle. Many of them suffered severe anxiety and depression throughout adulthood.'

'You think Ben fits into this category?'

'There're similarities. Regarding his identity, yes.'

'He used to be so happy when we were young.'

'Kids adapt. They learn how to cover up and how to live with their lot. Then they grow up, and the world is not such a protective place.'

'Is this why he smokes so much weed?'

'Most likely.'

'Doesn't it bother you that he smokes so much? Being a doctor and all that.'

She smiled with confidence. 'He'll stop soon. I'm helping him.'

'He once told me that every morning when he woke up, he felt hollow inside – like something was missing – but when he took that first drag of the day, that emptiness disappeared.'

She shrugged. 'He feels deceived. He needs to understand why his mum and dad abandoned him. He feels a need to develop his relationship with your mum. And find your family. Especially your dad.'

I sighed. 'What if I don't want to?'

'That's your call, Eva. You must do what's right for you. Did he tell you that he and Tammy are going to start family counselling together?'

'He did.'

'He said he was going to talk to you about it. For him, Tammy talking about her life, and why she did what she did, will help him come to terms with everything. I've introduced them to a friend of mine, Karen. She's an incredible counsellor. They're going for their first session tomorrow. Before we take Tammy out to lunch.'

'Is that her birthday present?'

She laughed. 'It was the only day Karen could fit them in.'

'He wants to find our father, too. Who knows who else will appear? We could have a whole other family out there. That scares me.' I took a sip of coffee. 'Really scares me if I'm honest.'

Her pager beeped and she made a call. I stared at mums pushing their children on the swings, thinking about the number of times Ben had hinted about finding our mother, and our father.

Once when I'd visited him in Barcelona a few summers ago. He was working two jobs then – labouring on a building site by day and serving in a beach bar at night – saving up for his trip to Peru. Because apparently, he'd told me, something was waiting for him there. 'Peru is my calling,' he'd said. Even back then he'd been talking about it.

'You always were such a fantasist,' I replied, sipping potent sangria from his hip flask.

'You've got to dream, Eva,' he said. 'Just like I dream about being with our parents again. Just to see.'

'See what? It won't alter a single thing'.

We'd been lazing on the beach at the time, admiring a father building an elaborate sandcastle. 'Bravo, fantástico,' his wife and two kids, a boy and a girl, called out, clapping their hands in awe as he planted a red and yellow flag on the turret of the tallest tower.

'Don't you want to see her again? I always wonder what she looks like now. And what she does for a living. She could've got married. We could have other family out there.'

I jutted my chin out. 'Shut up.' The two children ran up to their father and wrapped their arms around his thighs. He stroked their heads, gazing down at them adoringly.

'We could find out why she left us and, more importantly, why she didn't come back for us.'

I threw a handful of sand at his feet. 'No. I never want to set eyes on her again. Never.' Another handful brushed his knees.

'And our father. Haven't you ever wondered about him?

'No. Never, ever,' I said, flinging more sand at his shoulder. 'What good could ever come out of them reappearing in our lives?'

Emmy finished her call. 'I need to dash.'

I continued talking as we walked back to the hospital. 'I feel guilty because Tammy's so ill. And I feel I'm letting Ben down if I don't go along with what he wants. But I can't bring myself to see her. I don't know why, but I have this foreboding that it's all going to go horribly wrong. Please don't tell Ben I said that. I need to work it all out for myself.'

'Trust is an issue for you because of the degree to which Tammy let you down. Mothers are meant to protect their children. Tammy didn't, and so subconsciously you're scared she's going to disappoint you again. You don't feel capable of getting close to her. That's understandable.' We stepped into the hospital, entering the hot and stuffy forecourt. 'You'll know when the time is right to face your demons, Eva.'

Chapter 15

EVA

As I recovered from my own surgery I became restless, spending hours watching distressed parents fussing over their babies all day. Or not, in some cases where, surprisingly, parents only showed up in the evenings and at weekends. When I wasn't pumping milk or enjoying our daily dose of kangaroo care, which I'd grown to savour, I was sitting by Joe's incubator researching his condition. It began to skyrocket my anxiety levels, so I ordered a couple of books and started prepping for my return to uni.

'Are you seriously thinking about going back in September after all this?' Jim asked.

'You can always take a year out,' Ben suggested.

'Don't put that pressure on yourself, darling,' Jim said.

Dan displayed more understanding. 'Your choice, but if anyone can do it, it's you,' he said one evening. Jim was away on business and Dan had stopped by to see Joe and take me home.

'I feel torn. I should be with Joe every minute, but I'll be honest, sometimes it's suffocating.'

'I get that. It must be tough sitting here day after day.'

When I'd overcome the guilt at leaving Joe for longer than a cup of coffee, I started going for walks around London. It allowed me time to think. I felt misplaced when away from him, riddled with guilt and emotionally shattered, but on the days when I ventured out for an hour or two, I found injecting some normality into my daily routine a welcome distraction. Away from the crashing doors, the alarming monitors, and the trauma circling around me. Not to mention constantly counting every time the hand sanitizer by the ward door squirted another shot of gel into someone's hands.

*

One evening Ben and I were chatting around Joe's plastic cot when Dr Miles stopped by. I jumped up from my chair, wringing my hands together. At that point a washed-out Jim turned up. He had a deadline to meet and had been getting up at silly o'clock each morning. 'Could it be hereditary?' I asked.

Dr Miles head flinched back. 'Sorry?'

'The heart defect – could it have come from us, our parents? Or even our grandparents?'

Dr Miles covered his chest with Joe's files. 'Possibly. We'd have to carry out chromosome analysis to look for any abnormalities that could cause additional complications in a child with a congenital heart problem.' He rolled down Joe's sheet to look at the operation site. 'You may consider genetic counselling in the future should you think about further children,' he added as an afterthought.

'Can't you do that now?' I asked.

'As I said, we can look into such matters later.' He swiped the curtains around the bay. 'For now, I'm a little concerned about the raised potassium levels in his recent bloods.'

'What does that mean?'

'I've ordered some additional tests.'

My heart leapt to my throat. 'Potassium is related to kidneys, isn't it? He has something wrong with his kidneys too?'

'I can't say at this point, which is why I've ordered some additional tests. We'll reconvene when the results are through. No need to worry ourselves until then. Premature babies do run the risk of kidney complications in later life, so we need to ensure that we have all angles covered. It could just be an infection.' He snapped Joe's file shut. 'Like I said, no need to worry for now,' he added before moving on to his next patient.

Jim touched my arm. 'Come on, let's have a break. Coffee?'

'Good idea,' said Ben.

*

'What if he has something wrong with his kidneys?' I asked Jim as we queued in the hospital café. It was the usual scene. A group of doctors poring over medical papers, a couple I recognised from the NICU engrossed in conversation. A few patients attached to drips, seated with their visitors, relieved at having someone to talk to.

'You heard Dr Miles. We can't jump to conclusions. Let's wait for the results and worry about that later.'

But it was too late. Dr Miles's words had given me a train of thought I couldn't stop. 'What if he needs a transplant in the future? Kidneys or heart?'

Jim took my hand. 'Then we'll face it together. Let's get some perspective here.' He ordered three coffees and some sandwiches, and we took them to Ben who waited at a table. But despite hunger pangs, I couldn't eat. Images of malfunctioning kidneys and broken hearts had stolen my appetite.

All three of us sat silently sipping our coffees until Ben spoke. His words sprang up out of nowhere just like Joe's apparent kidney problem. 'Our aunt Bella died last year.'

'What?' I asked.

'A heart attack; she died instantly.'

'How'd you find that out?'

'Through a childhood friend of Bella's who Mum told me to look up. Bella was a doctor, too – the same as our grandfather. But she specialised, would you believe it, in cardiology. She never married or had any children.'

'So, she had something wrong with her heart?'

'It appears so.'

I slammed my hand on the table. 'Does Tammy have a heart problem?'

He flinched. 'I don't know.'

I jabbed a finger at him. 'You need to ask her. We need to find out.'

He sat back in his chair, squinting at me. 'Why don't you ask her?'

'What about her parents? Where are they?'

'She hasn't seen them since she was a child. I started to look into them, but got waylaid.'

I grabbed Jim's wrist. 'What about your parents? Do either of them have a heart problem? Or a kidney problem, come to that.'

'Not that I'm aware of, no.' He tried to free his arm from me. 'Calm down.'

'Go and call them,' I said, my hand still gripping his wrist. 'Tell them what Dr Miles told us. They might have a problem we don't know about. They need to get tested. What if there is a problem that runs in our families? What if Joe needs a kidney transplant? What if we have more children? The same could happen again, or worse.'

Jim shuffled along the bench and slipped his arm around me. I nestled my head in the folds of his shirt. 'Calm down, darling. You're reacting to something we don't have the full picture on.'

I trembled.

The time had come to face my demons.

I pulled away from Jim's hold. 'I need to find my family.'

Chapter 16

EVA

When Jim arrived to take us to Dollis Hill, I was chatting to Gill. She had agreed to sit with Joe for the afternoon. After kissing me and embracing Gill, Jim slipped his hands into the portholes of the incubator. 'How you doing, little man?' He rearranged Joe's woollen hat. Sarah had knitted a number of them in different shades of blue as soon as Joe was born.

'You'll need these in the coming weeks,' she'd told me. 'I worked in the NICU for a while when I was training. The babies wore them all the time. Helps keep them warm.'

'Ben texted,' I said. 'He's running late. He's going to meet us in the foyer.'

With his hands still on Joe, Jim twisted around. 'You don't have to do this, you know.'

'No, I do have to. Anyway, we'd better get going. You know what they're like about more than two visitors at a time.'

He closed the incubator doors and perched himself on the arm of my chair. 'You do have a choice. It's not urgent you find your family now. Emotions are too high. It's not the right time. Don't you agree, Gill?'

Gill raised her hands in a not-my-call kind of way.

'We went through this last night and the night before,' I said.

He sighed heavily. 'Don't do this to yourself. You've got enough on here.'

'I have to.'

'I get that, but not now. You've got Joe to consider. I understand it's important for you, but you don't have to do it yet. Gill, help me here.'

She smiled sympathetically but raised her hands again.

'Let's go.' I shoved my books in my bag. 'We'll be late.' I stood and grabbed my denim jacket from the back of the chair and pecked Gill on the cheek.

'I'll be gone by the time you get back,' she said. 'Don't forget my offer.'

*

Sporadic showers pelted down as we drove to Dollis Hill, resulting in a bumper-to-bumper traffic jam and roads resembling a grid of small rivers. The delay in getting there only added to my torment. Ben stuck his head between the headrests. 'Do you know seventy-eight per cent of distance travelled per person per year in the UK is by car? That's why we see this blimin' congestion all the time.' He tutted. 'I'll call her.'

'We should see a rainbow sometime soon,' Jim said, squeezing my knee, as we crawled along the A41.

I'd made a mistake. I didn't want to do this anymore. I had to fight the urge to ask him to turn back. The wipers scraped against the windscreen, which kept fogging up. I crossed and uncrossed my legs, shifting about, unable to find a comfortable position.

'What was Gill's offer, then?' Jim asked.

'She said she'll come and stay for a while when Joe comes home. To help out for a few weeks. She's fostered loads of babies in the past, a couple of preemies too, so she knows what she's doing. What do you think?'

'Up to you, darling. The help will be good for you. For us.'

'I think it will. What with you being away so much.'

'I'm sorry.'

'Can't you cut back on some of the travel?'

'I'll try my best. I promise. It's just that with the company having expanded so much in the past year, I know Warren's prepping me for promotion. If I can make it, it will secure our future.' He took my hand. 'We'll never need to worry about money again.'

I'd rather you were around for us, I wanted to say, but he looked whacked and I didn't want to burden him with any more pressure.

'We're going to be late, Mum,' I heard Ben say. 'How long do you think we'll be?' he asked, poking his head between the seats again.

'Hard to say.' Jim frowned at the dashboard. 'It's four miles away, but the satnav says it'll take another hour.'

My heart was racing. I stared out of the window and counted the drops of rain running down the glass like tears. Jim kept turning the radio on; I kept turning it off. Not even Rihanna could raise my spirits. Another forty-five minutes and one hundred and sixty-eight beads of water later, we veered into her road. I tapped Jim on the leg. 'Slow down, will you?'

A flash downpour dimmed the sky as Ben called out, 'This is the one,' and we pulled up outside a run-down 1930s terrace. We sat for a while, waiting for the rain to stop. I stared up at the roof of the car, my emotions pulling me in all directions. For so many years, I'd never considered I might meet up with her again. It was beyond the realms of possibility, as absurd as thinking she and my father would someday reunite. But I wanted this now, didn't I? I wanted to meet her and know more about my family, for Joe's benefit, and mine too. But now the time had come, part of me wanted to turn back home. Yo-yoing thoughts, spinning me upwards and downwards to the extremities of emotion.

'What the hell am I going to say to her?'

'You aren't about to meet the Queen. Be yourself. The rain's easing up; let's make a run for it,' Ben said.

Ben led the way up the path, and Jim pulled me along behind him like a mother dragging her child to the dentist. Slabs wobbled beneath our feet, and mud squelched up from where grouting had worn away, splattering my blue and white Nikes with dirt.

We approached her chipped front door. Flakes of crimson paint sprinkled the doorstep like drops of blood. Ben threw his arms around me as if I'd just given him a million quid. 'Oh, Eva. You won't regret this. I know we can make it work.'

Jim removed his blazer and draped it over me, but he needn't have bothered because only seconds passed before she yanked open the door and ushered us inside.

She no longer resembled the woman I had buried in my memory. The woman who had pushed me on swings in Victoria Park, bought me a quarter of liquorice every Saturday morning, and read me stories in bed at night. She wore a too-little-sleep look – dark circles and colourless skin, and her head was too large – all out of proportion against her stick-thin torso. And she was bald. She looked all wrong. A giant lollipop clothed in jeans and a silky shirt patterned with stripes, like a zebra. Ben had told me the chemo had stolen the pounds; he'd never mentioned her hair. I tried to speak, but expecting someone so much younger, the weary-looking woman standing before us stunned me into silence. Ben made one of his comments, something about the rain and global warming, which she didn't acknowledge.

There was an awkward silence as we stood, bunched together in her hallway, until she spoke my name. 'Eva.' She went to hug me, but I stepped back. I didn't mean to appear rude, but I needed to find a lifetime of forgiveness from somewhere before we went that far. 'Come on through,' she said. She had a cockney twang, her East End roots still apparent in spite of her North London postcode. I glanced over at Jim for reassurance. His face was as white as his shirt. Being there was doing neither of us any favours.

A stagnant odour – that of an ex-smoker – accompanied us as we shadowed her down the dingy hallway to the lounge. Her shoulders curved together like she might vanish inside herself, and her legs were like branches that might snap any second. As we walked in, my breath caught in my throat. The brownness of the room was overbearing: the worn sofa, the patterned carpet in swirls of beige, and a bronze-finished chandelier which was missing half its bulbs. With a trembling hand, she gestured for us to take a seat at the dining table. 'Drink, anyone?'

Jim nodded, but I shook my head. I pulled out a faux leather chair, hesitating before sitting down. The covers were like lizard skin, scaly and ragged, and looked like they held years of dirt like the air in the room. I watched her walk to-wards the kitchen. Bootcut jeans – at least two sizes too big – gaped at her waist even though she wore a belt. They were expensive jeans. I knew that because Jim had bought me a pair of the same brand for Christmas, and had left the price tag on by mistake. Ben stopped her, placing a hand on each of her bony shoulders with such compassion I recoiled. 'Mum, you sit and talk. I'll make the drinks.'

She lowered herself into the chair next to me. I froze. I hadn't known what to expect, but this wasn't it. She asked after Joe, then made small talk concerning the weather, the house, the neighbours. I sat and listened, wringing my hands in my lap, and when Jim gently prodded my shin beneath the table, I contributed the odd word. I tried my hardest, seri-ously I did, she wanted me to like her, and part of me wanted to like her too, but the only thing I felt was the heat on the tip of my tongue from the questions I was burning to ask.

Ben returned with tea in old china mugs. 'Here we go,' he said, beaming. 'How's work, Mum?' he asked, handing her a mug.

She told us about her work in the bookies on the High Street. 'I've been with the same company for ten years now. Not my choice if I had my time again, but it keeps the wolf from the door, so to speak. They've been good to me through my illness. I've started going in for a few hours a day when I'm up to it. It gets me out of the house. Stops me staring at these four walls all day.' She cracked a joke about her boss, an overweight forty-something biker called Martin, but only Ben and Jim laughed.

'Ben, didn't you see the sandwiches I made us all for lunch? By the toaster,' she said, looking at Ben adoringly. I had to turn away. How had they got so close? Forgiveness, Eva, a little voice whispered in my head. He's forgiven her, and so should you.

Ben pushed his chair back. 'I'll go and fetch them.'

She stood, raising a hand to wave his offer away. 'Don't worry. I'll go.'

Something I found odd was that, despite the dilapidated state of the house and the outdated furniture, signs of affluence lay evident around the place. When we'd entered her hallway, I'd spotted a row of brand new shoes, and I couldn't help but notice the Mulberry handbag sticking out from the space between the sofa and the armchair. *She can't earn that much working in a bookies, can she? Probably all counterfeits.*

Looking at Ben, I nodded to an ashtray on her wooden sideboard. 'She smokes, and she's got cancer?'

'She gave up when she was diagnosed.'

She returned carrying a selection of sandwiches on an old willow-patterned serving plate. A large chip dented the rim. 'Help yourselves.' She removed a stoneware vase full of artificial flowers caked in dust from the centre of the table and replaced it with her offering. My stomach turned at the curling edges of the crusts. Jim took a cheese and tomato one. I threw him a look – a don't-be-so-damn-stupid glare – but he just shrugged, closed his eyes and stuffed it into his mouth.

'So, tell me about uni,' she said to me.

'I've finished my first year.'

'Do you have to go in every day? My neighbour Bob's son only has to go in three days a week.'

'Same. Could change in September.'

'Is there a lot of work?'

I nodded.

126

'Do you know what you want to do when you've finished?'

I shrugged my shoulders.

'Who will look after Joe when you start back?'

'Not sure.'

'What do you do when you're not at uni?'

'Funnily enough, a baby in the NICU doesn't give me time for much else.'

She continued asking me questions, but I was antagonistic, goading her to erupt. Into what I wasn't sure – maybe a mess of begging forgiveness for the past which had brought us to the point we were at, two decades down the line. I didn't want to feel this way. It wasn't like me. I wanted to forgive her, didn't I? I wanted us to be a family. I shouldn't have come. I wasn't ready. I stood up. 'I need some air.'

Jim touched my arm. 'Want me to come with you?'

'You're OK.'

Ben directed me to her overgrown garden, which was long and narrowed down to what looked like a neglected greenhouse. Its aluminium frame was bent and had several panes of glass missing. I scoffed. She excelled at abandoning things, then. I wandered over to the low, rickety fence bordered by stinging nettles and peered over. Her garden was a depressing sight in comparison to the colour and well-manicured lawns of her neighbours. A spot of rain landed on my cheek. I glanced up to the sky. A black blanket as dark as my mood. I took some deep breaths, telling myself to give her a chance. She deserved that, didn't she? 'She's my mum, she's my mum,' I muttered to the overgrown brambles with their vicious thorns.

When the rain started for real, I returned to them. And then it came – the eruption. As if she'd bottled up a lifetime of frustration, and I had flipped the top off. She propelled herself out of her chair and announced she needed to talk. She startled me, Jim too. He sat bolt upright as though she'd woken him from an afternoon nap.

'I need to tell you so much.' Taking a measured, deep breath, she paused as if relishing the joy of the moment she'd believed would never arrive. 'I hope you'll understand.'

We sat in anticipation. Loud music pumped through the paper-thin walls from next door, which broke the stifling silence as we waited to hear her story.

Chapter 17

EVA

She walked over to the armchair by the window and eased herself down, the grey light accentuating her ashen face. 'I got married ten years ago.' Her fingers fiddled with a frayed strand of denim on the knee of her jeans where a small hole had started to form. 'To the area boss, Paul Rochford.'

'Shall I get us another drink?' Ben asked.

She drew her brows together and flapped a hand at him. 'A few months after we got together, he asked me to move in here. It was his mum's house. He'd lived here with her until she died the year before. I was so happy with him.'

The music from next door intensified as though the neighbours could sense the discomfort lurking on the other side of their wall.

'I didn't take the Rochford name. I hoped one day you would look for me.' She gave me a rueful grin. 'Paul and I made a nice life for ourselves. For three years, I was content with my lot. Then one day, he never returned from work. He died instantly, they told me; a stroke, no warning.'

The veins in my neck started pulsating. I glanced over at Jim for some comfort, but he had none to give. His shoulders sat tight, as did his jaw. He shared my torment. More colour had drained from him.

'I know you must wonder why you were taken from me all those years ago, and why I never came back for you.'

I gave several unfaltering nods. My insides were clenched tight with pain. Pain fused with desire. Wanting to discover the truth mixed with an awareness that whatever she said was going to hurt.

As she leaned forward in her chair, the story about the parents she'd detested began to unfold. Felicity and Patrick Mitchell had never been around for her. They had been too engrossed in their careers and her older sister, Bella. She spat the words out as if they were profanities. A frenzy of uncontrollable coughs followed, like a chesty smoker's hack, but it could have been the cancer. It continued for ages.

A fleeting moment of sympathy stalled my anger. 'Are you all right?'

'They treated me so badly. And I became an alcoholic. I couldn't look after you.'

I stood. Where had that sympathy gone? 'So, you blame your parents for your life's mistakes?' She was frightening me – or rather the feelings I had for her were. Breathe, Eva. I wanted her dead. I did. An overpowering urge to kill her raged through me. If Ben and Jim hadn't been there, I would have grabbed one of the grubby cushions from the sofa and held it over her face, constricting her airways until she gasped her final seconds of life. My legs wavered. I sat back down. In, one, two, three, four. The game was waiting for me to play. I began counting the brown flowers on her eighties-hung vinyl wallpaper, fighting back tears. I didn't want to feel like this. I didn't. It wasn't healthy, I knew that. I wanted to be more like Ben. I wanted to forgive her. But painful childhood memories stood in the way.

'Eva, please.' Ben clicked his fingers in front of my eyes.

I swiped them away. 'What happened to our real dad? Was he even the same man? Are Ben and I even real brother and sister?

'Eva!' Ben said.

'Is there anyone else?' I refocused on the wall. Seventeen brown flowers. 'Please just be honest with us. I need to know.'

Jim took my hand, but I wrestled it away.

'I understand this is hard for you,' she said.

'I'm here because I need to find all my family. I need to find out if anyone else has a heart or kidney problem. If it's genetic then we risk the chance of Joe's problems happening again if Jim and I have more children. And who knows what he may need in the future.'

'I didn't know Joe had kidney problems?'

Jim butted in. 'We don't know for sure. We're waiting further test results.'

I nodded to Ben then turned to her. 'Was our father the same man?'

She didn't hesitate to answer this time. 'Of course. Yes. Of that there's no doubt.'

'And where is he now?'

She shook her head. 'I don't know. I haven't seen him since he walked out on me all those years ago. When I was pregnant with you.'

'I need to find him. Where do I start?'

She shrugged. 'I wouldn't have a clue. I met him when I worked down in Surrey for Jim's family. He worked in a garage in Croydon.'

131

'What garage? What was it called?'

'Frank Billinghurst or Billingham, something like that.'

'And there's no one else? No other family on your side?'

She faltered, then captured our attention as she revealed to us another baby. The one she'd had as a teenager but had abandoned as well, although she blamed that on her parents too. 'I never agreed to it, I wanted to keep him, but my mother found him an adoptive family, and I never saw him again. My parents thought he was better off without me and as time went on, I knew they were right. The same as I knew you were better off without me.' A tear fell from her right eye, one single tear, as lonely as the image of her all those years ago.

'Who was his father?' I asked.

'A one-night stupid mistake.'

Ben's eyes were filled with disbelief. 'We have a brother?'

I corrected him. 'Half-brother.'

'How come you never mentioned him before?' Ben asked her.

I looked at the pain engraved in the lines of her leathery face, and I considered holding my hand out to her. Bridge the gap. Heal the hurt.

Jim distracted me from my musing. 'You OK?'

I jolted back to the moment. 'What about our dad?' I asked. 'Did he have any brothers and sisters?'

Ben slapped his hands against his cheeks and took a sharp breath. 'What'd you call him? Our brother?'

'Christopher. I named him Christopher Peter Mitchell.'

'Where's he now?' Ben demanded. 'How come you've never told me about him?' A red rash crept up his neck.

'It's not important. I just wanted to let you know how hard I've had it, so you understand why I did the things I did.'

I asked again. 'What about our dad?'

Her gaze remained on Ben as she bit her lip.

Why was she ignoring me? Where had our dad ended up? What about his family? Claustrophobia was overpowering me. I had to get out of there. But what had happened to our dad? I needed to know. I needed to find him.

She swallowed hard, looking in Ben's direction.

Ben shifted in his seat. His voice cracked. 'Carry on.'

'What about our dad?' She would answer me. I wouldn't leave there until she did. 'What was his real name?'

Her voice quivered. 'David Benjamin Pilgrim.' Her eyes flickered between Ben and me.

My stomach lurched, a sway of rapid movements, as she uttered my dad's full name. Ben had only ever referred to him as Dave.

'His parents were from London,' she said. 'That's all I know. I only met them a couple of times. I never went to their house. They came to visit us when Ben was born and a few times afterwards.'

Ben thumped the table in front of me. 'I'll fill you in on him later.'

I stabbed my index finger at Tammy. 'No, I want to hear it from her.'

Ben was frantically winding curls around his index finger, letting them spring free before grabbing another. 'I've already talked about Dad with her. I can tell you on the way home.'

'I often asked the social services people about you. They said they could arrange a meeting, but I knew you were better off without me.' A tremor took hold of her hands. Torment and torture, remorse and regret, I wasn't sure. She looked alternately at us, her eyes sunk in desperation for for-giveness.

'My life's been hell, Tammy.' The word *Mum* couldn't sur-face through the hurt twisting inside me. 'Do you realise what you put me through? I was kicked from pillar to post, from one foster family to another, never belonging any-where. You ruined my childhood.'

'I've paid double, treble for what I did, and I'll never for-give myself. I always thought you'd be better off without me.' She sat forward in her chair. 'I live with regret every day, but I want to make amends. Stay and talk further. Please. Has Ben told you about our visit to the counsellor?'

I nodded.

'Perhaps you could join us for a session. I think it would help us all. And whatever tests you need me to do for Joe, let me know.'

'What about this Christopher, then?' Ben asked. He was as ravenous as an unfed pet for further information on this half-brother of ours, but Tammy had little else to feed him, which frustrated him. His eagerness in scavenging for more made me want to leave.

What would happen next in the movies? Did we kiss and make up, declare absolution and undying love? No. But I'd made progress. We'd made a dent in the pent-up anger I'd held onto for most of my life. Only slightly, but unquestion-ably. Gill had once told me that if I didn't release this anger, I'd end up obsessively counting things for the rest of my life. If it didn't kill me first, that was. Only I could let it go.

Was there a chance us Mitchells could survive the tragic events of our lives? Who knew? I'd heard enough for one day, though. I had work to do. I had to find my dad and brother.

The music from the neighbours cut off as if that was my cue. I looked at Jim. 'Please take me back to the hospital.'

Tammy pushed herself out of the armchair. 'Don't go yet. Please stay. Let's talk this through.'

I slung my bag over my shoulder and tugged at Jim's sleeve. 'Not today, Tammy. Not today,' I said. But I did hug her on the way out.

Chapter 18

EVA

'What about our dad, then? I asked Ben when I climbed into the car. I glanced behind to see Tammy waving from her front door. I waved back.

'What about our half-brother?' Ben said.

'Him too!'

'Mum's never told me any more than she let on today.' He swung around and waved to Tammy until we turned out of the road. 'I asked the private detective who found her to look for Dad too, but his sister was taken ill after Christmas, so he's had to go back to India for a while.'

'Is he still looking?'

He shook his head. 'I spent the money on the business. Plus, you've been so upset with Joe, I kind of stopped.'

'What about this brother?'

'She's never mentioned anything about him. Nothing. I was as shocked as you to hear about that.'

'What else do you know about Dave Pilgrim, then?'

'I've already said. Nothing more than she let on today.'

'What happened with this counsellor?'

'We've talked about the past and about Dad. I really think

it would be good for you to join us,' he said. I turned away and looked out of the window. 'I'll ping you her number. Our next session is on Friday.'

I bent down to take my phone out of my bag when suddenly, Jim braked. My head smacked on the front of the glove compartment. I sat up to a swarm of lights reddening before my eyes as the car skidded, stopping only inches short from the brake lights of the lorry in front.

He reached over and grabbed my shoulder. 'Sorry, sorry. You all right?'

'You're going to have us a serious accident one day,' I said, rubbing my head. 'Slow down.'

After we dropped Ben off at Edgware Road tube station to meet some friends, we headed back to the hospital. I was yearning to see Joe again, to touch my flesh and blood. It was like that when I wasn't with him, like a piece of me was missing. As soon as we got to the ward, I rushed to open the portholes and cradle his head in my hands.

Jim dropped into the chair. He hadn't said much all the way back, but then again, neither had I. For the next hour, we remained lost in our own thoughts soaking up the drama of a new baby who had occupied the cot beside Joe's in our absence. The frantic parents reminded me of when we'd first arrived at this new chapter of our lives. Little did they know what the next instalment involved.

'You're quiet,' I said as we waited for the lift after the nurses' change of shift signalled our time for us to go home for the day. 'What's up?'

He took my hand, twisting his lips.

I nudged him. 'Spill the beans. You haven't been right since we arrived at Tammy's this afternoon.'

It took him a while, but he answered in the end. As we left the heat of the hospital, hurrying to the car, he told me that seeing Tammy again had unnerved him. 'She looked so different to when we were kids. She used to be such a happy person. No; sunny, that's the word. She used to be a sunny person, always smiling, but today she looked the polar opposite.' He clicked the remote and opened the car door for me. 'And that name, Christopher Peter Mitchell, I'm sure I've heard it before.'

'Where?' I asked when he climbed in and closed his door.

He shrugged. 'It just sounds familiar.'

'Another shock?'

'I guess you'll want to find him too now.'

*

'I'm starving,' Jim said when we arrived home. He switched on the lights, and we went to the kitchen and raided the fridge. The remnants of a tuna bake Gill had cooked earlier that week when she'd stayed stood lonely on the middle shelf.

'Shall we order a takeaway?' I asked.

'I can't wait that long,' he said, so I chucked the leftovers in the microwave and found some peas in the freezer. Jim uncorked a bottle of Chablis and filled two glasses.

'Where've you heard of this Christopher before, then?' I asked, laying the table.

He shrugged.

'It's bugged you, hasn't it?'

He hesitated and gulped his wine. 'I haven't a clue. I get the feeling it was from when I was younger. When I was at school.'

'Stay here.' I nipped back to the hall and picked up my bag. Walking back to the kitchen, I removed my laptop. 'No time like the present.'

'What're you doing?'

I left the laptop to power up and walked over to stop the microwave pinging. 'We're going to start looking for him.' I got two plates out of the dishwasher. It hadn't been switched on, so I had to wash them up.

'Are you sure you want to get involved in all of this?' He took another gulp of wine and refilled his glass.

'One hundred per cent. Can you log into your Facebook account, please? We're going to look for him.'

He pushed the laptop away. 'I don't know. It doesn't feel right.'

I drained the peas, dished up, and took our dinner to the table. 'For me, please?'

He hesitated before hitting the keys.

'She said he was born in July 1979, didn't she?'

'I remember that. July the twentieth.' He turned the screen to me.

'That would make him, what, thirty-three now?'

I typed Christopher Peter Mitchell into the search engine. 'That can't be right,' I said. 'There's no one in the world with that name.'

'No one with a Facebook account, that is,' he said.

'Fair enough.' I took out the middle name as I stabbed a piece of pasta with my fork and put it into my mouth; it tasted old. Hundreds of Christopher Mitchells scattered about the globe packed the screen. We scrolled through the random collection of people – predominantly Americans – from all walks of life: an art director, actor, musician, golfer, security officer. One by one, we scanned their pages, but none of them matched who we were looking for: too young, wrong skin colour, too grey. I tried shortening the name to Chris and then Peter, but nothing.

'This feels wrong,' he said, pushing the laptop away.

'What's wrong about it? We need to find him.'

'Feels bloody creepy to me.' He shivered and emptied his glass again as if he were drinking apple juice, not wine.

I pushed my almost-full plate across the table. My appetite had never recovered from the birth. As though it were waiting for Joe to get better. 'Why?'

'I think we have bigger fish to fry at the moment.'

'What could be more important than our son?'

He slapped his hand on the table. 'That's exactly what I'm talking about, Eva. We need to get him well. Then we can get him home.' He reached over and tucked a piece of my hair behind my ear, then stood and took our plates to the dishwasher.

I plugged variations of the name into Google and clicked onto images. I gasped. There staring at me were several Peter Mitchells.

'What've you found?' Jim asked, coming back to sit down beside me. He replenished his glass of wine then slipped an arm around my shoulders.

I studied the screen and sighed. 'Too old, aren't they?' I'd already answered my question but still selected each image to double-check, working my way through the winner of the 1978 Nobel Prize for chemistry, a politician, and an actor, for starters.

Frustrated, I continued surfing, playing around with the name, riding the wave of hope that I'd find who I was looking for. But who was I looking for? Jim sat patiently by my side, commenting here and there, the wine prompting him to make unhelpful comments.

I got him to log into LinkedIn, and I entered the name again. A freelance designer from London appeared promising. I squinted at the screen. 'This could be him.' I checked his profile.

'Too young.' Jim pointed to his qualifications. 'Look, he left school in 1990.'

Another couple of potentials appeared, but after scrutinising their credentials, I soon realised they were the wrong age. 'What're you going to say if you find who you're looking for? Then what?' he asked.

I hadn't thought that far. What would I say? 'Hey, I'm your half-sister. Fancy meeting up.' I tutted and rubbed my eyes. They stung, but I carried on, scanning through the pages like a detective. Nothing. I frowned at the screen, tapping my fingers on the edge of the keyboard.

'Come on, let's catch some TV,' Jim said, pulling me up. I followed him into the lounge with the laptop tucked under my arm. He started aimlessly flicking through the channels. Nothing grabbed our attention, just the same old rubbish which seemed to dominate the TV at that time of night. He settled for the Black Eyed Peas on MTV as he drank my remaining wine.

I returned to Facebook and keyed David Benjamin Pilgrim into the search engine. Nothing. I removed the Benjamin. A couple of names appeared, but Jim laughed. 'They look more like your granddad than your dad.' He switched off the TV. 'Let's go to bed.'

'Be there soon.' I changed the name to Dave Pilgrim which widened the search. But as I scrolled through all the pages, it became apparent that this was not going to prove easy. There were several middle-aged men who could have fitted the bill. I googled the name, but nothing came up. Tammy was going to have to help me with this one.

What next?

I keyed "How to find your estranged family" in the search engine and, after about an hour, realised that this was going to take some planning. The routes to find missing family were plentiful, but the fact that Christopher was most likely given a new name on adoption, and could live anywhere in the world, made it clear that finding him wasn't going to be a walk in Kew Gardens. I needed Tammy to sign up to the Adoption Contact Register to start with. An official government directory, so if this brother of ours wanted to find his birth family, he could put his name on there too and a connection could be made.

I carried the laptop up to bed and, removing my make-up, I looked in the mirror. Dark rings circled my eyes. I needed to buy some concealer. After getting undressed, I joined a sleepy Jim. Nudging him, I asked, 'Where was that garage Tammy said my dad worked when they were together? It began with C, but I can't remember where she said it was.'

He sighed and rolled over. 'Let it rest now. You need to sleep.'

I nudged his back. 'Can you remember?'

'Croydon,' he said, tugging the duvet over his head.

It didn't take me long. Within a minute, I had an address for Billingham's Garage in Croydon.

Chapter 19

JIM

The Manhattan Plaza Hotel, New York
October 2011

Tammy Mitchell wasn't at all as I remembered. True, I hadn't seen her for some twenty years – two decades which had aged her remarkably – but still, seeing her again disturbed me. Her skinny frame reminded me of someone I'd lived with in halls during my first year at the LSE. Rachel Jennings – a frail girl of five-feet who had eaten lettuce leaves for lunch and drunk diet shakes for dinner.

Half-way through the visit, you excused yourself to go outside for some air. As Tammy chatted away, I started to feel unwell. Everything became out of focus as if I'd taken off my glasses. She bombarded me with questions – about my parents and my sisters, you and Ben and Dan.

'You two were such a pair of rascals. Tormented the life out of Christina and Victoria. What's he up to these days?' She kept clenching and unclenching her fists as if warming up for a fight, her white knuckles prominent against the yellow stains on her skinny fingers. 'Still a mischief-maker?'

I nodded, laughing, and we discussed Dan for a while. I

think we all needed a subject other than each other. 'He's a photographer now. Works all over the world in the fashion industry.'

'Does he, now? Clever boy. Both of you, such clever boys. Kept me on my toes, I can tell you.'

*

The morning after our visit, it was still dark when I woke. I'd slept fitfully, my mind a bundle of dilemmas like a ball of elastic bands. Joe was still worrying me sick, you too with your fierce determination to find your family. And Warren had summoned me into his office before I'd left work the previous night, clicking his fingers like a restaurant's worst customer. 'Jim. Have a seat,' he'd said, rolling up his sleeves, plonking his elbows on the desk and steepling his fingers. 'Now then, New York, New York,' he announced in the dry, demanding voice he often used when a problem or two needed sorting. And usually when I was the one he intended to carry out the sorting. 'We've got some financial shit going down in New York again. An IRS audit is due in October, and I need someone I can trust out there to take a look at what the hell's going on, clean up the crap and put a lid on it before the markets screw us. I've got other problems I have to focus on. You up for it?'

I couldn't believe it. He had a cohort of dedicated early risers and late stayers at his disposal, gagging for such an opportunity, but me – he'd chosen me! It had felt so good. So damn good, until I thought of you and Joe and knew that I wasn't the one who was going to be sorting his crap out this time. I just needed to find the right time to tell him, and it was stressing me out.

And that name, Christopher Peter Mitchell, had stuck in

my mind like a bad dream. Perhaps it was someone Dan knew? I glanced at the alarm clock. 5 a.m. He was in New York on an assignment. No doubt he'd still be up. I crawled out of bed, put on my dressing gown and crept downstairs. In the kitchen, I flicked the kettle switch, picked up my phone and dialled his number. His voice boomed into my ear. 'Hey, Jimbob, how's things? How's Joe doing?'

Voices buzzed over jazz music in the background, and I felt a momentary pang for how I'd once spent my Saturday nights. Life before you. I updated him on Joe and asked him what he was up to.

'Dinner party with someone I worked with on a shoot this week. Wait up, I'll go outside. I can't hear you in here.' I heard a door slam, and the sound of conversation and music morphed into the steady flow of traffic. He carried on. 'The host is hot. Burning hot, hot, hot, Jimbob. But alas, she's taken. The hot ones always seem to be these days.' He let out a hearty laugh. 'How did the family day go?'

You'd shared the plans to see Tammy with Dan the week before, which had niggled me at the time. Despite a rocky start, your relationship with him had blossomed. I'd never been the green-eyed type of guy, but I couldn't help myself when sometimes I'd arrive at the hospital, and you two would be chatting like best friends. Or sometimes I'd get home and you two would be sitting on the sofa, laughing and joking around. I knew it was me being stupid. Dan and I had grown up together, been best mates close to thirty-three years, shared the highs and the lows of males growing up in the nineties and early noughties. I trusted him with my life.

'Do you remember us ever coming across a guy named Christopher Peter Mitchell?' I asked.

He shouted over the wail of a police siren. 'Why?

'Do you recall that name? I'm wondering if it's someone we came across when we were at school or uni, or in Australia; or America, perhaps. Christopher Mitchell is a popular name for Americans if Facebook is anything to go by.'

'Not off the top of my head, no. Who's this guy, anyway?'

I filled him in.

He sighed. 'Jim, what're you doing? Seriously, think about it. Don't go fishing for this bloke; you don't know what you might catch.'

I couldn't explain the tightness in my chest and the grating in my head I'd felt since arriving at Tammy's the day before. 'Eva wants to find all her family now. She's made it her mission. She wants to find out if Joe's medical conditions are hereditary.'

Dan continued, 'Leave well alone, mate. You could come across a nut job for all you know.' He hissed like Hannibal Lecter.

'I'll catch up with you later,' I said, ending the call.

He didn't understand.

Chapter 20

EVA

'All tests have come back clear,' a doctor I'd never seen before informed me during morning ward round later that week. Plaited hair, make-up-free face and large round glasses, Dr Smith looked like she should have still been at school, not updating me on my baby's medical conditions.

I rested my book on the table. 'His kidneys are OK, then?'

She nodded. 'We'll keep monitoring, of course, but for now we'll leave things as they are.'

I leaned back into the chair. 'Are you sure? Are there any more tests you need to do?'

She smiled warmly. 'No. Everything's on track for now.'

For now? What else could go wrong? I was going to ask, but she'd already moved on to the next baby.

*

Ben arranged a taxi to bring Tammy to our first meeting with Karen Fleming, and I took the Tube. Karen ran her practice from shared premises above a bakery along Hampstead High Street. Four chartered clinical psychologists working together to create the Awareness Institute. "A non-judgemental, transparent and sympathetic centre where clients feel secure enough to open up about their problems" so their mission statement pronounced.

I'd spent a few hours with Joe before going. Things were looking up. After a dip in the scales, that morning they had announced a gain of a few ounces. His steady progression up the charts was meeting with the neonatologist's approval. Best of all, though, he'd come off the CPAP machine which was helping him breathe. They'd tried to take him off a couple of times before, but his oxygen levels had plummeted, so they'd put him straight back on. But now he'd been off for three days, and we could fully appreciate his endearing features. With dark hair and eyes and a miniature straight-edged nose, he was Jim's mini-me.

I arrived at the Awareness Institute an hour earlier than Ben and Tammy. Karen had requested to see me first for an "introduction" session. 'Welcome, Eva,' Karen said, gesturing for me to take a seat in one of the five armchairs which surrounded a glass-topped table. Beside each chair stood a solid wooden block with a box of tissues on top. The peaceful ambience of her carpeted room created the air of a space safe from the outside world. It smelled of cucumber and mint, vanilla and lemon. Plenty of natural light shone through two large sash windows, and a sprawling plant lived in the corner, the sun casting shadows of its leaves across the white walls.

Karen had a kind face, relaxed, with rosy cheeks and smiley features even when she wasn't smiling. 'Ben briefed me on your son. I'm sorry you're going through such a difficult time.'

The session commenced with run-of-the-mill questions. Her soft voice took some getting used to. I had to strain to hear the introduction to her services and what she believed she could do for me. She asked about my background, then smiled fondly when I said, 'Have you got all day?'

'So, what brings you here, Eva?'

I bit my lip. 'My brother wants to reunite us as a family.'

She scribbled on her pad and asked, 'Any other reason?'

'I won't lie to you. I need to find my family, too. And Tammy is the starting point.'

'Need to or want to?'

Between the sash windows hung a painting of a group of Buddhist monks robed in orange. There were seventeen of them.

Karen coughed.

'Need to. Joe has a heart condition.'

She nodded. 'Ben mentioned that.'

'Until yesterday, we thought he might have something wrong with his kidneys, too.' I bit my lip to stop it quivering. 'What if he ever needed a transplant? Maybe not now, but in one, two, five years' time, and there was a family member out there who could help him? He deserves for me to find them.'

Silence trickled awkwardness into the air. For me, anyway. Her empathetic stare provoked me to continue. 'But there's something about her that I don't trust. I don't know if that's because of her failure as a parent...' I paused before adding, 'or my gut instinct that rarely lets me down.'

'We can explore these points. And do be honest, Eva. It really is the best policy.'

There was a fifteen-minute gap between sessions, so I nipped down to the bakery for a coffee. I took it outside to wait for Tammy and Ben. A soft chill was moving the clouds, allowing the sun to beat down on my face. There were several tables, sectioned off from the pavement by yellow-painted railings, with containers bursting with flowers hanging over the edge. With the floral cushions scattered over the metal chairs, it was a kaleidoscope of summer colour. A heavily pregnant woman was sitting at the table diagonally opposite me, drinking herbal tea and browsing through a magazine. She had that radiant glow of someone soon to give birth. My stomach tightened, and so did my chest. I rubbed my hand across my belly where Joe should have been still growing and looked away to the blur of people scuttering along the streets.

When the cab pulled up and Tammy stepped out, I noticed she was limping. 'I tripped yesterday. Nothing to worry about,' she said, but it highlighted her fragility.

'You ready?' Ben asked brightly, as if we were going to a concert, not for a counselling session to try and find a way forward for our fucked-up family. He hooked one arm through mine and the other through Tammy's, and led us up the stairs. My heart banged against my chest with each step, and my legs grew heavier as though trying to stall me from what lay ahead.

'Good morning, Tammy. Ben. Why don't you sit opposite me, Tammy, and Ben and Eva either side of you? Does that work for you all?' She nodded at each of us. 'Get yourselves comfortable. I won't be a minute.' She left the room and Ben started rambling on about the price of cabs these days until Karen returned with a tray of four glasses and a large jug of water with shavings of cucumber floating in it. She placed it on the table, alongside an elegant sculpture in a bronze finish which depicted five different-aged hands joined together in a circle, each hand holding the wrist of the next – a family ring of unity.

'The best place to start is always at the beginning,' Karen said, lacing her hands together on her lap. I stared at the imposing array of self-help books on the shelves behind her which I hadn't noticed during the previous session: *Adult Children: The Secrets of Dysfunctional Families*, *The Family Crucible*, *The Genogram Journey: Reconnecting with Your Family*. At the end of the row stood a porcelain Buddha figurine acting as a bookend. 'Tammy, why don't you begin by telling us all a little about your childhood.'

'It was sad and lonely,' Tammy blurted out as if she had known in advance how the meeting would commence. She sat with her bag on her lap. It was new. I could tell by its brand-new-leather-mixed-with-chemicals smell which did nothing to complement Karen's cucumber-infused water.

'Do you want to talk about it?' Karen asked, then cast her eyes around the three of us. 'Can I just make it clear that no one has to talk about something they feel uncomfortable with.' She gave Tammy a reassuring smile. 'Carry on, Tammy. If you want to, that is.'

'I haven't seen my parents since I was fifteen. That's when I ran away from home.' Tammy shrugged. 'They were workaholics.' She stopped again as if she needed Karen's encouragement to carry on.

Karen gave her a gentle nod.

'My father was a doctor, and my mother a journalist. Well, that was her day job, anyway. She also served as a Tory councillor, so she was never around. At weekends she was either representing the constituents of the local community or dealing with the mounds of post which landed on the doormat every morning.'

I found it strange hearing her talk about her family. In

151

my eyes, she didn't come from a middle-class background, raised by the likes of doctors and journalists. She was poor and uneducated. *What had gone so horribly wrong for her?*

'My mother had plans. Big plans. I often overheard her discussing them with my father when they ate their late-night suppers together. She wanted to secure a parliamentary seat at the next general election.' Her sad voice continued to tell us about her parents' careers, which came first, last, and everywhere in between.

'At least you had parents,' I said. I couldn't help myself. Ben shot me a look as if to say, "Give her a chance". Tammy really did bring out the worst in me.

'Eva, you must let others talk without interruption. We'll get to you,' Karen said, her tone gentle but stern. 'Tammy, please continue.'

'They weren't around a lot.'

'How did that affect you?' Karen asked.

'They left my sister in charge of me most of the time. Bella, Miss Goody Bloody Two-Shoes. I know I shouldn't talk about the dead in such a derogatory way, but you need to know the truth. She bullied me and made my life a misery.' The bitterness in her voice was cutting. 'She was the one born with the brains. And as if that wasn't enough, she was also the belle of the ball and I was the ugly sister.' Tammy gave a derisive snort. 'She had it all, did beautiful, clever, popular Bella. Ten A grades, she achieved in her O levels.' She looked around us all as if, all these years later, she still couldn't believe such an accomplishment. 'Ten more than I could ever hope to achieve. She used to taunt me all the time. Never in front of anyone else, mind you. Oh, no, she wouldn't have ruined that perfect façade of hers.' Her voice turned high-pitched. "What? You're in the CSE stream? You didn't even make it to the O level classes?" she used to mock me with on the way to school every day.' She snorted again. 'My best friend, Deborah, always said that some girls were destined to be doctors and astronauts, but we'd have to settle for the checkouts. She was right. I was just plain little Tammy, with few words to say, and bugger all to offer.'

Her tone shocked me. Clearly she had hated her sister.

'It wasn't for lack of effort. I tried, honestly I did. I spent my primary years battling to join Bella coasting at the top of the class, but from an early age I knew that things weren't as they should be. Words confused me. Lessons baffled me.' She shrugged her shoulders as if they still did. 'No matter how hard I tried, I couldn't keep up. I was dead sure some-one tampered with the blackboard to wind me up. Swapping letters around and wiping random ones out as I tried to make sense of them all.' She looked at Karen and lifted her shoulders again. 'My husband spotted something was wrong. He made me go for tests. It took forty-five years for me to find out I was dyslexic.'

'How did that make you feel?' Karen asked.

'Useless. Worthless,' Tammy muttered. She went on to describe that while Bella carried on trailing the heels of her beloved father's footsteps, cramming for A levels in maths, physics and chemistry, she chugged along like an old steam train running out of coal.

'And I always had her hand-me-downs. One Christmas, Bella wanted a new stereo. She already had one, but she wanted a newer one. I wanted one, too. So, I put it on my Christmas list. And there it was on Christmas morning, all wrapped and ready, a new stereo. But guess who for? Bella, of course. And I got her old one. And I never got new clothes. It was always Bella's cast-offs for Tammy.' She screwed her mouth up and shook her head. Her story continued to spill as if Karen had finally allowed her to turn on her inner emotional tap, and she was finding it hard to turn it off again.

'On my ninth birthday, my mum came home from work early. It was a Saturday, and I was so happy. She was carrying a C&A bag.' She glanced from me to Ben. 'You've probably never heard of that shop. It was like a department store, where we used to get our clothes from. I remember the bag because it had a multicoloured stripe running down the side of it, and I thought, that looks like a rainbow. I loved rainbows when I was a kid. Anyway, she pulled this beautiful pleated dress out of it. It was yellow, and I was so excited thinking she'd bought me something new for my birthday party. But guess what she did next?' Tammy looked between the three of us. 'She handed it to Bella, then ran into Bella's bedroom and came out and thrust this old dress of Bella's at me. "She only wore it once. Go and try it on," she told me. It was too small. It scratched around my waist and dug into my armpits. I told her that I hated it, but she just slapped me. I'd been right, though. At the party, when my friends twirled me around in a game of pin the tail on the donkey, the buttons all popped off. They flew in all directions and completely ruined my day.'

She glanced in my direction. 'Do you two want to talk now?'

'It's still your turn, Tammy. Ben and Eva will have time to have their say.'

Tammy flapped her arm at Karen. 'They can talk now if they want to. They don't need to know all this stuff.'

154

'Small talk can unearth big discoveries. Let's stay with you. Carry on when you are ready.'

'I grew up way too early. Deborah was a year older than me, and I hung around with her a lot. She got me into clothes, dancing and boys. Every Saturday morning, we would catch the bus up to Oxford Street, browse the shops all day then return late afternoon each with what we both had agreed had earned the title of "outfit of the day". We'd take them up to my bedroom, craftily remove the security tags and pose for each other.' She looked from Ben to me. 'Yep, we nicked them.'

I looked at her aghast. Like mother like daughter – teenage years plagued with anxiety issues and dodging shop security.

She sat silent after that as if she didn't know how to continue. Her eyes dull, empty eyes and her slumped shoulders painted a clear picture of her troubled life.

Was my back as rounded as hers? I shifted in the armchair and corrected my posture, pulling my shoulders back and stomach in.

'Where did you go when you ran away from home?' Karen finally asked.

Tammy let out a large breath of air. 'That's a whole other story.'

Ben interrupted. 'Shouldn't you finish telling us what happened before you ran away from home?'

'What do you mean?' Tammy asked.

Ben raised his voice. 'You had a baby. You told us about him, Christopher, but you've refused to speak about him since. I've asked you to, but you won't. Why? What happened there?'

'I've told you, Ben. There's nothing more to say. I got pregnant. My mother made me give the baby up for adoption. It was the most distressing time of my life. I couldn't bear to be in her house another day, so I walked out.'

'But we have a half-brother out there.' My foot tapped the floor. 'I want to find him and our father.'

'How about we come back to this part a little later? Let's move to when you left home, Tammy,' Karen suggested. 'Take your time.'

Tammy fidgeted. Stopping to take deep breaths to fuel her story along, she described how, as Bella continued to wear her parents' crown of pride, Tammy trudged along drowning in utter despair. Bella left home to start a medical degree at Oxford University. Her mother couldn't contain her excessive delight as she told Tammy how Bella was still achieving straight As, in addition to courting a fellow medical student whose father was a member of the Conservative Party and owned a holiday home in the Algarve. Escaping the suffocation of the walls closing in on her, before they squeezed the last ounce of oxygen from her lungs, became Tammy's priority. Little by little, so as not to raise suspicion, she took what money she could from her mother's purse and father's wallet and stashed it away in a pouch she hid inside the cup of a bra at the back of her underwear drawer. She didn't even make it to her sixteenth birthday before she left the cold collection of rooms her parents had called their home.

Chapter 21

EVA

Karen booked us in for the same time the following week, and after we'd said goodbye, Ben, Tammy and I stopped for coffee. I wanted Tammy to complete the Adoption Contact Register form I'd printed off that morning. 'I'll do all the leg work, and I'll pay. I just need you to give me the information.'

'You're wasting your time, Eva. I remember my mother telling me that he would've been given a new name when he was adopted.'

'You never know, he may come looking for us. For you, anyway. He wouldn't know Ben and I existed,' I said, fumbling around in my bag for a pen. I fished one out and passed it to her, surprised to see my hand shaking as much as hers. My nails tapped the table as I watched her complete the form. There weren't many questions, but she paused at each one as if she had to consider the answer. Her pinched face looked drained, as if it were a considerable effort for her. Maybe that was because of her dyslexia. Or perhaps her reluctance to complete the task.

When she'd finished, I downed my coffee. 'I must go.'

There it was again. That irrepressible yearning to be with Joe. The magnetic pull of motherhood forcing me back to my baby. I grabbed a twenty-pound note from my purse and slipped it in the bill holder. 'See you next week,' I said, and ran to hail a cab back to my son.

*

After tending to Joe, I started the search for my grandparents. With careers accelerating under the spotlight, it didn't take long, making me wonder why Ben hadn't found them already. Felicity had succumbed to motor neurone disease nine years ago, and Patrick to prostate cancer, six months later. He had been a highly respected member of the medical profession, contributing to a pioneering treatment for a children's blood disease and winning countless clinical awards. Articles he'd written packed the British Medical Journal. I scanned through them, fascinated by his achievements. And my grandmother, after her career in journalism, had worked – or wormed, according to Tammy – her way into politics in her early forties. A right-wing Conservative, she had caused quite a stir in her day with her strong views on equality. I thought about everything Tammy had revealed about them that morning with Karen. *How had they produced Tammy?*

I spent the next two hours registering with every website that could possibly lead me to my father and brother. A collection of organisations promising their utmost to deliver you to your loved ones. There were enough of them. One particular adoption agency piqued my interest. A countrywide organisation, it reunited families by mutual consent without the need to access adoption records. I spent ages trawling through the reunion registry:

Johnmartinrinder: searching brother adopted at birth, born 6th June 1966, Whipps Cross hospital. Birth name, Simon Partridge, Mother Margaret Partridge, Father unknown. Please get in touch.

Sandra1968: I gave birth to a baby boy at King's College Hospital, 27th April 1979. I registered him as Samuel Southgate. He was adopted straight away. I'm desperate to find him.

There were pages of them. Entry after entry of desperate people hunting for missing and estranged family. I swallowed the lump lingering in the back of my throat. It took a couple of attempts to be rid of it. And then, at the bottom of the page, stories of happy reunions. I registered with them, entering all the details I knew about Christopher, but nothing relevant appeared. I tried my dad after that, only to receive the same result.

Mia's appearance made me jump. She swiped the curtains around our bay. My questioning face asked her what was happening.

'Nothing to panic about. Joe needs a blood transfusion.'

'Not another one. Why?'

'Tests have shown he's anaemic. Don't worry. Nothing sinister. We're going to start straight away, though.' She handed me some paperwork. 'You know the drill. I need you to sign where I've put the markers.'

Here we were again. Back on the emotional rollercoaster of the NICU. One I couldn't get off, because it wouldn't slow down to allow me to.

'How long will it take?'

'A few hours.' You look tired, Eva. Go home for the day. I'm on until change of shift.' She glanced down and lifted her fob watch. A beam of sunshine through the windows shined the top of her red hair a brilliant golden shade, like a halo. 'I'll still be here when the transfusion finishes, so I can call you if there are any problems.' She reached across and plucked a pair of latex gloves from the box on the wall. 'Not that there will be.' When I didn't move, she said more forcefully, 'Go.'

'I'll be back later,' I said, pulling on my jacket.

'Just rest at home. Or take Jim to dinner. You're going to need all your energy when this wee man gets out of here.'

I shoved my things into my bag. 'I'll be back in a couple of hours.' I said. She shook her head like a schoolteacher.

*

I called Billingham's garage before I'd even left the ward. I knew Frank still owned it. I just wanted to check he was there. I then dialled Ben's number as I marched home. He answered on the first ring as if he had sensed the urgency of the call. 'What you up to?' I asked.

'Constructing a marketing plan. Well, trying to, at least.'

'Meet me at Clapham Common station in forty-five minutes.'

'Where're we going?'

'Croydon.'

'You are kidding me.'

I stopped at home only to pick up the car keys and grab a bottle of water from the fridge. There was an eerie feeling of emptiness in the house. Or was that the emptiness in me? I jumped in the car and counted the minutes all the way to Clapham Common station – eighteen – where Ben was waiting for me, shaking his head, as Mia had forty-five minutes earlier.

'Are you mad?' he asked, climbing into the car.

'It feels like it some days.'

'I can't believe we're doing this.'

'Neither can I.' I pressed my foot on the accelerator. A rush of speed threw me back into the seat as I pulled away from the station.

'You did call first, I take it?'

'Frank is there.'

'You spoke to him?'

I nodded.

'Why didn't you just ask him?'

'If he knows something about Dave Pilgrim, he's more likely to tell us face-to-face.'

'You're not thinking straight.'

'I've got something to tell you,' I said, ignoring his unhelpful comments.

'What?'

'Tammy's parents are dead.'

'I know.'

I shot him a look. 'Since when?'

'A few days ago.'

'Why didn't you tell me?'

'Wanted to wait until I saw you.'

'Does Tammy know?'

He shook his head. 'I'll tell her later.'

My stomach turned faster than the car wheels during the forty minutes it took to reach the scruffy workshop with "Billingham's, family business since 1979" branded across its brickwork. 'Looks like we made it,' Ben said taking a deep breath. Second-hand tyres, entwined with ivy, were piled up by the corrugated frontage, and an antiquated petrol pump stood desolate by the entrance. I stopped the car on the opposite side of the road, my heart pounding like a drum. Ben was right. I wasn't thinking straight. *What are we doing here?*

'Did you know that four thousand five hundred children passed through the adoption process last year compared to twelve thousand one hundred in 1978?'

I thought about this statistic for a moment as I wrung my clammy hands together. 'That's a vast difference.'

He nodded. 'It surprised me too.'

'Come on, then; let's do this.'

I pulled onto the forecourt and parked between two old bangers. Stepping out of the car, I took several deep breaths, trying to stop my stomach from spinning. Inside we found busy mechanics exchanging banter over music blaring from an old transistor radio. The intense stench of grease caught in my throat, making me cough. 'Can we help you?' someone called out.

Ben stepped forward. 'We're looking for Frank.'

'Boss, some people here for you,' the mechanic bellowed towards the back of the workshop. A bull-necked man appeared, late fifties at a guess, dressed in grease-soiled overalls and a faded baseball cap. He limped towards us with a curious look on his face, banging a spanner against his oil-stained fingers. 'Your car broke down?' His voice was as rough as his hands.

'Frank?' Ben said.

'Who's asking?'

'My name is Ben Mitchell. I'm hoping you can help me. I'm searching for my dad, David Pilgrim. He worked here back in the nineties.'

Frank clenched his fingers around the spanner. With raised eyebrows, he studied Ben for a while. 'Correct.'

'Where's he now? Do you know?'

The banging and crashing faded as the mechanics ear-wigged our conversation. They pretended to work under the bonnets of the cars, glancing up now and again.

Frank laughed scornfully. 'You kidding me? How should I know? He walked out of here over twenty years ago. Left us right in the lurch. My dad hit the roof. He took Dave on as an apprentice when he left school. Then Dave called one Sunday night and said he had to go away for a while.'

'Where? Why?'

'Bother at home like. Not that that surprised us. Right nutter he'd hooked up with. No wonder he left her, the crackpot.'

'Do you mean Tammy Mitchell?'

'That's the one. She looked after the kids of some well-to-do family out in the sticks. Not right in the bonce, her. The stories he shared with me. We waited every Monday morning for months thinking he'd show up, but we never saw him again.'

'Where'd he go?' Ben asked.

'London. To friends in Hackney, on the Holly Street estate. Right dodgy old joint. My aunt lived there before she passed. They demolished it a few years ago. Can't say I'm shocked.'

'Did you keep in touch?'

'I tried to find him myself when my aunt checked out. But he'd moved on, the mob there told me. With some bird with two kids. They moved out towards the Essex coast. Colchester, somewhere around there.'

'Anything else you know?'

'Sorry, can't help you.' He paused and glanced from Ben to me then back at Ben again, frowning. 'He used to bring you in here when you were a nipper.' He smiled at the recollection. 'Some Saturday mornings. He used to explain to you how car engines worked. You were too little to remember, though.'

Ben twisted his lips and seemed about to say something, but didn't.

'Would you know anyone who might have an idea where he ended up?' I asked.

'Sorry I can't help you more.' He walked off to the direction he had come from, turning briefly to say, 'I wish you luck in finding him. If that's what you really want.'

'Let's go,' I said, grabbing Ben's sleeve.

'Thanks for your time. Much appreciated,' Ben called after him.

Frank raised a hand.

On the way back to the car, Ben squeezed my shoulder. 'We've got work to do.'

Completely deflated, I felt like one of the old bangers parked next to us. Like I had a puncture which had sucked out my spirit. 'This could take forever.'

'When we were kids, we lived near that Holly Street estate. You probably don't remember. I had a friend who lived there. Another Ben – Benjamin Clarkson. His flat was on the sixth floor, and he always made me go in the lift with him. It stank of piss and was covered in graffiti. Disgusting it was, but he still made me go in it because his mum wouldn't let him use it on his own. I guess you'll want to go to Colchester now?'

I nodded. 'Once I find him.'

'When we lived with Mum on Well Street in Hackney, our dad only lived a mile or so away. All that time and we didn't know. I wonder if she knew?' He crossed his arms over his chest and in a low-pitched, steady voice added, 'We will find him, you know.'

'I know,' I said. Because my baby needed me to.

Chapter 22

EVA

'Sorry, shall we carry on from where we left off last week?' Karen said when we were all seated ready for our second session. 'Firstly, Eva, how is your son?'

I beamed. 'All good news. He's reached four pounds. The doctor is pleased with his heart. They are talking about transferring him to an open cot and moving him to SCBU, the special care baby unit.'

Karen clapped her hands together in front of her chest. 'That's wonderful news. Congratulations. You'll be getting him home soon, then?'

'Let's hope so,' I said, fanning my face with a leaflet I'd picked up off the table, titled Family Mediation. 'It's stuffy in here today.'

Karen walked over to the large sash windows and partly opened one of them, which let in a flow of air along with a steady buzz from the traffic and street below. 'So, over to you, Tammy,' she said, sitting back down.

Tammy carried on. A week's interlude had not stopped her flow. 'So, I ran away from home.'

I butted in. 'We've found some news out since we were last here.'

Karen arched her eyebrows at me.

'Our grandparents are dead.' I briefed Karen on the details.

Tammy carried on as if I'd casually shared the news that it was raining outside or what I'd had for breakfast that morning. 'I stuffed a few things into a suitcase and boarded a bus up West. It was cold and raining, and I was so scared, but I knew I never wanted to see my parents again.' She shrugged. A shrug that said how little she had cared about them. 'I wandered the streets for ages as if waiting for someone to rescue me. Later that same morning, I found myself in some dingy café in Soho. I ordered a cup of tea and sat staring out of the window, wondering what to do. I needed a job and somewhere to stay for the night. I saw a bloke on the opposite side of the road selling fruit and veg from boxes resting on a curtain of fake grass on a cart. All he had to do was weigh them, tip them into brown paper bags and twist the corners, and I thought to myself, how hard can that be? He had customers queuing around the corner into the next street.'

There was a pause as Tammy encountered one of her coughing fits. Karen leaned forward and refilled Tammy's glass. 'I'll open another window,' she said, 'When you're ready, Tammy, we're all listening.'

When the coughing calmed, Tammy continued. 'I remember it as if it were only yesterday. I ordered another tea, trying to pluck up the courage to go and ask the bloke if he would give me a job, when this voice made me jump. I'll never forget his well-groomed moustache and garish kipper tie, or his opening words to me. "What's a cute-looking lady doing in a dump like this?" he said, offering me a cigarette. "Robert Ray. Pleased to meet you." Within ten minutes, he'd offered me work. "Entertainment industry," the dirty bugger said, rubbing his hands together. "I have an opening in one of my shows at this very moment, which will suit a young lady of your character." He had such a smug smile. "A job for you pretty one, and a palace where you can lay your weary bones at night." I remember it all so clearly.'

'He gathered up my belongings, threw some coins on the counter, and escorted me out of the café as if he already owned me. I knew I shouldn't have gone with him, but I was scared I wouldn't have anywhere to sleep that night. He pulled me along, smiling and muttering to himself words I couldn't make out. Then I found myself outside a building wedged between a sleazy sex cinema and a tattoo parlour in Walker's Court. "Come on, girl. Follow me," he said.'

Ben and I sat mesmerised by her story, Karen too. How clearly Tammy could recall the details astonished me.

'He led me up two flights of rickety stairs to a dark landing so small there was only room for him and my suitcase. He knocked on one of two doors but didn't wait for an answer. He shouldered it open and burst in, dragging me behind him. It was a drab old bedsit, save some signs that someone had tried, at least, to brighten it up. Fading Polaroids of smiling girls stuck on the fridge, flowers in a vase on the table, that kind of thing. It stank of hairspray and cheap perfume. I remember it as if it were yesterday. This voice shouted out. "Bloody well wait for an answer before you barge in here, will you?" That was frizzy-haired Katie.' Tammy gave an affectionate smile. 'She became my friend; I don't know what I'd have done without her. "This is Tammy. Explain my expectations and make sure she's working by tomorrow night." That's all Robert said. Then he lit a cigarette, winked at us both, and left.'

She stopped talking for a while and fiddled with the strap of her handbag. Karen encouraged her along. 'You have such a vivid memory of those times. Do you want to tell us more?'

'Katie led me back down the staircase and into another large room. "Welcome to our dressing room. You can have this seat," she said, showing me a pink padded chair with suspender belts and fishnet stockings hooked over the arms. It faced a dressing table, crowded with crumpled, lipstick-stained tissues, and above it hung a large mother-of-pearl framed mirror with a string of red bulbs hanging around the edge.'

Karen shifted in her seat, and Tammy's voice broke at this point as she told us about the dozens of unpaired shoes lying dotted about the floor and clothes piled over every visible surface like a chaotic jumble sale. She never saw Robert Ray again. He vanished without notice, leaving the girls to run the establishment served by one muscled knucklehead who worked the door and another who managed the music. It didn't turn out as difficult as she'd first imagined. Before long, Katie, an acrobatic performer who could strip off a camisole while hanging upside down with her toes curled around a stainless-steel pole, had taught her to perfect the art. Ben burst into laughter at that description, which made Tammy and me laugh too. Even Karen couldn't help a giggle. It cleared the air somewhat.

They made a team – ta-dah – the Katie and Tammy show. Katie looked out for Tammy and Tammy for Katie. Within weeks, Tammy's parents and Bella were just a blur Tammy conversed with only in her dreams as she developed a love-hate relationship with the busy and noisy Soho that became her home. She detested the peep shows and private booths, and the flashing illuminations from the façades of the seedy porn shops with their sex aids on open display, but she grew fond of the pubs and clubs where she and Katie hung out in their spare time, drinking Alabama Slammers and B52s.

As I sat in that hot and stuffy room listening to my mother – the woman who gave birth to me, at least – it occurred to me, with a pang, that despite the degradation and bad decisions, she had lived, really lived, and often on the wrong side of morality.

I felt nothing but overwhelming compassion for her.

Karen had been right. Small talk can unearth big discoveries. Leaving me wondering what else Tammy's words were going to unbury.

Chapter 23

EVA

'Sorry, I forgot to take my keys when I left,' Dan said when I opened the front door later that night. I'd not long been in from the hospital myself.

'How're things? How's Joe?' he asked, throwing his coat over the banister. He kicked off his shoes and dropped his holdall at the bottom of the stairs and followed me into the lounge.

'Good news. I'm hoping we'll get him home soon.'

He dropped onto the sofa. 'Then the fun will really begin.'

'You know my friend Gill? She's offered to come and stay when we bring him home. To help me out.'

'Sounds like a plan.'

'You don't mind?'

'Why would I mind? If it helps you, go for it.'

'Where've you been this week? I can't remember.' Nothing was registering in my brain tonight. It was too crammed with Tammy's revelations from earlier on.

'Poland and Belarus.'

'Good time?'

'Not really. They were outside shoots and the weather shockingly cold. What time's Jim back?'

'He's not. He flew out to Madrid yesterday. Not back until tomorrow night.'

'He didn't tell me.'

'He didn't know himself until Monday night. That bloody boss of his. He's turned Jim into a workaholic, just like him.'

'You need to be a workaholic to work for Warren Price. You ever met him?'

I nodded. 'You want a drink?'

'What're you proposing?' He raised an eyebrow and smiled. The smile that I'd once found offensive, but had come to accept, over the last eight or so months, as part of his endearing personality. I'd made a real effort with him and discovered he was more than the obnoxious prick I'd originally taken him for. Which came as a relief. No woman wants to find herself on the wrong side of her fiancé's best friend.

'Tea, coffee?' I asked.

'But it's hump day, and I've been hanging around an airport or on a plane for most of it.'

'Bottle it is, then.'

'Only if you'll join me.'

I went to fetch some drinks.

He called out to me in the kitchen. 'The plane food was dreadful. Always is with the Eastern European airlines. I've barely eaten all day.'

I grinned and searched for something quick to eat; the kitchen cupboards were in desperate need of a decent food shop. I hadn't really bothered since Joe's birth. Food was a necessity rather than a pleasure, and I'd taken to grabbing what was on offer from the hospital canteen, or a chuck-in-the-oven from the forecourt M&S. Especially when Jim was away. Luckily, I found a tube of Pringles amongst a lonely can of tomato soup, some noodles and tins of tuna. I grinned. Gill wouldn't stand for this.

When Jim had asked if Dan living with us bothered me, I'd lied when I'd said no. 'He's not around much, so he won't be any bother,' Jim had said. 'It'll only be temporary until he has more of a clue as to where he'll end up workwise. He may go out to New York again. We've talked about me buying him out at some point.' Jim had been right. We hardly saw Dan. He worked away a lot and partied like a wild beast. Ever since I'd found out I was pregnant, Jim and I were usually in bed by the time he found his way home. And when Jim was away on business, Dan tended to get back earlier, and I found his presence in the house comforting. Coming home to an empty house after a day at the hospital was as depressing as sitting by Joe's cot waiting for him to get better. I just didn't see Dan making any effort to find somewhere more permanent.

I grabbed a couple of bottles of Bud from the fridge. Luckily Jim kept the fridge well-stocked in that department. Balancing the Pringles under my arm, I returned to the lounge. 'What're your plans? I could call for pizza if you fancy it.'

'Sounds tempting, but I've got a date.' He gulped his beer and shoved a stack of the crisps into his mouth.

'Now there's a surprise.'

We both laughed. Dan's obsession with the sparks of a new relationship had become a standing joke between Jim and me, and we often teased him about his short-lived relationships. 'Don't tell me. You met her on the plane today.'

'Who's Miss Clever Clogs then? She was one of the air hostesses and a very friendly one at that.'

'What's her name?'

'Zofia. Zofia Nowark.'

'Why do you always go for the foreign ones?'

He laughed playfully. 'They're easier to get rid of when I've had enough.'

I flumped beside him and slapped him on the thigh. 'When're you going to stop this serial dating?'

'When I find the right woman, Eva. When I find the right woman.' He took another gulp of beer. 'Jim told me your exams went well.'

I nodded. 'A first.'

'A first for your first year. I really admire you, you know. Being pregnant and achieving a result like that.'

'I needed to have something to show for the debt the fees have saddled me with. Besides, I do want a career at some point.'

'You're a tough cookie, Eva Mitchell.'

'Luckily Joe didn't come any earlier or I wouldn't have got to take them.'

'I heard things are going well with your mum?'

I sighed heavily.

'They're not?'

'Not sure how much Jim has told you, but my long-lost family is creeping out of the unknown. Grandparents, an aunt, my dad, a brother – it's like a frickin' episode of EastEnders.'

He laughed. 'Think you'll find there're scores of families out there as complicated, if not more so. What's the latest?'

'I found out that my father used to work at a garage in Croydon. Then one day, when Tammy was pregnant with me, he just walked out, and she never saw him again. How can people do that? Just disappear from their lives?' I didn't tell him about the trip to see Frank. I hadn't told Jim yet and it felt disloyal.

'You don't know the circumstances. He would've had his reasons. Maybe Tammy chucked him out.'

'What if he shuns me when I find him?'

'Or maybe he'd love to see you now.'

'Do you ever think about finding your dad?'

He sneered. 'Never in a million years.' He crossed his arms over his chest. 'But it's different.'

'Why? What's different about it? Your dad walked out. My dad walked out.'

'I had twelve years with mine. Although my parents divorced when I was ten, he was still a big part of my life. Then, when I needed him most, when I was nearly a teenager, he moved halfway across the world without giving me and my brothers a second thought.' He stared blankly at his bottle of beer before necking the rest of its contents.

'That must've been tough for you all.'

'I understood the divorce. I mean, there's no convenient time for your parents to split up, is there? People don't get on, right? So what's the point in staying together? I get that. My parents fought every day for as far back as I can remember. Neither was to blame. Things were better when they parted and he moved out. Yes, we lost the big house and the big garden and the lavish holidays, but at least we didn't have to listen to them squabbling every five minutes. But to move to the other side of the world and completely wipe us out of his life is pretty heartless, wouldn't you say? I felt betrayed.'

'You never heard from him again?'

He shook his head. 'Nope. We never even had a phone number for him.'

I never thought I could feel sorry for Dan. He just wasn't that type of guy people spared pity for, but my heart pumped an extra beat for him at that moment, and I found my head on his shoulder. 'What did they argue about?'

'My mum was unstable, is one way to put it.'

'Snap.'

He laughed. 'She had a difficult delivery with me and nearly died. Then afterwards, she suffered postnatal depression. From which, according to my dad, she never truly recovered.'

'So, there was no contact whatsoever after he left?'

'Not even a card at Christmas. We never heard another word from him. My brothers were traumatised. It took them years to get over it, and I wonder if Noah, the youngest, ever has. He's been in and out of trouble all his life. A habitual shoplifter, he even spent a year in a youth detention centre.'

'What's he doing now?'

'Not a lot. He still lives with Mum and works in a bar in Guildford. I had to be tough for their sake, so I acted like I didn't care.' He rested his chin on my head.

I closed my eyes. We hadn't realised that we shared a mutual understanding of what it was like to be betrayed by someone who should have protected you and looked after you. We remained that way for a while, his chin on my hair, silent and still. I found it comforting – a solace amongst the mayhem of our childhood memories.

'Life can be shit,' he whispered before gently pushing me away. 'What's next, then? You going to find your dad and this brother of yours?'

Chapter 24

JIM

The Manhattan Plaza Hotel, New York
October 2011

I should've listened to Dan when he told me to leave well alone. But things are never as straightforward as we want them to be, are they, Eva? You know, more than anyone, that life has a habit of throwing hurdles in your path when all you want is to jog along in peace.

All I wanted was to smother you in love and make you happy.

*

Ben called me at work one morning. 'I'm up in the West End today, you free for lunch?' he asked, then added, 'Please,' when I didn't answer straight away. Eyeing my overflowing in-tray and the file Warren had slapped on my desk earlier, I tried to find a polite way of saying no, but then detected an inkling of desperation in his voice. He was my future brother-in-law, I reminded myself, so gave him directions to a small Italian I knew a few streets from my offices near Bond Street underground. I often took clients there. Pricey, but the service was quick and their seafood risotto second to none.

I had an hour to spare, at a push. Listen to me – I sounded more like Warren every hour! He'd landed yet another unrealistic deadline on my desk that morning – a trip to Zurich the following day to present a report to one of our influential clients. And guess what? I had to source a mass of data to prepare said report by close of play that day for him to approve. Ever since he'd promoted me to Director, when I'd completed the New York project at Christmas, he'd drained me dry. Sticking me on planes and delegating heaps of his projects my way. 'I'm prepping you for my shoes. You do know that, don't you?' he'd told me over dinner at the Ritz one evening that week while we were waiting for a client who was about to sign a major deal with us.

For years, all I'd ever aspired to was to be the next Warren Price – to head the European arm of the company. I was so near, so damn close. He'd started his move into the Pacific Rim. I'd overheard Janita talking to another secretary that week, about some property viewings she'd booked for his upcoming trip to Singapore. The door was almost open enough for me to slip in and sit in his chair.

The goal I'd strived to achieve for so long was waiting for me to pass the finishing line and grab the prize. But as I got closer, I couldn't quite reach it, and I couldn't quite work out why. Maybe fear that I wasn't capable of matching up to the oh-so-mighty Warren Price? 'You need to kick your impostor syndrome,' you often told me. I knew you were right; I just couldn't seem to strike hard enough to score the winning goal.

I was running late, and when I arrived Ben was already there, killing time with a Peroni at the bar. The host grabbed two leather-bound menus and led us to a small table in view of the kitchen where chefs were busy spinning pizza dough and slicing meat and vegetables. I pulled out a leather chair, amid the wafts of roasted garlic and bubbling tomatoes. The waitress tapped our order into her device.

As soon as we sat down, I detected a hidden agenda to the casual lunch I'd assumed it to be. Twiddling a leather wrap bracelet around his wrist, Ben began his usual abstract prattle – something about Italian cooking and the calorie difference between a pizza and a risotto. After the waitress returned with our drinks, we chatted about his business before he revealed the real reason he had called me that day for lunch. 'I need your help, Jim.' He ran his hands around the collar of his T-shirt. 'Can you lend me some money?'

I coughed. 'How much do you need?'

'Can you spare me five grand?'

Five grand. Five bloody grand, for Christ's sake. I whipped off my glasses and rubbed my eyes.

'I know it's a lot, but I've got no one else to turn to.'

'What do you need it for?'

A blotchy rash started to crawl up his neck. 'I'm in a spot of bother. I owe some people money.' He was silent for a moment as if assessing the impact of his next sentence. 'Also, I want to hire a private detective to find my dad and this brother of ours. Eva's desperate, you know.'

I stared at him; my jaw dropped at his audacity. I'd lost interest in the search for Christopher Peter Mitchell and your father. I knew you wanted to find them, and I'd listened to your concerns about Joe's potential need for a transplant and future genetic testing. But I failed to see the urgency. The timing was all wrong, so I'd put it to the back of my mind. Not forever – more like relegating a half-read book to

179

the rear of a shelf with the intention to pick it up and finish it one day. In my view, we just needed to get Joe well enough to take him home. That had to remain our priority.

The waitress appeared with our food, granting me time to think. Not that it made any difference. I still didn't know what to say. What would I tell you, Eva? The waitress served the food and asked if we wanted another drink. I shook my head. I had too much work waiting for me back at the office. Ben downed his beer, handed her his empty bottle and nodded his request for another. He started to slice his pizza. 'Say no if you can't. I've got five hundred quid that Mum gave me for my birthday, and I've got a couple of hundred saved, but I need five thousand.'

'Tammy gave you five hundred pounds for your birthday? That's generous.'

'I think she's making up for all the birthdays she's missed.'

'Have you spoken to Eva about this?'

'No.'

I sighed heavily. 'Give me your bank account details. I'll transfer it over. I'll have to tell Eva, though.'

'Could I possibly have a grand in cash?'

Loading my fork, I drew it to my mouth, but a sudden bad taste brushed the back of my throat. I dropped the food back on the plate. 'OK, I need to go to the bank, though.' I scraped the risotto around in a circle.

'Thanks, Jim. I owe you one,' he said after I'd raided the cashpoint and we exchanged goodbyes at Grosvenor Square Garden. I felt queasy as I watched him wander off. I blamed the risotto until it struck me that it was him. I shivered as goosebumps slid down my spine. What kind of trouble was he in? I entered the garden and hurried over to an empty

180

bench near to the steps of the Franklin Roosevelt memorial statue. I loosened my tie and buried my hands in my pockets. For Christ's sake, what was happening? It wasn't the first time I'd lent Ben money. He'd asked the same favour of me many times – five to be exact – to sub him a few hundred here and there. And only he and I knew about the plane ticket and new life I'd bought him to escape the delinquent gang he'd got himself involved with all those years ago. But five grand? I'd always caved easily. Given him whatever he'd asked for, despite my resolution not to as he'd never fully repaid my generosity. Each time he'd started with the right intentions, handing over the correct amount on time. However, after the first couple of repayments, his attempts became sporadic until they dwindled to nothing. But I'd just let it go. There had always been something about Ben.

Two Japanese tourists parked themselves on the bench beside me, shortly joined by another munching on a freshly-baked Belgian waffle. I usually loved that sweet vanilla smell. It reminded me of being a kid. Biting into the warm, gooey mouthful of heaven my mother used to make on special occasions. Or had that been Tammy? I shifted along to the end of the bench. Today, the sickly smell turned my stomach.

Apprehension accompanied me back to work like an unwashed stranger. Ben was broke. How could I let him pay to find your family? You were going to be my wife. You were my responsibility. I was the one who needed to sort this for you. I scrolled through my phone for Jake Harrison's number. He owed me big time.

Chapter 25

EVA

One night the following week, on the way home from the hospital, I met Carrie for a drink in Marco's. Jim was away – so was Dan – and I couldn't face going home to an empty house, so at the last minute, I'd succumbed to her offer. I'd not seen her for a month. She'd been holidaying in Costa Rica, visiting her father's family. 'Come out with us this evening,' she said, opening a bottle of Sauvignon Blanc she had waiting. She'd arranged a get together for the few students from our course who had stayed in London for the summer. 'Everyone would love to see you. They keep asking after you.'

It was lively in there, glasses clinking, a loud buzz from people chatting, the ding of the kitchen bell to signal another meal to serve. I felt misplaced, a sharp sense that I no longer fitted in anywhere anymore. Guilt raced through me. My place was now beside Joe. It somehow felt ugly to be in a carefree scene of pints of lager and bottles of wine.

Carrie clicked her fingers in front of my eyes. 'Anyone there?'

'Sorry, miles away.' I felt like crying. I wanted to go home. I wanted to go back to the hospital. Actually, I didn't know what I wanted, only that it was to be somewhere other than there.

She slid a large glass of wine across the table as her eyes scanned the room, pausing at a group of guys with gym-loving biceps sitting diagonally opposite us. She clinked her glass against mine. 'Cheers. So, are you going to come out?'

'Sorry, my head's not in the right place.'

'Knew you'd say that but still wanted to ask. How's Joe?'

'A constant worry.' I glanced at my watch. 'But good news. He's graduated to the SCBU.'

'What's that?'

'The special care baby unit.'

'Still sounds serious.'

'Yes and no. He no longer needs intensive care, which is positive, and he's out of the incubator. He's still got a feeding tube, but a lot of the lines have gone, so it's easier to cuddle him. But he's still not feeding right, and he needs to gain a bit more weight.'

'He's on the home stretch, then?' She looked pleased for me, but she didn't understand the significance. Only mums who had sailed the turbulent waters of life with a preemie could relate to the relief this news brought. It wasn't all plain sailing ahead, but Joe was on course for home.

'And how's Jim?'

'He flew off to Zurich for a meeting this morning. Not back until tomorrow.'

'He's always flying off somewhere.' She shook her head. 'God, how do you do it?'

'Do what?'

'Be with one guy? Even if he is a catch as worthy as Jim.'

'I can't imagine it being any different now.'

'Rather you than me. There's too much choice out there. I've got a date with Mr Leathers on Saturday.'

'Mr Leathers?'

Surreptitiously, she pointed to the bar where a man with a ponytail, dressed in black biker's gear, sat sipping a bottle of beer.

I rolled my eyes. 'You should be with Dan. He's a male version of you. A perfect pair of sluts.'

She laughed with me. 'The photographer? Now he's one superior specimen of the male race. He hasn't been in Marco's for a while. He still living with you and Jim?'

I nodded.

'Doesn't he get in the way?'

I shook my head. 'When Jim's around he makes himself scarce, and when Jim's away, he keeps me company.'

'I didn't think you liked him?'

'I didn't when I first met him, but he's grown on me. He's been so kind with Joe. Comes up to the hospital to visit a lot. Sorts out stuff at home.'

'Things have changed, then. Don't you fancy him?' She held her thumb and index finger and squeezed them together in front of my face, giggling. 'A teeny-weeny bit? I mean, come on. How could you not?'

'Cut it, will you? He's my husband-to-be's best mate.'

'Wouldn't stop me.'

I giggled. 'No, I doubt it would.'

I sipped my drink as two guys passed with a tray of shots. One of them – tall, with a trimmed beard and well-gelled hair – stopped and high-fived Carrie and they briefly chatted. I gazed around the place. I hardly recognised anyone. Even Jason had shifted a few pounds and now helped out behind the bar. Evidence that time didn't stop or wait when you found yourself confined within the walls of a hospital ward.

'How's that brother of yours? Still with the doc?'

I nodded. 'Still with Emmy.'

'Shame. What a waste.' She winked at me. 'And your mum, how's that going?'

'Ben still sees her a few times a week. I've seen her a couple of times, too.'

'How was it?'

'I'm getting used to it. We've had some family counselling.'

She sat up straight. 'You never told me about that.'

'I haven't seen you properly for weeks. The therapist, Karen, is really nice. We've only had two sessions. She's away on holiday for three weeks now, but we'll have another one when she gets back.' I briefed her on Tammy's revelations from the meeting.

'Wow, she's had quite a life.'

I nodded. 'She has finished chemo now.'

'How's that been?'

'Surprisingly she's sailed through it, given she smoked a packet a day before she got diagnosed. She's lost her hair but not had any of the sickness.'

'Now what?'

'The chemo has shrunk the tumour. They're operating next week. Then radiotherapy.'

'And if that doesn't fix it?'

'Not sure.'

'How're you feeling about her now?'

'Things have moved on. She's had a really rough life.'

'Things *have* moved on. I can see it in your face.'

'I feel sorry for her.'

'But? There's a but, I can hear it in your tone.'

'There's something about her that I don't trust.'

'Why?'

I shook my head and shrugged.

'I'm sure the trust will come. She's got to work on it. How's the rest of the search going?'

I filled her in on my trip to Croydon. 'I've been looking online, but it's like looking for a needle in a haystack.' I scoffed. 'According to Directory Enquiries, there are one hundred and twenty David Pilgrims in the UK. I narrowed it down to four with the middle initial B, but none of them are Benjamin. Sometimes you can see their age category, but not always. Tammy can't even remember his date of birth. Only that his birthday was sometime in September, and he was three years older than her.' I shrugged. 'What hope do I have?'

'How do people go about finding missing family members?

'Some look for years with no luck. Or it costs a couple of grand to get an agency to do it. And I don't have that kind of money.'

'Jim would pay for it, surely?'

'It's a touchy subject. Every time I mention it, he gets funny. He just wants to concentrate on getting Joe home. I haven't even told him about going down to Croydon yet. He thinks I should at least wait until things settle down with Joe. Besides, there's this half-brother to look for, too. And any other family that might appear. The cost could mount up.'

She finished her wine and slipped on her leather jacket.

'You sure you won't come up West with me? I think you need it. Come on, Jim's away. Time to relax.'

Relax, I thought. It was only just revving up for me. The car was now in gear. It was time for full throttle. Joe would soon be coming home, and I had a family to find.

Outside, she hugged me. 'Call me if you change your mind. And keep me up to date with Joe. I'll pop in and see you both when you're back home. Or you pop in here and see me. Get Jim to babysit. Things aren't the same since you left, you know. I miss those days. We all do.' She blew me a kiss and wandered off.

A year had passed since I'd moved into Walcot Square, I thought as I walked home. I shivered despite the summer rays. I should have been happy, Joe was on the mend, but all I could feel was an impending sense of doom seeping into my bones like a winter chill.

A year ago, life had been so easy.

*

Jim didn't return from Zurich until the following afternoon. He stayed the Friday night for a client dinner and met me at the hospital on the Saturday afternoon, arriving in his suit, swinging his briefcase. 'That was a hell of a couple of days,' he said, his eyes dark circles in his pale complexion.

'You looked drained,' I said, getting up to kiss him. I gestured for him to have the comfy chair and handed Joe over to him as we caught up on the previous few days.

'Don't forget my parents are stopping by,' he said, the joy of seeing his son relaxing the muscles in his face.

'How could I?' I said, sharing a smirk with him.

'They said they would text me when they get here. Don't worry, they're running late. And they're meeting their friends at six, so they won't be staying long.' His phone beeped from his pocket. 'That's them.' He stood and put Joe back in his cot, sighing. 'No peace for the wicked.'

I could tell something was up as soon as I saw Sarah. A mere trickle of affection – a small wave and a tight-lipped smile – replaced her usual gush to see us. We exchanged pleasantries until they finished their drinks and trotted off to see Joe. 'What's wrong with your mother?' I asked.

He shrugged. 'Bit quiet, wasn't she?'

I went to queue for coffee, plucking up the courage to tell him about Ben and my trip down to Croydon. Once seated with our lattes, I let it all spill out.

'You did what?'

I looked at him, waiting for the fallout. I'd thought he might explode at some point.

'You can't just go around searching on your own. This bloke could be anywhere.'

'I need to start somewhere.'

He hesitated before continuing. 'I've been looking into this for you.'

My jaw dropped.

'I know a guy from when I first started working for Warren. He was the boyfriend of one of the girls in my cohort that year. Jake Harrison. He's an ex-copper who researches missing people. I called him. He owes me a favour, so I've arranged for him to look for your dad and brother for you.'

'What favour?'

'I helped him out with a small loan a while back.'

'But it costs a fortune to find people.'

'Let me worry about that.'

'But you've been dead against it.'

He took my hand, gently, as if he were scared he might break it. 'I want to see you happy again, Eva. I've not seen that special smile since before Joe was born.' He ran his thumb along my forehead. 'It's been replaced with this perpetual frown. Let's do some positive stuff. Let's find your family.' He held my hand a bit tighter. 'And let's start organising our wedding. How about early September before you start back at uni? It doesn't have to be anything big.'

'Sure,' I said, stunned at both suggestions. He'd been surprisingly unsupportive in my quest to find my family, and, with Joe so sick, we'd put the wedding on the back-burner.

'How much will Jake cost? I'll pay you back.'

'It doesn't matter. I've sorted it. Anyway, it's irrelevant.'

'Why?'

'Eva, you're the love of my life. We're going to share our future. What does it matter what it costs?'

A lump formed in my throat as I stared at the love in his eyes. He really would have done anything for me. 'What happens now, then?'

'We can go and see Jake, or you can chat to him over the phone, and he'll explain what he does. Then, if you're happy, he'll start the search.'

'How long will it take?'

'Anywhere between a couple of days and a couple of months,' he said.

'When can he start?'

Chapter 26

EVA

Apart from an efficient secretary named Cindy – 'With a C, not like the doll,' she'd pointed out – Jake Harrison was a one-man band. He operated out of spatially challenged premises tucked away in the bowels of London Bridge. When Jim and I arrived at the dark, two-roomed offices, Cindy – tight pencil skirt, bubblegum pink lipstick – seated us on the worn sofa alongside her workstation. 'Can I get you two a drink?' she asked, brushing the sleeves of her suit jacket. 'Tea, coffee, orange juice, coke – regular or diet. Or water.' She draped our jackets over her forearm. 'Mr Harrison's with a client, but I've told him you're here. He won't keep you long.'

She tottered off in her stilettos behind a room divider at the far end of the office, and I heard the flick of a kettle switch and the clattering of cups. 'What was the small loan you gave this guy, then?' I whispered to Jim who was texting on his phone. I nudged him. 'Did you hear me?'

He put his phone in his jacket pocket. 'He was working for a big organisation and hated it. So I helped him get this business up and running.' Another person he'd helped out. 'I bought into this.'

'So, it wasn't a loan. You actually own part of this business?'

'You could say that. Only a small part, though.'

'A silent partner.'

True to Cindy's promise, within a minute a suited man with a red hot face exited the room next door, storming to the exit with his head bowed. Another man, medium height and stocky with receding hair and a greying beard, followed shortly after. He was wearing trainers, jeans and a T-shirt with a faded motif of some rock band I didn't recognise which clung to his forty-something neglected belly. 'Jim, it's been too long,' he said, then turned to me. 'You must be Eva. Jake Harrison, pleased to meet you. Come with me.'

Shelves jammed with A4 files lined the walls of Jake's cramped office. It reminded me of Gill's crooked cottage. That was what had struck me the first time I'd walked into her small lounge. Books, books, books, they had lain everywhere, stacked in neat piles on every surface, dominating the room like a library. "Books take you everywhere, Eva, without you having to go anywhere," she had told me. "They feed your creativity, boost your imagination, motivate and educate. Their power is endless."

Jake's battered desk was stacked with files too, as if he had built a wall to protect himself from any dissatisfied customers. He picked up a half-eaten, giant sausage roll. 'Don't mind if I finish this, do you? Didn't manage to fit breakfast in this morning.' Not waiting for a reply, he ripped a sizeable chunk out of the pastry.

Cindy knocked on the door and entered carrying a tray of tea and a plate of plain biscuits. A file labelled EMJuly2011 was tucked in her armpit. She turned aside, unclenched her arm and dropped the file, along with a sheet of paper typed with several questions, into Jake's waiting hand.

After warning me of the emotional impact of finding estranged family, Jake wasted no words outlining the steps he would take to trace David Pilgrim and Christopher Mitchell. He then fired questions at me as if I were a defendant in a court of law with Cindy perched on a stool in the corner of the room noting the conversation like the court stenographer. Jim sat beside me, saying little, just squeezing my hand now and then as I parted with all the information I knew to help Jake fulfil his quest.

Jake finished with, 'Any questions?'

'How long will it take?' I asked.

'No two searches are the same, and unfortunately a magic wand is not part of my toolkit. All I can guarantee you is my commitment. I know how important this is for you. Jim's got my number; you can call me at any time. Middle of the night, if you want.' He picked up a water bottle from the floor and glugged down its contents, then wiped his mouth with the back of his hand before continuing. 'But don't you worry, I've been finding people all over the UK for...' Frowning, he glanced over to Cindy who piped up with, 'Over twenty years now.'

'I've never failed. Sometimes it's as little as a couple of days. In the more difficult cases, it can take a few weeks and even run into a couple of months. But don't you worry. I always get there in the end. I doubt Dave's going to cause me too many problems. You've given me something to go on. Might even get back to you within the week. It's Christopher who's going to keep me here late at night. The adoption cases always prove trickier. Much more protocol to follow.' He winked at Jim. 'But as Jim and I go way back, I know a few people who could bend a rule or two.'

*

Jim's phone buzzed at ten thirty the following night. We were in bed. He groaned as he rolled over and answered it, handing it straight to me. 'Dave Pilgrim. DOB fifteenth of September, nineteen sixty-nine. Married to a Laura Pilgrim. Address thirty-four, Kirbine Crescent, Clacton-on-Sea, Essex. Two step-children from Laura's previous marriage. Joint owners of a jewellery shop in Colchester. I'll text this all to you along with details of his parents who live a few streets down from him. I've got a telephone number, too. I just wanted to give you the news verbally. No luck with Christopher, but it's early days.'

'And?' Jim said when I was still silent a minute after handing him back his phone.

'Thank you,' I whispered once I'd repeated Jake's findings.

'I guess you'll want to visit Clacton now, then.'

I nodded as my shaking body leant into his open arms.

Sleep evaded me after that. But that was nothing new since Joe had arrived. Nights often stretched long as I lay anxiously waiting for an unwelcome call from the NICU. I crept downstairs, made a cup of tea and called Ben. 'That's brilliant news. And, so quick, too. You going to call him, then?'

'Will you?'

'Would love to.'

*

Ben made his intentions explicit as soon as I shared the long-awaited news. The following afternoon he came to the hospital, bright-eyed and revved up. 'I want a relationship with him. Emmy says I should develop the bond slowly, but I don't care,' he said.

'You should listen to Emmy. She's a psychiatrist in training. She knows about these things.' I don't know why I bothered.

193

The resolute look on his face expressed his intentions.

'I'm going to visit him on Sunday. You want to come?'

It's what I wanted. What I'd been working towards for weeks, but now it had come to it, I wasn't so sure I was ready. My bags of enthusiasm and dogged resolve had morphed into a suitcase of twitchy nerves. 'Let me think about it.'

Jim turned up at that point, chatting to Dr Miles. Ben grabbed his jacket, preparing to leave.

'I see this little one has had another weight gain,' Dr Miles said, flicking through Joe's file. 'Breathing's good.'

'He's almost two kilos now,' I said proudly. 'One point nine four.'

Saying it out loud it didn't sound a lot. My baby weighed less than two bags of sugar, but given his traumatic beginning, it was still a sweet achievement.

'Don't forget the four,' Jim laughed affectionately. Only those in our situation understood the significance of such minuscule gains.

Dr Miles nodded without looking up from the papers. 'He's feeding better, independently maintaining his body temperature.' He glanced up at us and smiled. 'He's holding his own. I'm pleased.' He whipped his stethoscope from his neck and gently unrolled the blanket from Joe's chest. 'Let's listen to this heart,' he said, unfastening Joe's sleepsuit. Inserting the earpieces of the stethoscope into his ears, he placed the diaphragm onto Joe's chest.

My breath paused in my lungs until his words allowed its release. 'All sounding good. We now need to strengthen this little chap up, and at this stage, the best place for this to happen is at home.'

I shot a look at Jim. Could we dare hope?

'I'll start the ball rolling with his discharge papers. I want to do a final scan before you go. I can get that arranged for Monday. And I need some fresh bloods, so, if Joe carries on in the same direction, let's aim for you to leave early next week, shall we? He'll have to attend my clinic for the fore-seeable future. My secretary will arrange appointments for you.' He snapped Joe's file closed, nodded his satisfaction, and marched over to a family three cots down.

*

'Ben's been exchanging texts with him all day. He's sent me some photos,' I said to Jim as we sat down to dinner that evening. A three-course special courtesy of Gill from when she'd stayed earlier that week. Jim had stopped at M&S on the way out of the hospital earlier, emerging with a carrier of beer and Chablis. He had put on some relaxing music and dimmed the lights.

'You want to go with him on Sunday?' Jim asked. 'You know I have to go into work tomorrow for a team meeting, don't you?'

I rolled my eyes. He had told me, but I'd forgotten. 'Look.' I passed him my phone. 'My father and his wife and her two kids.'

Pulling the tab on a can of lager, Jim gave me a sympa-thetic smile. He'd given me a lot of them lately. 'I suppose that's to be expected. It's understandable that he's had an-other life since Tammy.' Pouring a large glass of Chablis, he passed it to me. 'We should be drinking champagne.'

'Let's get Joe home first. I don't want to jinx things.' I clinked my glass against his can and took a large sip. It had been a long week. 'So, I'm going to meet my father.' I took another sip.

'How do you feel about that?'

I shrugged. 'It's all moving so fast. It's what I wanted, I know, but it's more unnerving than I expected.'

Jim piled my plate with rice while I served up the chicken casserole. 'So, do you want to go on Sunday with Ben?'

I picked up a stick of garlic bread and split it in two uneven portions. Shrugging, I placed the bigger half on his plate.

'It's totally up to you, but once we get Joe home we're going to have to keep him inside for quite a while, so I won't be able to come with you.'

'Let's go Sunday, then.'

Chapter 27

EVA

I decided against meeting Dave at his house. 'It's too personal,' I said to Jim. 'Where do people go in these situations? I mean, come on. You hardly want a rendezvous on a seaside pier with the dad you've never met, do you?'

'Leave it with me,' Jim said, and, the following day, after exploring several possibilities while at work, he booked us into a casual restaurant with sea views. A modern, high-ceilinged place, popular with Sunday lunchtime diners. Pleasant enough, but downmarket in comparison to the places he usually took me to. He said the options had been limited. Clacton wasn't somewhere he would go if he had a choice.

Ben had decided to take the train up the day before. As soon as we walked in, I spotted them, seated at a circular table for four in front of large bi-folding doors with views of the waves. A strong waft of roast beef and Yorkshires flowed from the kitchens. A smell that ordinarily would have triggered hunger pangs only served to kill my appetite. Chitchat and the clinks of cutlery filled the air, interspersed with parents ordering their kids to keep quiet.

Dave Pilgrim was wholly different from the image I'd conjured up – that of an overweight, aggressive-looking man with a comb-over wearing ill-fitting jeans. In reality he was slim with an abundance of dark hair, like Ben, and was dressed in chinos and a smart blazer. Ben was leaning towards him and they were chatting like they had known each other for years.

I felt a look of distaste flash over my face. *How have they become so close so quickly?*

I gingerly walked over to them with Jim steadying my shaking hand. Dave stood up and walked around to the front of the table. 'Hello, Eva,' he said, tapping his fingers against the side of his legs. After an awkward silence, he held out a hand to me which I shook briefly and I gave him a half-smile. We all sat, and a bubbly waitress appeared. She handed around menus, recited the specials of the day and scribbled Jim's order for sparkling mineral water and a bottle of their best white. He'd read my mind. Something was needed to calm the atmosphere. Or rather, something was needed to calm me.

I had to give it to the guy. No one could have faulted him for his efforts. He strived to make conversation, bringing up a variety of current topics as if he'd swallowed every Sunday paper that morning. He asked questions such as, "So, what's your view on Osama bin Laden being buried at sea?" Questions which I hadn't expected. I didn't know why, but I thought the conversation would centre around the Premier League or reality TV. I couldn't pair him with Tammy; which made me wonder how they'd ever got together in the first place.

'So, what do you hope to do with your law degree, Eva?' He smiled at me. A smile curved with kindness. Ben resembled him in so many ways; it was like looking at an older version of him. Powerful emotions hurtled through me. I realised I couldn't help liking him, which wasn't what I'd expected.

'Eva?' he said, bringing me back to the moment. He unfolded his napkin onto his lap and repeated his question. His tone was gentle, encouraging me to answer.

'I'm interested in family law, justice for children, so maybe a family lawyer. I've thought about joining the police, too.'

'I'm a volunteer for the NSPCC.'

'What does that involve?' I asked.

'I'm a Deaf Childline volunteer counsellor. I have a stepdaughter who is deaf, and my wife and I decided to do something to help other children less fortunate.'

'I used to volunteer at a local homeless shelter until Joe was born. Jim still does. I plan to start up again when Joe gets a bit older.'

He beamed. 'We have something in common. It's very rewarding helping those less fortunate than yourself, isn't it?'

The waitress arrived with our drinks. She unscrewed the cap of the wine and poured us all a glass then scribbled our orders for food. Dave and Ben discussed Ben's business. I tipped my glass towards Jim. Hesitantly, he poured me another.

My next question shocked everyone. 'Do you have any heart problems?' It was the way I said it. I didn't mean to, but even the people at the adjacent table turned to stare.

Dave frowned. 'No, why?'

'Our son was born with a heart condition.'

'Ben told me.'

'I want to find out if it's hereditary.'

'I've been as fit as an athlete all my life. No injuries, no illnesses.'

'What about your parents?'

'Not that I'm aware of. They're in their seventies, swim twice a week and belong to a walking club and a lawn bowls club. Maybe we can arrange for you to meet them one day too? Your grandparents.'

'I just need to find out if any of you have heart problems.'

'I'd be happy to have the tests you need. I'm so sorry to hear about Joe. It must be hard going,' Dave said. 'I'd love to meet him one day.'

Jim stepped in when I didn't answer. 'We're hoping to bring him home this week. He's doing much better, but we need to look at genetics if we're going to have another child.' Jim spoke more about our difficult times with Joe, and Dave listened, making all the right noises and facial expressions. The fact that this man was my baby's grandpa I found hard to comprehend. Mixed emotions overwhelmed me. The father I'd never met was sitting opposite me, sharing a bottle of wine with me, talking about my son, his grandson.

I needed air.

'I won't be long,' I said, grabbing my bag and walking towards the door. I heard Ben say, 'Give her time, Dad. She'll come around. It's been difficult for her, reconnecting with Mum and now you.'

'Eva, come back,' Ben called after me and apologised further on my behalf to Dave.

'Let her be. All in her own time,' I heard Dave say.

And there we were – another episode in the emotional drama of our broken family.

Jim found me leaning against a wall, staring across the beach, counting the people walking along the shore and children playing in the sand. Seagulls screamed overhead. I counted them too. It was a beautiful day. Sunny with a strong breeze dispersing the fragrance of the salty sea and blowing my hair in all directions. Jim enfolded me in his arms and rested his chin on my shoulder. 'He seems like a decent guy.'

'I know.'

'He's making a real effort.'

'I know.'

'What's wrong, then?'

'I thought it'd be easier than this,' I said. 'I didn't think he'd be so nice.'

Ben had picked up the reins of a father-son relationship and was cantering along as if Dave Pilgrim had always been part of his life.

'You need to take things slowly.'

I nodded and leaned into him.

'Let's not leave yet. Give him more of a chance. Come back in and at least stay for lunch. We can head straight off afterwards. Come on, another hour, tops.'

I turned to look at him, overcome with love for the only person who truly looked out for me, every minute of every day. Tears pricked my eyes. I glided my fingers across his cheek and gently kissed his lips. 'Give me five. You go back in.'

He touched my cheek. 'You still look beautiful, you know. Despite the angst.'

I stood there counting for another few minutes, as memories surfaced of Tammy taking Ben and me to the beach when we were kids. It had been a cold summer's day. There had been a man with us too, but I couldn't remember him in detail. Only that he had bought Ben and me a stick of rock each. We had been sitting on metal chairs outside a pub, crunching away while he and Tammy guzzled pints of cider and scoffed a bag of salted peanuts.

I found a tissue in my pockets and wiped my eyes, telling myself to be a better person and give this man a chance – if only for Joe's sake.

Back in the restaurant, Dave gave me a tentative smile. 'I didn't think I'd see you again today.'

'I'm sorry, I'm finding this harder than I thought I would.'

'I understand.' He paused and smiled. 'We can talk about the past another time. How about we start slowly and get to know each other? You're free to leave at any time.'

I nodded and allowed him a half-smile.

'Tell me more about your studies.'

I got through the next hour; it didn't prove as difficult as I had imagined. I didn't say much, instead observed, listening to their lively chatter and jovial banter as they discussed a range of topics from Team GB's chances at the London Olympics to the history of Clacton Pier. When the bill arrived, Jim and Dave had a friendly argument about who should pay. I inwardly laughed because I knew who would win.

'I remember when Tammy looked after you as a child. She always said you were a determined young man,' Dave said to Jim.

'Why did you leave?'

Ben and Jim shot me looks of surprise. So did Dave. I hadn't planned to ask it. It just burst out of my mouth like an unexpected sneeze. 'Tammy. Why did you walk out on her? You had a son. The photographs showed you were happy. She was pregnant. It doesn't make sense.'

'Maybe this conversation is best for another time,' Ben said, scraping back his chair.

'No. No,' I said. 'I need to know now.'

'Let's end today on a high, Eva. I was young. Your mother and I didn't get on. Let's leave it at that for now. We can discuss these things another time.'

He was lying. I could tell by his change of tone and choice of words. Tammy had told me the same when I'd asked her, and I had thought she was lying too. There was something both of them weren't telling us.

'Eva, all I can say is, I'm truly sorry for any impact my actions have had on you and your life.'

And from the sincerity in his expression, I could tell he meant every word.

Chapter 28

EVA

On the day we took Joe home, the sky was a sheet of azure blue, the sun a ball of shining brilliance – a perfect page of summer bliss. Once settled, and it took a while, we sat in the garden in deckchairs with Joe in his car seat, and Jim brought out champagne, and a bottle of milk for Joe.

'To our little family,' Jim said, handing me over a glass and picking up Joe to start his bottle.

Our little family.

What more did I need?

Joe changed Jim and me. His arrival strengthened our bond. The superglue making us forever inseparable. After the initial chaos of his arrival in Walcot Square – interrupted sleep, countless nappy changes, and feeds twenty-four-seven which seemed to roll into a never-ending bottle of formula – we established a routine and learned to cope. Gill moved in on a part-time basis, arriving Monday afternoon and leaving Friday after an early lunch. 'Just until you get yourself sorted. It's tough bringing a baby home at first, let alone one who's been so ill.'

We spent the rest of the summer helping Joe restore his health while planning the wedding Jim was insistent would take place before uni started again. Some days I was more worried about Jim than I was about our baby. What with the anxiety of Joe and trying to juggle the pressure of Warren's ever-increasing demands, stress ate away at him. It manifested itself by him nipping into the supermarket on his way back from the office and returning home with a six-pack every evening he was in town.

Slowly, we introduced Joe to the outside world. Starting with a Sunday drive out to the countryside for a walk in the fresh air, we gradually progressed to afternoon strolls up to Geraldine Mary Harmsworth Park. I often walked Joe up there when Jim was at work. Sometimes with Gill, sometimes alone. Stopping at the Tibetan Peace Garden, I'd sit on one of the meditation seats near the pergola draped in branches of jasmine. I'd count the scented roses as I sang made-up lullabies and rocked Joe in my arms.

Our nerve-racking visits to the cardiologist failed to show any deterioration in Joe's heart problem. 'The surgery has fixed what it needed to,' Dr Miles informed us as he probed and prodded, and asked us endless questions about our baby's development. Overwhelming relief choked me when he gave us the line, 'I don't need to see Joe for another three months.'

We discussed genetic testing, too. I was much keener than Jim. 'Let's just concentrate on getting married and being a family,' he repeated whenever I broached the subject.

*

I opened the car door and secured Joe's Britax into the rear seat, triple-checking that I'd tightened the harness to the max. Jim's sister, Vic, her husband, Ted, and son Alex had arrived from Australia for the wedding, and we were off to Surrey for a family reunion.

'Please drive slowly,' I said, opening the car window for some fresh air. There was something about trips to Elm House that always stifled the air – even before we got there.

'That's the third time, you've said that,' Jim said, pulling out of Walcot Square.

'Because you still drive too bloody fast.'

'Not anymore.'

Granted, he'd curbed his need for excessive speed. And he'd sensibly bought us a family car, saving his Porsche 911 for solo outings. But he still drove too fast.

When we arrived at Elm House, Vic, a petite woman like her mother but with ginger hair cut in a pixie-style, answered the door and threw open her arms. 'And this is my gorgeous nephew. I must have cuddles.' After hugging Jim and me, she took the car seat from Jim and fussed over Joe as we walked to the lounge. 'How old is he now?'

'Nearly four months.'

'Look at those gorgeous eyes. You take after your daddy, beautiful baby,' she said, stroking his cheek. She looked up at me. 'I guess you don't remember me from when we were kids?'

'Christina asked me the same when I met up with her again. I don't, but she's filled me in.'

'You know, my fondest childhood memories are of Tammy bringing Ben and you to visit. I used to pretend you were my little sister because I was fed up being the youngest child. You were a super cute kid, you know. And how's Ben?'

'Good. You'll see him at the wedding.'

'I can't wait. I still can't believe my brother's finally getting married.' We walked into the lounge. 'They're here, everyone!'

'Uncle Jim, Aunty Eva, is that Joe?' The kids ran over and crowded around the car seat, begging me to get him out for them to hold. Nervously, I told them he was still too little, but to save that wish for Christmas and Santa would deliver for sure.

Sarah's well-organised family gathering began in high spirits, her treat-laden trays stacked ready for a celebration. A bottle of Moët, juice for the kids, and a selection of fancy hors d'oeuvres she'd no doubt spent the week planning and prepping. Sarah called over, 'James, do the honours, will you?' She passed him the champagne before handing around her mouth-watering goodies.

'Just look at my mother,' Jim said, topping glasses with bubbly, 'constantly smiling as if she's taken some of my father's happy pills.'

I slapped him playfully. 'It's been a long time since she's had her children all together. It would please any mother,' I said, then felt a tug of sadness wondering how Tammy had coped all those years not seeing Ben and me. 'Anyway, she looks happier than the last few times we've seen her. She's lost weight, though.'

'I thought that too,' he said. 'My father seems in a bright mood. He must've upped his dosage.'

'Dosage of what?'

'His happy– oops, I mean his back pain pills.'

Banter filled the room, growing in volume, especially with my five future nieces and nephews scampering around like excited puppies and Vic's voice resonant over everyone else's.

Jim handed around drinks. 'A toast,' he called out. 'To Vic, Ted and Alex, welcome, and...' He took my hand. 'To the sister-in-law, aunty, daughter-in-law and wife-to-be.' He tenderly kissed my lips to enthusiastic cheers.

'My big brother is, at last, tying the knot,' Vic said. 'Here's to Jim and Eva.' She raised her glass to toast us, the happy couple soon to take our vows. 'OK, now I'm going to embarrass you, Eva. Because I'm good at that. We're going to play the *Guess Who* game.' Her voice had an Australian twang, her bossiness steering the show. 'I made it up when we were kids, and I always made everyone play it. Christina, Jim, do you remember?'

Jim rolled his eyes and laughed. Christina too. 'How could we possibly forget,' Christina said with a mischievous smile.

'We take it in turns to guess a person from a list of one-word descriptions provided by each family member.' She put her arm around me and laughed out loud. 'I'm going to go around everyone, and they all have to summarise you in one word.'

There were times when you wished the ground would open up.

'Father, you start.'

When he didn't answer, Vic's voice rose. 'Father?'

The prolonged wait for his reply clogged the room with an awkward silence and tension rose around the room like razor wire. I glanced around, willing someone to speak, to say something, anything, even a word would have done, but all I could see were blank looks of surprise. When the embarrassment became intolerable, Vic was half-way through repeating her question when Richard rose from his chair.

Reddish-purple blotches crept above his shirt collar as he cleared his throat and tugged his cardigan over his hips. One of the kids giggled as Richard stormed out of the room, leaving several mouths agape.

Jim excused himself. Sarah and Christina exchanged grave looks. 'What's wrong with Granddaddy?' Hannah asked.

I asked Adam to keep an eye on Joe and excused myself too, calling after Jim, who was racing up the hallway in the direction of the kitchen. He turned to me. 'The watershed has arrived. For most of my life, he's managed to crawl under my skin, but I can no longer tolerate the way he's inched his way so deeply beneath it.'

I tried to calm him, but my efforts achieved diddly-squat against the rage racing through him. I'd never seen him so angry. I stood in the utility room next to the kitchen, listening as he hit his father with a verbal thwack. 'What's your problem with Eva? You've never welcomed her into this family, and I want to understand what your bloody problem is.'

Before Richard had a chance to answer, I heard Sarah burst into the kitchen as the sound of smashing crockery ricocheted around the room. She slammed the door behind her, silencing Jim's outburst. I could still hear the shouting. 'Mother, stay out of this. It's between him and me.'

'Richard?' she said in a begging voice.

'Mother, be quiet. Please. Is this because of her upbringing? Because her background doesn't meet your expectations? Is that it?'

Richard's voice was calmer than Jim's, but still loud enough for me to hear. 'Partly. She's too young for you. It won't last. She's only with you for your money.'

My hands flew to my mouth as I gasped.

'How can you say that? She's given you a grandson,' Jim said.

'Because I see it from an outsider's point of view. You'll end up getting hurt.'

Sarah intervened, trying to break up their fracas. She started sobbing. 'Calm down, you two. Please. Please.'

The bellowing continued, both of them resorting to a game of slanderous ping-pong, the insults becoming so hurtful Jim finally stopped playing.

'At your peril, James. You're making a big mistake,' Richard called out as he stormed out of the room like a bolt of thunder.

'Always have to have the last word, don't you?' Jim called after him.

I stepped into the kitchen. Jim was standing with his arms ramrod straight, his fists on the table. His head was dropped, his eyes staring to the floor. Sarah collapsed into a chair, cupping her heavy head with her trembling hands. A stab of compassion hit me, as I knew how much the precious evening had meant to her.

Vic appeared. 'You all OK in here?' She looked at her mother, then me, then at Jim. 'I take it the answer's no. What the hell's going on?'

'I've got to get out of here.' Jim walked over to me. 'I'm so sorry.'

Vic started arguing with Sarah as Jim escaped into the hallway.

I followed him past the sound of noisy kids and laughter floating from the lounge – everyone in there oblivious to the commotion in the kitchen. When we got to the front door,

Christina appeared. 'Whatever's happened? Mother and Vic are arguing in the kitchen, and Dad's just passed with a face like a slapped arse.'

Once he'd gained enough self-composure to answer, Jim's words spilled out. 'He doesn't believe in this wedding. He thinks Eva's too young and only with me for my money. I'm not a millionaire for Christ's sake. And we've got a son together. What is his problem?'

She groaned and scoffed. 'Come on. You must know Father by now. Ignore him. Remember how he was with Adam and me?' She looked towards me. 'Has Jim ever told you? He didn't want me to marry Adam. Eighteen and pregnant, oh, how I'd shamed him. The local GP's teenage daughter was with child; what a disgrace I was to him. He spared no feelings when expressing his opinion that my potential marriage partner was a pathetic loser. But hey, I stood my ground and look at us now, ten years and four kids later. Ignore the grumpy old bugger. Stick to your guns. He'll surrender.'

'Why's he such a grouch? Ever since we were little he's been the same? Always working at the surgery and when he did come home, so snappy and forever complaining about something.' He paused. 'Me most of the time. He can go screw himself.'

She tried to appease him, but I think Richard had pushed him too far.

'Get Joe, darling, we're going,' Jim said to me, opening the front door. 'I'll wait in the car.' He grabbed his jacket, and I watched him march across the driveway, his hands in his pockets, kicking the gravel like a football.

After an awkward round of goodbyes, I took Joe out to the car. The temperature had dropped, not that Jim seemed any cooler. Vic appeared, looking distraught. 'Jim, come on, come in and make up with him,' she pleaded, but his face told her to back off. The day was over as far as he was concerned.

Sarah came running out, begging us to stay between the involuntary sobs she was trying her hardest to conceal. Jim opened the car window and touched her hand. 'Let's leave it for now,' he said, gently pushing her away. We exchanged repentant goodbyes. Gripping the steering wheel, he slammed his foot on the accelerator. The engine roared like an animal possessed, skidding the car out of the drive.

*

He didn't see Richard again until the night before the wedding. They didn't speak, either. Richard sent him an email that he read out to me – a pathetic attempt at an apology. A short paragraph dotted with phrases such as "regrettable night" and "we must move on".

'I could put that evening behind me if my mother's hand weren't so evident in his lines,' Jim said with no remorse whatsoever.

*

When the day arrived, the sun was out and the air fresh with a tang of autumn. The bells rang as Gill, Ben and I walked through the quaint churchyard scattered with late summer blooms. Emmy was waiting at the church doors, cuddling Joe. My baby had been out of hospital for eight weeks and was thriving. I gave him a quick kiss.

Ben escorted me down the aisle, a ukulele version of Bruno Mars' 'Just the Way You Are' playing from loudspeakers on stands at the sides of the pews. Jim had insisted on that song. He'd said I didn't realise it, but the whole world was always stopping and staring at me.

White silk ribbons, candles and fragrant lilies decorated the small church, sending a sweet honey scent accompanying us to the altar. Jim peeped around, and I thought I saw relief in the quick smile he gave me. He later confirmed I had been right. His wait at the altar had been plagued with nerve-racking thoughts as if he were on a self-sabotage mission. Was I going to turn up? What if I'd changed my mind? Should he just leave now? Dan was standing patiently beside him. The perfect best man spruced up in a black tie and red rose buttonhole to match the groom. He shot me a quick look and smiled before facing forward and dropping his chin to his chest. When the music stopped, and Ben released my hand, the message in Jim's smile was as clear as the sunshine radiating through the stained-glass windows. He would always have my back.

Life was perfect.

Who was I trying to kid?

Chapter 29

EVA

'Thank you for these mugs; they're beautiful,' Tammy said as we lounged in her garden, chatting and sipping tea. She was in a good place. They'd operated and dug out the shrunken tumour, and over the summer she'd undergone a course of radiotherapy. She still looked tired, but her complexion was starting to lose its previous corpse-like pallor.

I shifted in Tammy's new wooden chair, experimenting with the five reclining positions. Finding the most comfortable one, I closed my eyes. The late-September sunshine, obstinate against an impending autumn chill, and the whir of a neighbour's lawnmower had flicked my drowsy switch. Beside me, Joe grunted in his car seat as though he were about to stir. I opened my eyes and replaced his dummy.

'You've all given me hope, you know,' she said. 'I don't think that I'd have fought this cancer if it hadn't been for Ben and you and now Joe.'

I smiled.

'Do you think we should see Karen again?' she asked.

We'd had to cancel our third session with Karen. What with Joe coming home, then the wedding, I hadn't had the time. Or the mental capacity. 'Maybe. The garden looks pretty,' I said, screwing my eyes up against the brightness of the sun. I pointed at the towering spikes of cobalt-blue flowers stretching down to the greenhouse. 'Those delphiniums are striking. They're Gill's favourite.' The lawn glowed in the sunlight, and the beds were stacked with colour. Such a contrast to the unsightly overgrowth of blackberry bushes, thorns and stinging nettles when Jim had brought me here nearly four months ago. At the end of the garden, her once-abandoned greenhouse had received some TLC, the glass replaced, and the frame straightened out. 'You've fixed the greenhouse,' I said.

'Bob, my neighbour, has helped me with the whole garden. Mr Green Fingers. He said it'll look even better next year when it's more established. He's put in extra annuals to add some colour this season. He's been a lifesaver – worked on it part-time for most of the summer.'

'That's kind of him.'

'I've paid him. Come and have a look.'

The smell of freshly mowed grass trailed our stroll to the bottom of the garden. 'Your lawn is almost as perfect as Bob's now,' I said.

She laughed. 'Nice of you to notice. Bob's worked on that too while I've pottered. It's given me something to do on the days when I've had the strength.'

The greenhouse smelled earthy and was awash with greenery and flowers of varying sizes. She proudly listed the names of each of them and her plans to plant them around the garden.

She is capable of salvaging broken things, then?

Bob had also laid some decking and constructed a heavy-duty gazebo which housed a new wicker table and chairs set and a state-of-the-art barbecue which resembled a gigantic egg. He'd built a serving area too, with a fridge underneath like a mini outside kitchen. *Where does she get her money from?*

'Let's see these pictures, then,' she said when we returned to the chairs.

I dug a small album out of my bag and handed it to her. It was a selection of the best of Dan's shots from the wedding. She lifted the folding panel on the side of her chair to rest her mug. 'I was so upset I couldn't make it. Of all the days to be sick.' She slowly turned the pages. 'Wow, Dan is very talented, isn't he?'

'I know. They're great photos, aren't they? These are only a selection, too. He took thousands. He's working his way through them all to put professional albums together. But he wanted us to have some in the meantime.'

'Very talented.' She flipped the pages, her eyes glazing over. 'So very talented.' She choked on a sob, and two tears slipped down her face. She wiped her eyes with the back of her hand. 'You look beautiful. I can't believe I missed it.'

'It was only a small affair.' In the end, I'd been relieved when I'd picked up the message to say that she wouldn't make it. I think I'd invited her more for Ben than me. I was working on the forgiveness thing, but wasn't fully there. It was like making a cake. I'd constructed the base but had yet to finish icing the top layer. And I still had to source the cherry for the top.

She gasped as she turned the page, lifting the album up and turning it to show me a picture of Richard and Sarah holding Joe. 'Hasn't Richard aged?'

I snorted. 'No one can preserve youthful looks being so grouchy all the time. Was he so moody when you knew him?'

She nodded. 'Always been the same. People don't change, you know. However much we want them to.'

But you have, haven't you? You didn't want Ben and me, and now you do.

Her eyes narrowed as she lifted the album closer to her face. 'Gosh, Sarah's lost a lot of weight. She looks upset in these photos.'

'She wasn't herself all day. They argued at the church. I don't know what about. Did I tell you it's their ruby wedding anniversary next weekend? Forty years together! Jim often says he doesn't know how she's stuck with him this long.'

After commenting on most of the photos, she handed the album back to me. 'When does uni start again?' she asked.

'Next week.'

'Are childcare arrangements all sorted now?'

'It's all worked out well. I only have to be there twelve hours a week. Gill has agreed to come up once a week, and Ben is going to do Fridays.' I touched Joe's foot. We'd looked at employing a nanny, but when it came to it, I couldn't bear to leave him with a stranger.

'I could always help look after him?'

'Thanks, but it's all sorted now.'

We'd grown closer. But not that much.

'Thanks for bringing him today. I appreciate you making the journey. How's Jim?'

'We've hardly seen him since the wedding. He flew off to Frankfurt yesterday.' I grimaced. 'Unplanned, so we had to cancel a genetic counselling appointment booked for Thursday.'

'So you're thinking of having another baby? What wonderful news.'

'Not yet, of course, but I need to know if there's a risk another baby could be born with the same heart condition as Joe's. We can't go through that again. It could be fatal next time. Annoying we had to cancel. I researched for hours to find the best clinic.'

'Do you get a choice?'

'We're going private.' I stared at Joe. He'd gained weight, the skin and bone of his harrowing start giving way to signs of chipmunk cheeks and chubby bracelets of folded fat.

'What are the chances of that happening?'

'There seems to be differing opinions, depending on who you talk to. Genetic testing can estimate the odds of us having another child with a congenital heart defect.'

'Have you booked your honeymoon yet?'

I shook my head. Gill having Joe for the night of the wedding was as close as we'd got to getting away. Being apart from Joe any longer than that was too painful. 'We'll do something next year.'

'Ben told me about seeing your dad again.'

We'd made another trip to Clacton the week before. Just a Sunday afternoon drive with Joe, but we'd met Dave for a cuppa which had turned into afternoon tea.

'Why did he leave you?' I had to know.

A gush of wind started her coughing. 'What?'

'Why did he leave you before I was born?'

'We were young. He wasn't ready for a family.'

'But you'd been together a while when he walked out. And you already had Ben.'

'He wasn't ready for another child.'

'Why did you get pregnant, then?'

'You weren't planned.'

Neither was Joe, but Jim hadn't walked out. I stroked Joe's palm. His delicate fingers opened and closed, grasping my thumb. I looked up at Tammy. 'What was he like?'

She took a big sigh. 'Let's just say, he didn't treat me anywhere near as well as your Jim treats you.' And with that, she hauled herself out of her chair and hurried off inside.

My phone beeped. A text from Jim telling me not to get caught up in the afternoon rush hour. I smiled. He never stopped thinking about me. I gathered my things and took Joe inside to her utility room for a quick change before we left. A tiny room at the back of the house, it housed the boiler and washer/tumbler on which she laid out a changing mat when we visited. And on the shelf above, in a wicker basket, she stored everything needed to change a nappy. I started organising the area when I noticed there was only one wipe left in the packet. That wouldn't be enough. I walked over to the corner cupboard where she kept some spares and opened the door. A green carrier tumbled out. The gold lettering on the side caught my attention, and the rich, earthy smell of new leather told me what it contained, but still, I had to look. Inside, I found a drawstring bag, its material soft to the touch. I opened it to the most beautiful Dior handbag. I glanced up. Another Harrods carrier met my eyes. I tugged the handles apart to find another designer handbag.

Does she have a thieving problem?

Her voice calling from the kitchen startled me. 'You OK in there? Need anything?'

I shoved everything back in the cupboard and found some wipes to finish what I'd come to start. As I changed Joe, I searched my mind for the best way to raise the subject of the handbags with her, but decided to chat it over with Ben later.

At the front door, which Ben had repainted a sunny shade of yellow, she embraced me. 'Come again soon. I feel so blessed for this second chance with you.'

'Goodbye, Mum.'

She pulled away from me. Her hand flew to her heart. 'You called me Mum.'

Forgiveness. *Is she worth it?* She handed me Joe's baby changing bag. I swung it over my shoulder. 'I know,' I said with a sense of pride. I'd come so far to stop the longing to smother her face with a cushion. But as I stuck the key in the ignition, the scepticism which goaded me every time I saw her surfaced. That familiar yet unknown hunch that something was amiss, tapping my skull like someone persistently knocking at the door.

Will it ever go away?

Always so many unanswered questions.

Chapter 30

EVA

'That's not fair. You can't leave this one up to me,' I said, my temper heating up like the tension in the room. It was gone ten o'clock, and Jim had not long arrived home from work. I was at the kitchen table – lights bright, a guitar melody strumming from Classic FM on the radio – working on the first assignment for my second year back at uni.

'I can't get out of this one,' he said.

I stopped typing to talk to him. 'I don't want to go on my own.'

'I've spoken to Dan. He's agreed to go with you.'

I crossed my arms. 'You don't get it, do you? This is an important event we're talking about. You can't miss your parents' ruby wedding anniversary.'

'I've told Warren that I'll go now.' His head dropped slightly.

'You can say no, you know. It's not a crime.'

'Sorry, but Warren's on the warpath at the moment.'

'What's new?' I said with the biting sarcasm I'd begun to use whenever his boss's name was mentioned. I didn't care what path Warren was on. Jim didn't need to follow the same one. 'It's our first night out since Joe was born. I want to go with you, not Dan.'

'I'll make it up to you. I promise.' He plonked a bag on the table. 'Their anniversary present – I got it when I was in Prague and forgot to bring it home.' Taking a box out of the bag, he opened it and unwrapped a ruby red glass bowl, held it up, and asked, 'What do you think?'

'That's got to be the most hideous thing I've ever seen,' I said poking my nose up at the jagged-edged eyesore. It looked more like some kind of weapon than the work of art it was supposed to be.

He laughed. 'It cost a fortune. My mother will love it.'

I turned back to my laptop and resumed typing. We rarely argued, but as far as work was concerned he'd become a record on repeat, and one I no longer wanted to listen to. He'd been away most weeks since Joe had got home, sometimes flying off Monday morning and not returning until Friday night. When he was with us, he doted on us. There was no doubt he adored us, but his preoccupation with conquering the corporate ladder was becoming a blind obsession.

*

He left Saturday morning. With a twenty-four-hour flight to endure, he needed time to recover before the meeting on Monday morning. 'I'll be back Wednesday night,' he said, giving me a lingering kiss, and off he went. Five days gone for a meeting in Sydney. Promotion may well have been dangling in sight, but the lengths to which he was having to go to reach out and grab it came at too high a cost to his health and his marriage.

Ben and Emmy had agreed to babysit, and that evening Dan and I jumped in a cab.

'Don't often see you in a dress,' he said.

'You look rather dapper yourself,' I said, reaching over and picking a piece of fluff from the jacket of his tuxedo.

'Where're you off to, then? A romantic night out?' the cab driver asked.

Dan and I looked at each other, aghast. 'You couldn't be further from the truth,' I replied, refusing to indulge his nosiness with any more details.

We were the last of twenty-four to arrive in the wood-panelled private dining room at the Royal Society of Medicine where a Vivaldi violin concerto was playing, complementing the formal atmosphere. A heavily made-up lady wearing a red suit took our coats. Once we'd handed them over, and a waitress swung a tray of champagne-filled flutes under our noses. Dan took two and handed one to me. 'You know it'll be official soon. You'll have to start calling him Sir.'

'Over my dead body. Anyway, it's an MBE. Thank God he isn't being knighted.'

'I was only winding you up.'

'No need to try. There should be a rule that only decent people can be awarded MBEs. You should get the chance to air your objections like at a wedding. "Speak now, or forever hold your peace." Or something like that.'

Searching for Sarah amongst the pockets of people, I spotted Christina and Adam engrossed in conversation, but apart from a couple who Richard and Sarah had invited to our wedding, they were the only people I recognised. I took Dan's arm and was about to walk over to them when a maître d' asked us to take our seats at the table. It was set Sarah style – everything beautifully laid out to complement the four-course meal. Dan found our place cards and pulled out my chair between his and Adam's. 'Guess we're not in for a theatrical drama tonight with so many important names and faces present,' Adam whispered in my ear, sarcastically.

'Who are all these people?' I asked.

'Mainly colleagues from the medical field. I've met some of them over the years. I thought we were coming to their anniversary party myself, not a show to celebrate his MBE.'

At that point I gasped so loudly that Dan turned from talking to the lady seated next to him. Richard was escorting Sarah to their seats at the centre of the table. 'What has happened to Sarah?' I said. An oversized dress hung off her as if it had been made for someone else. She seemed to have shrunk inside herself.

Christina leaned forward. 'She's been ill. She looks dreadful, doesn't she?'

'What's been wrong with her?' I asked.

'Some virus,' Christina said, clearly concerned. 'It's taken it out of her.'

I didn't get to speak to Sarah until after the meal when people started mingling. 'Happy anniversary,' I said, leaning over to kiss her.

She stiffened, her hands shaking slightly as she smoothed down the skirt of her dress. 'Ah, Eva. How are you?' She wouldn't look me in the eyes. *What have I done?*

'How are you, more like? You look dreadful,' I said, making a mental note to go easy on the champagne. It was the most I'd drunk since finding out I was pregnant, and Jim wouldn't be there to save me from the graveyard shift when Joe woke.

'Yes, yes, I haven't shaken this flu completely, or virus, whatever it is.'

'Have you been to the doctors?'

'All tests came back clear. You'll have to excuse me; I need to speak to the caterers.'

I pulled her hand. I wanted to talk to her some more. The sleeve of her dress edged up her arm. Fading bruises circled her forearm, shocking enough for me to keep hold of her arm and ask, 'Sarah, where did you get those marks from?'

She tugged her arm back. 'The garden,' she said, but I knew she was lying. She shook her arm from my grasp, and off she wandered as if she didn't know where she was going. I finished my drink. The night was turning stranger by the glass.

When the time came to leave, I couldn't get away fast enough. Richard and Sarah were standing at the door to thank their guests for their presence and presents, and I rushed to ensure that Dan and I were first to receive their gratitude.

'What a strange evening,' I said as Dan escorted me down the stairs like the Prince Charming he was.

'What do you expect with the Barnes family? You should be used to them by now.'

*

The following Friday, as I was dashing out to uni, Sarah rang. I declined the call. I'd stubbed my toe on the edge of the stairs in a rush to find my shoes, and Joe was wailing in Ben's arms. 'Hush, little fella,' Ben said, rocking his nephew. 'Go,' he said to me. 'He'll be fine when you're gone.'

'Thanks for this. I'll be back by one.' I blew them both a kiss, trying to ignore the wrench of leaving Joe, which twisted my stomach. 'You and Emmy still coming for dinner tonight?'

'Seven?'

I nodded and ran out of the door, when Sarah rang again. I was about to delete it, but visions of her in that tent-like dress last weekend at her party persuaded me to accept it. Her tone was flat as if she were disconnected from her body. 'I'm so sorry, but I'm calling to cancel next weekend. I'm still not feeling myself. It will be too stressful cooking and entertaining everyone.'

'That's such a shame,' I said, punching the air. It was Richard's birthday, and she'd planned one of her fancy family affairs.

'Do send my apologies to James. I can't get hold of him. He's not returning my calls.'

'He's been busy with work. Sarah, are you OK?'

'I'm fine. The doctor has checked me out again, and it's only some nasty virus taking its toll. I'm on the mend.' Her voice choked. 'Don't you go worrying after me. You have enough to think about.'

Ripples of compassion washed through me. 'Why don't you come to us? I'll cook dinner for everyone,' I offered.

'No, no. I'm going to stay put. Thank you all the same.'

'What about your birthday? Why don't you come to us for that?'

'We'll see. We'll see.' With that, she abruptly rang off. I stood staring at the phone for a while, sensing lies in her excuses.

Chapter 31

EVA

My phone rang again only minutes after Sarah's call. I slid it out of the back pocket of my jeans and ducked into a shop to shelter from the rain that had started sheeting it down. A number I didn't recognise flashed up on the screen. Inquisitively, I accepted it.

'Eva?'

I hadn't recognised the number, but there was no mistaking the voice. My heart started thumping.

Is this it? Has he found him?

'Jake. How're things?'

Like the first time I'd met him, he dived straight in. 'I'm having a few problems finding this brother of yours. His date of birth – twentieth of July, nineteen seventy-nine – is this a definite?'

'As far as I'm aware.'

'Check it out, can you? Speak to your mum. Ask her how sure she is.'

'I'll call you back.'

I dialled Tammy's number.

'It was definitely the twentieth of July, nineteen seventy-nine. How could I forget that date?'

I explained Jake's call. 'Maybe it's best you leave all this now, Eva. You've enough to worry about,' she said; her tone, I felt, relieved. I knew she'd only gone along with this search for my sake. She didn't want us to find the child stolen from her at birth the same as I'd never wanted to find her and my father again.

Why?

Always so many unanswered questions.

*

As promised, Jim left the office considerably earlier than usual that night, arriving home about seven thirty. I'd put his favourite chicken casserole in the oven and was rocking Joe's bouncy cradle with my foot while chatting with Ben, Emmy and Dan when he walked into the lounge. He bent over to kiss Joe, then me. I chose not to comment on the waft of alcohol on his breath. Stress often took him for a swift pint or two in Marco's before coming home. Carrie had told me.

'Beer?' Dan asked him, getting up.

Jim took the bottle Dan handed him and took a long gulp. 'Give me five to change,' Jim said then dashed upstairs, returning wearing jeans and a well-worn blue T-shirt with 'NEW DAD [Est MAY 2011]' printed across the front. A present from Dan when Joe was born. Jim selected some smooth R&B tracks to play on his iPod in the background and scooped Joe into his arms. 'Dinner smells great,' he said, kissing me.

I went into the kitchen to check on the casserole. It was hot in there, so I opened the patio doors to the bite of the early evening autumn air. I removed the dish from the oven, humming along to the music from the lounge. As I stirred the casserole, my phone rang. I reached over to the counter. My stomach leapt to my throat. Since that morning, I'd learned that number off by heart.

The leaps turned to cartwheels, ending with somersaults as Jake relayed his findings. It took me a good five minutes counting the number of seconds pass on the oven clock before I managed to find Tammy's number. Not that she could shed light on the situation.

I returned to the lounge.

'You OK?' Jim asked as I perched myself on the edge of his armchair.

'Christopher Peter Mitchell never existed,' I said loudly enough for everyone to stop talking.

Ben's bottle paused an inch shy of his open mouth.

'Or whatever his name is now,' I added.

'What's that meant to mean? Ben asked.

'Jake's just called me. He can't find him.'

Jim's body tensed beside me. He sat up straight. The colour visibly bled from his face as fast as he drained his bottle of beer. Dan flipped the top off another bottle and handed it to him. 'What're you talking about?' Jim asked.

'He doesn't exist?' Ben said.

'There's no trace of a Christopher Peter Mitchell in any form – Chris, Peter, Pete – on any official records. He's vanished.'

'He doesn't exist, or he doesn't want anyone to find him?'

Hairs rose on the back of my neck. 'All public and adoption records. That name's not on any of them. Jake said.'

'How come?' Ben asked.

I shrugged. 'He wasn't adopted.'

'But Mum said her parents arranged his adoption. I remember her telling us the first time we went to see her. That's definitely what she said.'

'I know. I've just been over it all with her again. As far as she is aware, her mother arranged for her child to be adopted. But he wasn't. Not legally, anyway.'

'What does *that* mean?'

Dan cleared his throat and stood up, holding up his empty bottle of Bud. 'Anyone for another?'

Ben held out his empty. So did I.

'One for me too,' Jim said, rubbing his frowning forehead.

'It means that if this Christopher guy was adopted, it wasn't through the official channels. According to Jake, anyway. Mum's parents must have handed the baby over with a fraudulent birth certificate.'

'How can that have happened? Why?' Ben asked.

'Jake said he'd uncovered a few instances where children weren't legally adopted – especially in the sixties and seventies.'

'Why?'

'Various reasons: forced adoptions, abductions, to keep the child's eventual whereabouts hidden forever.'

'How do we know he's even alive, then?'

'We don't. Tammy's parents are dead. We'll never find out.'

'But why would they have done that? Given their grandchild over to someone and not used the legal channels? Her father was a doctor. It doesn't make sense.'

'As far as Mum is concerned, they took the baby and told her he went to a suitable family who were desperate for children. That's what she told me,' I said.

'Did anything come from the Adoption Contact Register?' Emmy asked.

I shook my head.

'This is confusing. Someone, please explain,' Ben said glancing around like a lost child.

I let out a frustrated groan. 'I wish I could, but I'm as confused as you. I'm unsure where to go from here.'

'So, what's this Jake guy going to do now? Is there no other way of finding him?' Emmy asked.

'He said he'll carry on looking, but according to him, it's like looking for dog shit in the autumn leaves.' I threw up a hand. 'Who knows anything, anymore?'

Jim whacked the edge of the chair, making me jump. I turned to him. He looked exhausted. His eyes were bloodshot as if he'd skipped a night's sleep, missing their usual enthusiasm. 'You have to leave all this baggage now, both of you. Can't you see? This Christopher, or whoever he is now, doesn't want anything to do with you. If he's even alive, that is. You need to accept it.'

Ben removed a lighter from his pocket and started tapping it on his knee. 'I wish I could.'

The chair took another thump. 'Get on with your life. Your place is here now with your real family, with us, with Emmy.' Jim looked at me. 'Concentrate on the real, not the delusive notion of a huge devoted family awaiting you. We will have our own family.'

'Jim!' I tapped his leg, shocked at his outburst.

Ben fumbled in his jacket and pulled out a tatty leather pouch from which he removed the answer to all his problems. 'I hear you.' Emmy laid her head on his shoulder.

I nudged Jim. He looked lost in another world as if he'd

just smoked the joint Ben was preparing. He shuddered his thoughts back to the moment. 'Find a new purpose, Ben. Propose to Emmy, make a baby, or do both.'

Emmy blushed, and I apologised on behalf of my husband. *What has got into him?*

Ben gave a tight-lipped smile. 'I'm going for a smoke.' And off he walked, his shoulders slouched so acutely he looked like he could curl into himself.

'I'll join you,' Dan said, following Ben out of the room with Emmy on their tail.

'All a bit strange, don't you think?' I said, my stomach still turning with the turmoil.

'Maybe Tammy's parents thought it better for everyone if it was all done anonymously.'

'But why?'

'Beats me,' he said. 'There's nowt so queer as folk.'

We talked for a while until the buzzer called me to the kitchen. Putting beans on to boil, I stared out through the open patio doors to see Ben and Dan in the garden under the striped awning. An eyesore left by the previous owners which Jim kept threatening to rip down. Ben was cross, his head making jerky movements as he talked to Dan, who was listening intently. Taking knives and forks from the kitchen drawer, I laid the table, then went to ask Jim if he fancied red or white. As I approached the lounge, I saw Jim, hands in his pockets, pacing the room liked a stressed parent. Joe was back in his bouncing cradle, asleep. I took a step backwards and another sideways, hiding from view as I listened to him repeating the name Christopher Peter Mitchell over and over again as if he were chanting.

I poked my head around the door. 'What are you doing?'

I asked, startling him. He wore the troubled look of someone who had more on their mind than they could cope with.

'Joe was getting heavy,' he said. He was lying. Joe weighed barely four kilos, and Jim never put him down unless he had to.

'I heard you saying that name, Christopher Peter Mitchell.'

'You must have been mistaken. I was singing along to the music,' he lied, again.

Chapter 32

JIM

The Manhattan Plaza Hotel, New York
October 2011

Why hadn't I worked it out before, Eva?

Rihanna was singing with Calvin Harris on the radio, about how they'd found love. Of all the things to recall about that horrendous day as we drove to Surrey, absurdly, it's that song belting from the car radio which surfaces first. Life before realisation sliced my life in half then chopped it up into fragments of horror.

Neither of us wanted to make that trip, but it was my mother's birthday, so I didn't see we had much choice. She'd been in an odd mood for weeks, and I didn't want to upset her any further. As we drove along, you brought up the subject of genetic testing again. You'd arranged another appointment to start the process off, and I'd half-heartedly agreed to attend because you wanted me to. The thought that Joe's heart problem could be hereditary had plagued me no end, but I didn't have the bandwidth to search for causes, let alone do anything about them. My father had insisted that this kind of thing was just one of those things. And my mother had said, 'Many babies are born every day with heart abnormalities. Even after a normal, natural delivery. I've seen it many times during my career.'

We arrived much later than planned. My father was with Adam in the lounge, talking about horse racing, I think, or maybe football, and my nieces and nephews were darting around, arguing about whose turn it was to hide and whose it was to seek. My mother, still looking thin and pale, was serving up slow-cooked lamb.

'Dinner's ready,' Christina called out, and we all took our places to enjoy my mother's efforts.

Dessert followed the roast. The same my mother made for every birthday celebration – a Mississippi mud pie with a twist. Slices of calorie-laden goo drowned in amaretto and topped with mini chocolate eggs she sourced from a chocolatier in Guildford. It was a lively family occasion. After second helpings, the kids scampered off to play, and, for whatever reason, my father excused himself.

And my life came tumbling down.

A mighty roar from the lounge broke the cheer amongst those of us in the dining room. Loud and deafening, as if my father were witnessing a heinous crime. 'What do you think you're doing? Put that down at once.' He continued to shout words I couldn't make out, roaring along the hallway like a crazed animal, with cries from my nephew Harry accompanying them.

What the fuck? My heart started racing as the realisation gripped me, hurtling me back to a painful moment in my childhood. I felt as though I'd been teleported back in time, right back to the mid-eighties. My father had been watching football – or so I'd thought – while I sat at his desk. An old dining table which stood in a corner of the lounge at the time, before my parents built their extension and he got his own study. It was a strange area of the room, my father's makeshift study. The desk was bestrewed with all kinds of miscellaneous items because he believed everything had a purpose so threw nothing away. I loved sitting there, in front of his old-fashioned typewriter, amongst files and records scattered everywhere. Often, while he was at work, I would sift through his stack of research papers and piles of medical journals, mindful to return everything to its right place.

If I look back, Eva, I was always searching for something. I can see that so clearly now.

As eight-year-old me had sat there that day, absorbed in my father's world – his stethoscope hanging around my neck, shuffling paperwork and intermittently pretending to take my pulse – his yell petrified me to such an extent that wetness soaked my pants. 'What do you think you're doing? Put that down at once,' he had bellowed at me.

In one shaking hand, I'd been holding an envelope, and in the other a birth certificate. And, as clear as the glass paperweight eight-year-old me found the envelope beneath, hidden under a mound of documents were the details:

CHILD: Christopher Peter MITCHELL
FATHER: Richard James BARNES
MOTHER: Tammy MITCHELL

Chapter 33

EVA

Silence descended upon the family gathering as if one of the kids had sworn. Adam's lips twitched to stifle a grin. He nudged me and flashed a sarcastic look of here-we-go-again. Jim clutched the arm of my chair, and Sarah's delicate face looked as if it were about to crack. My gaze whipped from Christina to Adam, looking for an answer neither of them could give.

'What's Harry done now?' Christina rolled her eyes. She prodded Adam's elbow. 'Go and find out what he's up to, will you?' Adam clenched his jaw and exhaled an exaggerated sigh which made Christina bang her spoon on her half-empty plate. 'I'll go, then.' She slammed her hand on the table and stormed off.

Hannah started bawling. 'Can we go home, Daddy?'

Adam opened his arms to Hannah. 'Come here, sweetheart.'

'Why is Grandfather shouting so loudly?'

'I don't know. Mummy's gone to find out.'

I looked at Jim. He was as white as the starched tablecloth. 'What's wrong?' I watched in confusion as he folded his napkin into the smallest square possible and placed it in his pocket.

'Excuse me,' he said, pushing back his chair so hard it crashed to the floor, which made Hannah wail more loudly.

'Jim?'

He looked drained. I took his arm, tugging it to get his attention, but he shook me off. 'I'm OK, darling. I've come over a bit funny. I'll be back in five.'

A blunt knife could have cut through the strained atmosphere. Adam and I exchanged confused expressions. He shrugged and smirked as if to say, *same old, same old.* Sarah still looked dazed, as if she'd witnessed a car crash.

'Watch him, will you, please?' I asked, placing Joe by Adam's feet. I then followed Jim as he faltered along to the kitchen, steadying himself on the wall every few steps, trying to catch his breath. 'Jim, what's going on?'

He turned to look at me. A strange look I had never seen him give me before. As if he didn't know who I was. 'My head is pounding. I'll get some fresh air and come straight back in. Go and look after Joe.'

But I couldn't. I needed to know what was wrong with my husband.

He slipped out of the back door, both hands clutching his head. I dashed over to the window. It was spitting with rain, tiny drops falling faster. I watched as he strode up the garden path and disappeared behind the double garage. *Where is he going?* I rushed after him, leaving the sounds of Christina arguing with Richard over Harry's convulsive sobs resonating from the lounge. I stopped at the garage and peered around the corner. Jim was squatting against the brick wall, repeatedly slamming the palms of his hands into his eye sockets. I stood staring at him, feeling like I was in a dream about to turn into a nightmare. A downpour started, but he stayed put, blowing fierce breaths out through his pursed lips.

I ran over and crouched down to face him. Diagonal sheets of rain were pelting down as if they were trying to wash a layer of dirt off the path. I grabbed his arm. 'Jim, come inside.'

He looked up at me with a desperate gaze. Water bounced off his face and dripped off the end of his nose. A clap of thunder pounded through the air. 'Come on. We'll get struck by lightning at this rate.' I pulled him up. He didn't resist. Scared his legs might buckle, I linked my arm through his and guided him back inside.

Things were kicking off in the lounge, the kids crying, the adults bellowing.

'I need to get home,' Jim said. I edged him over to a chair. Water puddled at our feet as it dripped from our hair and trickled from our clothes. 'Stay here while I get Joe,' I told him.

'I've got a migraine,' he said, shuddering. 'I can't see properly.'

'Give me a minute.' I ran to the lounge. Christina was arguing with Sarah, who looked as stunned as Jim. Adam was jigging a wailing Joe with one foot while trying to console his daughters who were clinging to his legs like monkeys.

'What're they rowing about *now*?' I asked Adam as I picked Joe up.

'Who bloody knows?' he whispered, suppressed amusement tremoring his lips. 'It's been like this for years. The annual Barnes blow-up. I must say, though, I think this one tops the lot.'

'Eva, where's Jim?' Sarah asked, her voice shaking.

'In the kitchen.'

'What happened to him?'

'He's got a migraine. I think we'll go home now. Bye everyone,' I said, leaving the room, no pause to allow for persuasion to stay.

Sarah tore after me. 'Is he OK?'

'He'll be fine.'

'Let me see what I can do for him.'

'Leave it, Sarah. I'm just going to get him home.' Guilt stabbed me as she tottered back to the lounge, but I knew Jim wouldn't want his mother fussing over him.

As I drove away from the Barnes' tumult of shouting and confusion, relief overwhelmed me. 'What the hell was that about?' I asked.

His eyes were closed, but I knew he wasn't asleep.

'I'll stop and get you some tablets.' I shook his knee.

'Just get home as soon as you can.'

*

I spent a restless night, wrestling with an impending sensation that life as we knew it was drawing to a close. Several reasons why buzzed about in my head, but none of them made any logical sense. I woke exhausted, rolling over to cuddle Jim, but he wasn't there. I sat up. A mug of lukewarm tea stood on the bedside table. I ditched the duvet and shot out of bed, finding him in the kitchen already suited and booted, drinking coffee.

'Feeling better, then?' I asked.

He nodded. 'Don't wait for me for dinner. This one could go on into the evening,' he said with a smile that didn't reach his cheeks, let alone his eyes.

I wanted to hug him, but his usual warmth was missing. Something wasn't right. I could feel it in my veins and see it in his expression. An invisible barrier was between us, and I couldn't work out why. 'Not the office today, then? Where're you off to?'

'A meeting over near Gatwick. I'm taking the train.'

'You never told me about this.'

'Sorry, I forgot to mention it. Warren offered me up last thing on Thursday.'

'Let me make you some breakfast. Eggs? Porridge?'

He tipped the last of his coffee into the sink and placed his dirty cup in the dishwasher. 'I'll get something at the station. I'm late.'

'But you didn't eat last night, either. What *is* going on?'

He took me into his arms and buried his nose in my neck, breathing me in as if he'd never get another chance. I held him tightly, feeling the tension stiffening his whole body. We remained cuddled close, a typical morning good-bye, but then he abruptly pushed me away as if I were a stranger.

'Be honest with me. Are you OK? You've been strange since we were at your parents' house yesterday. Talk to me, please.'

'Work's getting to me at the moment. Warren's on my case.' He snatched up his briefcase. I'd never seen him so keen to get away. 'I don't need the third degree from you.'

His words stung like a slap across the face. That wasn't my Jim. My Jim was loving and caring, and every other word in that category. *What is wrong with him?* I looked at him, uneasy, searching for an answer. But his face was blank. Where were the flames that usually sparkled in his eyes, and the fire of enthusiasm he always had for life? Was this burnout?

I chose to ignore his hurtful words. 'Whenever is Warren not harassing you? You need to throw that job in. Now – today, just do it,' I called after him as he trudged towards the garden gate. 'Find another one. Do something you love.'

But he wasn't listening.

Chapter 34

JIM

The Manhattan Plaza Hotel, New York
October 2011

Lying to you gutted me, Eva, but I had to see my parents.

My parents? Who were my parents?

Crisp sunshine was trying to push through a scatter of dark clouds in the depressingly grey sky. I spun around to look at you; bright rays enhanced the whiteness of your cotton nightie as you yelled up the path something about finding another job.

I closed the wooden gate. My stomach flipped.

Who was I?

On the walk to the Underground, I dialled my parents' number. It took Mother a while to answer. 'Are you in this morning? I have to see a client down your way. I'm going to stop in to see you en route.'

'Your father is nipping into town to run some errands, but I'm here. Is everything all right? You sound odd.'

'See you later.'

'What time?'

I cut her off. I couldn't speak to her until I understood her involvement in the whole ordeal.

After taking the Tube to Waterloo, I stopped on the concourse to buy a coffee. Opening my wallet, I gulped as my world smiled up at me from the transparent fold at the front. A snapshot from late summer when we'd first got Joe out of hospital. You, my beautiful wife, smiling radiantly while cuddling Joe in the garden.

*

I hope that when you read all this it explains everything to you, Eva. Since meeting up with you again that August evening, just over a year ago, all I have wanted is the best for you. And Joe too. That's all I live for now, and that's why I work so hard. It isn't about getting ahead anymore, the power, the pride or the prestige, but the protection and best existence I can achieve for you, the love of my life.

*

The train journey dragged as I sat praying that I would wake up from the all-absorbing nightmare. Why had it taken me so long to face reality? To remember finding that birth certificate. It was like it had always been there deep in my head, but something had blocked its journey to my conscious mind.

A young guy was sitting across the aisle, drinking a can of lager, talking and joking on his mobile. 'Get real, Dad. The Gunners will knock you lot from the League, Sunday. Guaranteed.'

I left my seat to find a quieter area.

I took a taxi from the station, my guts as tight as my balled fists the whole journey. A torrent of childhood memories, darkened by untold truths, came flooding back. A haze of confusion had perpetually touched the surface of my life, even way back then. Tammy picking me up from school – Christina and Vic in tow – messing about in the garden with us, making us picnic teas. Dan always around ours because of his parents' constant arguing. Tammy, her belly enlarged with you growing inside, pushing Ben, Dan and me on the blue and yellow swings with Victoria and Christina swaying on the see-saw beside us. My father always grumpy, finding fault in everything I did, making me feel like I never properly fitted in. A family swaddled in fabrication and deceit, with me at the core of it all.

I'd always known, somewhere deep within me, that something was amiss. Like pieces of a puzzle which never all fitted together to make a pretty picture – edges frayed, joins unaligned. But now the truth had finally fallen into place as if I'd been waiting my whole life for it to do so.

When the cab turned into the driveway, I found my mother kneeling on a mat, digging weeds from the flowerbeds which skirted the front of the house. I paid the driver, not waiting for my change, and marched over to her. She knew I knew. I could tell by the way she recoiled when she saw me.

'Where's Father? I need to talk to you both.' I ripped off my tie. It felt like it was strangling me.

She eased herself up, removed her gardening gloves and dusted her trembling hands together. 'He'll be back soon. What're you doing here? Has something happened to Joe?' She fiddled with her hair which was already neatly tucked in a bun.

I kicked the shingle, propelling small stones onto her shoes.

'Come inside. I'll make us a pot of tea,' she said, as if a pot of bloody tea was the answer to our family deception.

'Cut the bullshit. How did we get here?'

'James, what are you talking about?'

I told myself not to be so stupid. I must have got it all wrong.

But I knew I hadn't.

Deep down, I'd always known something about our family was fucked. I looked across the front garden. There was my favourite tree. A large oak with autumn leaves carpeting the base of its trunk. Dan and I used to climb that tree all the time when we were kids, hiding in the mini treehouse and inventing ghost stories. One day, when Mother was at work, Dan and I were mucking about, and we fell. I was OK, a few scrapes, but Dan fractured his arm. Tammy was distraught. She called my father home from the surgery, and he told her if she couldn't look after us properly then he'd have no choice but to let her go. She cried all day as if one of us had died.

I charged up the steps to the front door, my heart like a battering ram trying to push through my chest. I thrust the door open so hard it bounced off the wall inside with a loud bang. Panting closely behind, my mother tried to keep up. Once in the kitchen, I turned to her and asked, with all the calmness I could muster, pausing between each part of the name, 'Who is Christopher Peter Mitchell?' I knew, but I needed to hear it from her.

Her right hand flew to her heart as if I'd announced the death of a relative. 'Oh, goodness, oh, dear,' she said, her lips quivering as she deliberated what to say next.

The tick-tock of the antique pendulum clock positioned

above the fireplace sounded like a gong in the silence between us. Wafts of homemade bread, cooling on a wire tray, reminded me of the rare days when I used to come home from school and she would be there beavering away in her apron, cooking and baking. Or had that been Tammy?

I seized a ceramic pestle from its mortar and pounded it up and down on the worktop. 'I need honesty.'

Her hand covered her mouth, her words muffled by her fingers. 'Oh, James, please, let's wait for your father.' Small whimpers escaped from her. The pathetic servant waiting for her master to come home.

Thud went the pestle.

'You've known all along, haven't you? Tell me. Now.' I started to scare myself as visions of grinding the pestle into her skull filled me with a sense of satisfaction.

Is that how you used to feel about smothering Tammy's face with a cushion, Eva? I never understood how you could have held such anger. But now I do.

I moved to lob the pestle at my mother's head but stopped mid-aim. I'd be punishing the wrong person, wouldn't I? I threw it across the worktop instead. We both flinched as it clonked onto the tiled floor.

'How did you find out?' she asked, her voice barely a whisper.

'You're in on all of this, aren't you?'

A stunned look fogged her face. She dug her fingers into her cheeks. 'Oh, no. Please don't let this be happening.'

There had to be an explanation.

But I knew there wasn't one.

I'd known it all along.

My family was a farce.

'I remember seeing it on a birth certificate I found on Father's desk when I was young. I'm Tammy Mitchell's son, aren't I? Father went ballistic then, precisely as he did with Harry yesterday.'

She shook her head and started whimpering like a helpless animal. 'No, no. Your father needs to explain all this properly. It's his sordid story.'

I had so much more to say, but my thoughts were all tangled up, confusing the hell out of me. The sound of my father's car disturbing gravel set her hyperventilating. She pulled on my arm. 'Let me talk to him first,' she pleaded.

A strong desire to see you and Joe overcame me; to hold you, to feel you. My stomach convulsed – to hold my half-sister? I shook Sarah off and marched to my father's study. Was he still taking them? The pills he'd stored in his top desk drawer for years. When I'd first found them, as a child, when I had been searching for some paper, he told me they were for his bad back. Then he stopped my pocket money for a month for snooping in places I shouldn't. Years passed before I learned that diazepam was not a medication used for back pain. I couldn't talk to him about it, so I'd asked my mother. 'Why does he take those tablets?'

'For his back. You know how he suffers so.'

'But they aren't for back pain. They're for anxiety. And he's on a pretty high dose.'

'They work for him. He doesn't suffer from his back pain when he's taking them. He knows what he's doing, James. Leave him be. He's better when he's on them.'

Better?

I ripped open the desk drawer, but they weren't there, so I carried on hunting in the other drawers. Where were they?

Eventually, I found the bottle amongst the disorder on his desk, under a newspaper behind the telephone. Snatching it, I shoved it in my pocket. I had to get out of there.

I ran outside, punching my hand against one of the hanging baskets my mother took so much pride in. She cried out in agony as it struck her in the face.

My father – a pathetic monster of a man – was getting out of his car. He looked confused. 'James, what's going on? What are you doing here?' He strode towards me, and I met him halfway. I ripped the car keys out of his hand and stared at the ground, wishing it would open up and suck him down to hell.

He prodded my shoulder. 'James, whatever's happening?' He looked at my mother. She was standing in the doorway, clutching her head, blood on her face, a pathetic sparrow of a woman.

I jumped in his car as he ran after me, calling out for me to explain myself.

I wound down the window and stared at them one last time, wondering how it was possible to know someone all your life but not know them at all. I took a deep breath to steady my voice. 'This is the last time you'll ever see me, Sarah and Richard Barnes,' I called out, then screeched out of their gravel driveway with him running after me.

The journey back to London was a blur. I drove for a while, then I took a train. Of that I'm sure because it stopped at Woking for at least an hour due to a security alert at Clapham Junction. But where I dumped their car and boarded that train, who knew? My phone rang as we pulled away from the platform. I looked at the caller ID. It was him, the monster. I pressed delete.

For the rest of the day, I exhausted myself in a fog, unable to find a way out, unsure what to do. Arriving back in London mid-afternoon, I thought about going into the office. Anything to resume normality, to get out of the haze, but I couldn't face anyone. Betrayed by the person I'd trusted the most all my life, my mother, and by my birth mother, who had abandoned me as she had her other children, I needed to work out my future. Did Tammy have any more children? I hadn't thought of that, or of Ben, my younger half-brother, in all the disorientation. Ben!

At Waterloo, I boarded a Jubilee line Tube train. I had to see her. For Christ's sake, she could have stopped all this. But when the Tube pulled into Dollis Hill, I couldn't do it. I couldn't stomach Tammy Mitchell. Not yet. I first needed time to calm the sickness resulting from the consequences of her actions. The train remained stuck at the station due to a passenger incident, doors wide open to a cutting gale. I stayed in my seat, shivering yet sweating. 'Go on, go and see her. Have it out with her,' the devil in my head demanded for the next twenty minutes as, shell-shocked, I debated whether or not to get off. When the driver tannoyed that the train couldn't go any further northbound and was turning back to London Bridge, waiting passengers hopped on, packing the carriage but leaving the seats either side of me free.

As the train bolted through the tunnels, I counted the number of stations on the entire Tube map, starting at Amersham and ending at Upminster. Count things when you're stressed, you've always told me, Eva. Distracts the mind. Helps you stay calm. Two hundred and seventy stations.

*

The fog has shifted, and I can see everything more clearly now. That's why I slog. All my life, I have absorbed myself in work. Twelve top GCSEs, four As at A level, a first class degree from the LSE, an MBA, and now following in Warren's footsteps. Constantly distracted by work, so my mind doesn't wander to the deceit underpinning my existence. All those hours I could have spent with you and Joe.

I'm so sorry, Eva.

*

At London Bridge, I forced myself to get off. I needed air. My phone beeped at least a dozen times as the escalator transported me to ground level. Twelve missed calls from the monster and as many texts. I deleted them and blocked his number. Then I messaged you, telling you not to wait up, and switched it off. I crossed the bridge, going nowhere in particular. End it here, right now, I told myself. I stepped to the edge of the kerb, the traffic whizzing past, whooshing wind into my face.

I don't know how long I stood there, subdued and shivering, counting the cars and vans, bicycles and black cabs.

A man rested a hand on my shoulder. 'You all right, mate?'

I continued counting. Buses. Motorbikes.

'You look a bit confused. Can I help in any way?'

I crossed the road as horns beeped and tyres screeched. The man called after me, but I carried on, circling the streets, turning it all over in my mind.

As day turned to dusk, desperation drained me. Just before nine o'clock, when the skies opened vehemently, I turned in the direction of my office block. Cold raindrops pelted into my face, stinging my skin as I ran to shelter in the fire exit alcove of the building opposite. Always the last to leave, Warren would be out soon. He never went home before nine. I started retching, but I'd not eaten all day, so nothing came up. My stomach was as empty as my feelings for the two people who, for my whole life, had called themselves my parents.

Half an hour or so later, when Warren darted out to a waiting cab, I entered the lobby, shaking the rain from my clothes. I flashed my badge at night security. The guard, used to me leaving, rather than arriving, at that time of night, nodded a what-you-doing-here greeting. I swiped my badge across the turnstile and took the lift to the second floor. My mind was set, my plan decided. I slammed my office door shut, switched on my PC and sent two emails. One to Warren, explaining some problems in New York and my intended trip out here to resolve them. The second to Janita, asking her to book me onto a flight to JFK the following day.

Afterwards, I texted you. The lies kept spilling, as did my tears.

Some issues have come up. Kiss Joe for me, and don't wait up, I'll be back late. And, sorry, I've got to go out to New York tomorrow. I love you, darling. X

I'd always detested liars, but my so-called parents had turned me into one.

Chapter 35

EVA

Despite feeling annoyed that he'd left us for so long this time – seventeen days in total – I couldn't wait for Jim to come home and wrap his reassuring arms around me. I knew something was wrong. Very wrong. He'd replaced his usual frequent texts and daily telephone calls with sporadic voice-mails during lecture times or the middle of the night. Complicated work problems and the time difference had been his excuses, but still, that never usually stopped him.

Air traffic congestion had delayed his flight, and I found myself restless, mooching about, pretending to tidy up, moving items from here to there with no particular purpose. Joe was lying on his playmat, bashing the plastic toys attached overhead. I'd bathed him ready for his daddy's homecoming, and he smelled of a heavenly mix of fabric conditioner and baby shampoo.

I picked up one of my law books. Flicking through, too distracted by Joe to take anything in, a firm knock at the front door startled me. Joe too. Ruffling his hair, I sang, 'Whoever could that be?' to the tune of Olly Murs' 'Please Don't Let Me Go' ironically playing on the radio. 'Your daddy? Your daddy's home.'

I rushed to the door, my tummy turning somersaults faster than an acrobat, the anticipation almost too much to bear. Then the thought struck me. Why hadn't he used his key? I opened the door, unable to contain my exhilaration, wearing a smile so broad my lips hurt. An excessive beam soon to fade when I saw facing me was not my husband, but a man and a woman both dressed in blue. They held up badges, but I didn't register the details. The grave look on their faces indicated that they were not the bearers of news I wanted to hear. *What have we done?* Visions of Ben flashed through my head. Something had happened to him. *Ben, oh no, please be OK.*

'Are you Mrs Eva Barnes?' the male officer asked.

I nodded, unable to speak.

'I'm PC Simon Holmes, and this is my colleague, Samantha Ferne, a family liaison officer.' He replaced his badge in his pocket and peered past me to the end of the hallway. 'Can we come in, please? There are some matters we need to discuss with you.'

Not thinking, I stepped aside and let them in. They stood opposite me, the three of us nervously staring at one another. 'Shall we go through?' the PC asked.

I gestured for them to follow me. At the end of the hallway, I stopped by a silver-framed photo of Jim and me on our wedding day. It was my favourite shot of the whole day. Dan had captured me smiling coyly as Jim whispered something into my ear. Turning to them, I let out a nervous giggle. 'It's nothing bad, is it? I mean, you're not wearing your hats. It can't be serious if you don't have them on, can it?'

'Let's go in, shall we?' the PC said, his tone weighty enough for me to know he wasn't here to tell us our car was in a compound for parking in a bus lane. Sickening dread pulsed through my veins. Just tell me, I wanted to scream.

In the lounge, they remained standing but suggested I take a seat. The PC looked around. 'Is anyone else at home?'

I pointed at Joe. 'Only my son.' All I could think of was Ben. Where was he? What had he done? My breathing changed, coming short and sharp. Memories of Ben and me together as youngsters hurtled through my mind: climbing in the playground, him teaching me to master the Rubik's cube, our time with different foster families. 'It's my brother, isn't it? What's happened?'

The PC coughed as he delved into his black canvas holdall. 'Do you recognise these items?' He held up a plastic bag containing a watch and a smashed up mobile phone both smeared with blood.

I gasped and cupped my belly as if to cover my growing baby's ears. He or she mustn't hear what was to come. 'They're my husband's. What's happened? Where is he?'

'I'm sorry to be the bearer of bad news, Mrs Barnes. I'm afraid to inform you that your husband has been involved in a serious motor vehicle accident. The attending paramedics did all they could, but he has sustained some serious injuries.'

His words didn't fully register, not to start with. He'd got the wrong person. Jim was going to walk through the door any minute, his arms laden with presents from duty-free. Perfume for me, a bottle of whisky for him and a bag bursting with cuddly toys for Joe. Detached from reality, as if I were floating above my body, I stared at the two of them and laughed nervously. 'He can't be.'

But the confirmation shone in his eyes like a light of truth. I swallowed hard. 'When did this happen?'

'We're not sure of the exact timings, but he was trapped in the wreckage for a considerable time. He had to be cut out.'

'Where is he now?'

The female officer handed me a piece of paper with a number scribbled on it. 'Call this, they will give you up-to-date details.' She spoke softly but with confidence. This wasn't the first time she'd had to deliver such devastating news. 'Is there anyone we can contact to come and help you with your son?'

I stared at the number. 'Is he going to die?'

'We don't have any more details. I'm so sorry. Can we call someone for you?'

It was surprising how composed I remained. Maybe because Joe was in the room, or because my thoughts were still protecting me from the gravity of the situation. 'I'll do it.'

Maybe Ben should've been at the top of my list, but it was Dan I called. He was out on a date – a rendezvous with some woman he'd met on a shoot – but I knew he would come straight home for me. Perhaps he would tell me not to be so stupid, that I was just dreaming, and Jim was with him.

He took a while to pick up. I struggled to find my normal voice. 'I've got a problem and need you to come home.'

He sensed something amiss. Why else would I have contacted him on a Saturday afternoon, when I knew he was on a date, and ask him to come home? 'Where's Jim? Isn't he back yet?'

'His flight is delayed.' I paused to steady my voice. 'I can't get hold of Ben, and something's come up. I need someone to help me look after Joe. It's a bit complicated, but I'll explain when you get here. Please be quick.'

'Give me half an hour.'

I hung up before he could question me further. I couldn't tell him the truth over the phone. His bestie was on his death bed. Spare him that knowledge another thirty minutes, I told myself.

'Would you like us to drive you to the hospital?' the PC asked.

I stared at the bloodstained items in the plastic bag, wanting to know which part of my husband's body the sticky red mess had bled from, but I didn't dare ask.

'I want to wait for my husband's friend to get here.'

'We'll stay until he arrives.'

*

I called the number they had given me, trying to remain patient as I was passed around different departments. Finally, a robotic voice on the other end of the line informed me that Jim had been transferred to Hammersmith Hospital and gave me another number to call. After confirming that I was indeed his next-of-kin, someone finally told me, 'He's currently in surgery. You should get here straight away.'

I dropped the phone on the sofa and walked over to Joe. He was jabbering away, laughing with such innocence and love that I started to shake. All I could see was a mini-Jim staring back at me and my life drifting onto another plane, the ride unbearable. I clutched my belly. How many times had I told Jim not to drive so bloody fast?

It wasn't until Dan turned up, flustered and hot, that I allowed myself to let go. When I sobbed the news out, the police officers took Joe into the garden. I clung to Dan and buried my head in his shoulder, deadening the howls of grief which erupted from my core like a wounded animal caught in a baited trap.

Chapter 36

EVA

I told the police I would make my own way to the hospital. After they left, Dan sorted a taxi then took Joe from me. I pulled on Dan's arm. 'Please, come with me. I need you.'

He shook his head, jigging a sobbing Joe on his hip. 'I'll stay here with this little one. It's no place for him. Where's Ben?'

'I can't get hold of him. I've left him an urgent message to call me.'

'Emmy?'

'Work. I've left her a message too. And Gill.' I grabbed strands of my hair and shook them. 'Why can't you get hold of anyone when you really need them?'

'Richard and Sarah?'

I scoffed. 'Not yet.'

'Eva, you must call them. He's their son.'

'Of course, of course,' I said. 'As soon as I get to the hospital and find out more, I will.'

'Leave it to me. Stay focused. Jim will need you to be strong.'

He was out of surgery when I arrived at the ICU and I didn't know whether that was a good or a bad thing. I could've done with more time to prepare for the unspeakable horror awaiting me. A nurse introduced herself, but I didn't note her name. She led me down a dimly lit corridor speaking words I couldn't truly understand, too stunned to take them in. I just stared at the posters on infection control, dispensers of hand sanitizers and boards of thank you cards, feeling an overwhelming sense of déjà vu.

I followed her to a noisy room and nearly walked straight back out because I thought she'd got the wrong patient. That mess wasn't my Jim. My Jim was strong and good-looking and always wore a smile for me. My open palm shot above my eyes to shield them from the harsh light as I squinted to take a closer look.

The nurse rested a hand on my shoulder. 'Don't worry. You'll get used to the brightness.'

My mouth dropped as my brain registered the smashed-up human sprawled across the bed. A pile of wires, tangled like cables on an overloaded extension lead, lay above his shoulder, each attached at one end to his body and the other to beeping monitors. Stomach-churning memories of when we first saw Joe in the NICU resurfaced.

His face was bloated and blemished with cuts and grazes, and his eyes were red and swollen – two bruised plums in a bowl of mashed fruit. What distressed me the most, though, was the thick tube protruding from his mouth and linking to a piece of apparatus to ensure his oxygen supply. The nurse moved to the end of the bed and adjusted the padded splints covering his ankles. 'It's a bit of shock to start with, but don't worry, Mrs Barnes, he's in the best place. You'll be able to speak to the doctor shortly.'

I leaned against the bed, trying to gulp in air. 'Call me, Eva, please,' I told her, as I guessed right then that we were going to spend a shedload of hours together in the long weeks ahead – if my husband survived. I looked at her name badge. Mary, Staff Nurse. It suited her, as did her winged cat-eye glasses, her dark hair swept tightly into a bun and the efficiency of her orders to the other two nurses in the room. Mary had her patch under control. A nurse bustled in and wrote on a chart. Another was emptying yellow liquid from a plastic bag hooked onto the end of the bed. I gulped. Of everything, Jim would have hated that the most. Me seeing someone having to empty his pee.

The clammy air in the room was suffocating. I struggled out of my coat then fell into a blue plastic chair. Shuffling it as near to him as the bedside would allow, I reached out and took his hand. The hand that usually radiated heat, protected me, thrilled me, was stone cold, like I imagined death to be. I dropped my head as memories of where Joe began his life filled me with the same hope and fear. Hope that I would get to take him home and fear that I wouldn't. Hope battling fear – a balancing act of swaying proportions. I wanted to kiss him, let him know his wife was by his side, but too many wires and tubes blocked the way.

After a while, a woman in a white coat entered the room, exuding both fatigue and sympathy. She held out her hand. 'Sandy Matthews, Head of Neurosurgery. Could we have a chat?'

I desperately wished Dan was with me. I could have done with him to keep me grounded as I drifted down the ward to discover my husband's fate. In her windowless office, Sandy dropped a file on top of a mountain of others. She sat opposite me, her elbows propped on her desk and her fingers steepled. She opened her speech, which felt rehearsed, although to be fair she had probably given it a thousand times, with the line, 'We need to focus on the positives here.' She smiled assuredly. 'James is still alive.'

My voice broke. 'Jim, everyone calls him Jim.'

She nodded. 'I apologise, I didn't realise.' She paused briefly as if to give her apology extra weight. 'As you've probably gathered, Jim's injuries are significant. We've had to put him into a medically induced coma. This is, in effect, controlled use of drugs to shut down brain function to reduce the swelling caused by the accident.' She went on to describe the drugs and type of injury in more detail, and all I could do was sit and listen as she described my husband's clash with death.

This was the NICU all over again, but instead of two powerless parents trapped in a maze of helplessness, I was alone.

'This is not a decision we've taken lightly, Mrs Barnes, but in extreme circumstances such as these no other options are open to us.'

'Eva, please call me Eva,' I said. Another person I was going to get to know in the coming weeks. I looked past her shoulder to a life-size skeleton standing in the corner beside a metal locker. A deathly chill shot up and down my spine.

'Our aim is to reduce the risk of long-term brain damage.'

Reduce the risk or eliminate it? I wanted to ask but couldn't brave any more gutting news. 'Is he in pain?' He couldn't suffer, especially in silence. That was the priority here.

She shook her head quickly. 'Rest assured. He's on too much medication to feel any pain or discomfort.' She continued with a detailed explanation of the process.

'What are his chances of surviving this?' I finally dared to ask.

'The next twenty-four hours are critical. Let's say, I've seen worse cases pull through. Sometimes going on to lead normal lives, other times not so positive. We'll know more in the coming days when we try and wake him up.'

Try?

He'd promised me until death do us part. He couldn't bail out so soon.

'I'm afraid it's a waiting game.'

Another game where the rules were bloody unfair.

What felt like days later, but my watch told me differently, Dan arrived, white and shaken, stressed and terrified like me. 'Ben's with Joe.' He gently ran his finger along Jim's plastered arm while I updated him. Then he came and sat on the arm of my chair. 'How long are they going to keep him in this coma?'

I leaned into him and repeated Sandy's lines. 'Until the time's right. Depends on his progress. Two days minimum. Longer than two weeks is rare.'

'Bloody hell.'

Mary came in, and we watched as she methodically changed one of the IV bags. 'Can I get you two anything?' she asked as she documented her actions on a chart.

I shook my head. There was only one thing I wanted, and no one could give it to me.

'It's all my fault,' I said when Mary left.

'Why would you blame yourself?' Dan asked.

'That day he left for the airport, he was preoccupied. Something was bothering him. Something bad, but he wouldn't tell me what. There'd been an incident at his parents' the day before. Did he mention anything to you?'

He shook his head, his face pale and eyes glazed with shock.

'It all kicked off, and we had to leave. Richard lost his temper with Harry. I don't know what about. Jim went all weird, said he had a migraine, but I'm not so sure he was telling me the truth.'

'I've never known Jim to suffer from migraines.'

'Exactly. I begged him not to take his car to the airport. "Let me drive you. Please, it won't take long," I said. "Joe would love to wave his daddy off at the airport." I even tried to take the keys out of his hand.' My chin dropped to my chest. 'Why didn't I listen to my gut instincts?'

He drew me into him, squeezing me tightly, absorbing my tears in the fabric of his jacket. 'Let's stop this right here. This is not your fault.'

'Why hadn't I insisted? Then he wouldn't have been driving back from the airport today. And none of this would have happened.'

Chapter 37

EVA

I could feel him creeping up the corridor as if he were crawling beneath my skin. 'Richard and Sarah are here,' I said.

Dan dropped my hand and swung around to the door. 'Where?'

Moments later, Sarah walked in, looking no better than I'd seen her on her birthday. Gaunt and frail, she'd lost even more weight. Richard followed with his usual air of self-adulation, reaching out to prop up his wife as she crumpled at the sight of her son. The air in the room thickened. It always did with Richard around. His presence made it more difficult to breathe.

I couldn't deal with their grief. I was swamped in too much of my own. So, after relaying Dr Matthews' précis of the situation, I pulled Dan's arm. 'Only two visitors allowed at one time. Let's get a drink.'

'Let's stretch our legs. The air will do us good,' he said as we entered the lift to the ground floor. 'There's a park a couple of streets away. Wormwood Scrubs.'

'That's a prison, isn't it?' *From one prison to another?*

'There's a park with the same name.'

'I don't want to be too long.'

'You can't bear to be in the same room as that man, can you?' he said as we left the medicated hospital air.

'I've said it before, and I'll say it again. He gives me the creeps. I'm sure he's got something to do with Jim's strange behaviour during our trip down there for his mother's birthday.'

We didn't make it to Scrubs Park. Overcome with anxiety as we strolled up the street, I had to turn back. I couldn't be too far from Jim. It felt all wrong.

'But he's not going to wake up for a while. You need to look after yourself,' Dan said, but he couldn't persuade me. We wandered silently up the busy road in the other direction. I counted each crack in the pavement until we found ourselves inside a fish and chip shop. The smell of frying reminded me of Ben's hatred of chips, which only added to my emotional vulnerability, so I waited outside, counting the passing cars. Dan ordered for us both, and we picked at our dinner like anorexics on the walk back to the hospital entrance where we dumped the hardly touched bags of food in the bin.

Back at the ICU, Jim's door was shut. Had something happened? I walked in, but slatted screens circled his bed, and I could hear a suction noise like a vacuum cleaner swallowing up something it shouldn't. Mary popped her head through a gap. 'We're just carrying out some procedures. We won't be long. You might want to wait in the visitors' room around the corner.'

One of the nurses had shown me the visitors' room earlier. A place where traumatised visitors sought relief, it was located just off the side of the ward, comfortably arranged with sofas, a TV, and a table stacked with last month's news-papers and out-of-date magazines. In the far corner were coffee and tea making facilities and a fridge with sad shelves holding sachets of milk and labelled food items shouting out, *Don't touch me, I'm not yours*. So similar to the family room in the NICU.

I heard my in-laws before I even got to the door, quar-relling in hushed voices. I turned to Dan with my finger to my lips and slid my ear up to the door.

'What if he dies? Then no one need know,' Richard said.

'You heard the doctor's words; he has a chance of living. He may well come out of this.' Sarah sighed as if she wasn't entirely convinced. 'Let's just wait and see, shall we?'

My body moved more quickly than my brain. I barged in. The air was hot and stale, stifled with deceit. 'What does no one need to know?' I asked, startling Sarah.

'Eva! Dan!'

'What do you mean?' Richard asked, his face flushed.

'I heard you say that if Jim dies, then no one needs to know. Know what?'

'You heard wrong.'

'I didn't.'

Richard refused to look at me. 'I said if he dies, we'll need to know why. As in what caused the accident.'

'Won't we need to know that if he lives, too?'

'Of course, yes.' He picked up his briefcase. 'We need to get going. I have a meeting I need to attend across town.' He folded his mac across his forearm and, nudging Sarah, pointed to her coat on the sofa. 'Hurry along; we'll be late.'

How can they think about being anywhere else at this mo-ment?

'We've spoken to his doctor,' Richard said. 'There'll be no response for at least a couple of days, so you best get home and get some rest. He'll need you more in the coming days. We'll be back tomorrow. Visiting hours are generous enough. Shall we work out a routine, so you don't have to be here constantly?'

His cold words fell on me like a bucket of freezing water thrown in the heat of the room. 'I want to be here all the time.'

'What about Joe? Children aren't allowed on this ward.'

'I'll get him covered.' I didn't know how, but I'd work something out.

'We'll be seeing you tomorrow, then.' He reached out and shook Dan's hand before he left with Sarah hanging off his arm like a piece of luggage.

'Please tell me you heard his words,' I said through tightly gritted teeth.

Dan shook his head. 'I didn't hear anything. What did he say?'

'He said, "What if he dies? Then no one need know." He was referring to Jim.'

'You sure you heard right?'

Nothing was going my way.

*

When ten o'clock arrived, and visitors petered out of the ward, Dan arranged a cab home. We travelled home in silence, both lost in disturbing thoughts too painful to share. As we pulled up to our house, I couldn't contain the tears I'd suppressed all the way home at the sight greeting me. I dashed out of the cab and ran towards the answer to my prayers. Maybe a God did exist after all? 'I'll stay and look after Joe as long as you need me,' Gill said as I hugged my guardian angel.

Chapter 38

EVA

Grief was like living two different lives. In one, I pretended all was OK, and I was making headway as usual; in the other, facing each day was like walking through muddy fields wearing flip-flops. That's how I operated those first two weeks. Each morning desperately hoping that when I arrived at the hospital, Mary would tell me they were going to be waking Jim up that day. I needed the not knowing to end. Not knowing if he would ever sleep in our bed again – if he would get to see his next child born – if Joe would get to spend at least one Christmas with his daddy.

Too many ifs.

From the second I'd first walked into that ICU room, I knew, whatever the outcome for Jim, we'd lost that perfect life we'd shared. We'd passed that station, and the train had decided not to stop. The grief was raw, exposing me to painful feelings I'd never experienced – not even when Joe was in the NICU. When people visited, except for Ben and Dan, I left them to it and walked the dreary streets around the vicinity of the hospital or sat in the bleak café staring into umpteen cups of cold coffee. 'Last year, eight hundred and thirty-five car occupants died in road traffic accidents,' Ben told me the night of the accident. I lived each day in trepidation that my husband would become one of the 2011 statistics.

I slept little, but when I did, I dreamed about him all night – dreams about him loving me in that perfect way of his. And each morning when I woke, tricked by grogginess, I would turn to cuddle him only to find the barren space he'd left behind. The realisation would then hit that he might never come back, and my tears would commence. They became part of my morning routine as habitual as painting on my eyeliner – along with my daily smile.

I often held his hand in that stuffy ICU room, whispering, 'Please come back to me, please, Jim,' over and over again as I listened to the steady pulse of the cardiac monitor, the rhythmic sound of the ventilator and the beep of the IV pump. A deafening band of machines playing their tunes, accompanied by the drum of my heart.

I would continually beg him for a sign that he was still with me. Squeeze my hand, twitch your lips, wiggle your toes, I asked of him only to end up with a gutful of disappointment every single time. Nothing moved other than the ups and downs of the monitors displaying his vital signs which I counted obsessively every hour.

Day twelve, they finally tried to wake him. Almost two weeks of gut-wrenching waiting, and all he treated me to was a minute movement in his little finger. And even that could have been a result of my jittery imagination. 'He's been ventilated for a significant time, Eva, and he's on a cocktail of drugs that we need to wean him off. You need to be patient,' Sandy told me. 'This is not a case of we switch on the light and he jumps out of bed. Rather, we turn on the light with a dimmer switch, and he slowly comes to.'

Two days later, the first flicker of hope emerged. But not in the form any of us were expecting. A dark shadow rather than a ray of brilliant sunshine. Nothing happened all morning until Richard and Sarah arrived early afternoon. The usual time for me to try and force something into my stomach and stare into yet another cup of black coffee. They hadn't been for a couple of days as Sarah had had a cold. 'How are things?' she asked when they walked into the room as Richard, his voice loud and unrelenting, bombarded Mary with medical questions I wouldn't have thought to ask.

Sarah leaned forward to kiss me when, suddenly, I winced. A sharp pain jabbed into the side of my thumb. I looked down to see Jim's fingernail piercing the skin. I gasped and jumped up, my hand still clinging to his. 'I felt that. I felt your nail. I'm here, Jim. I'm here. Wake up.'

Mary's eyes scanned the monitors. I continued talking, reassuring him. I needed him to open his eyes, give me some clue that he was coming back to me. But he didn't. Instead, he began grunting, shaking his head and thrashing his arms, smacking them against the side rails of the bed like he was trying to release himself from a strait jacket.

I'd once witnessed a guy suffer an epileptic fit. When I was in college doing my A levels. One minute he was sitting at the desk beside me, the next he had collapsed to the floor, his body convulsing and his arms flailing against the furniture. The teacher, trying to appear calm, cleared us all away and shoved his desk and chair aside. I'd stood watching, helpless and scared, willing the guy to open his eyes. Déjà vu, but this time the helplessness was magnified tenfold.

I looked at Mary, aghast. 'What's happening?' I flinched and stepped backwards as Jim pulled an IV line out of his arm, and the stand crashed to the floor. Monitors alarmed, machines beeped, and Sarah started wailing like an ambulance siren.

Mary calmly signalled to another nurse for assistance. 'This is not unusual, so please don't worry,' she said. 'Patients often wake up confused.' But I couldn't calm myself. Such aggression was not in Jim's nature. Jim was a tender and gentle man. He held doors open; helped people who were struggling; listened even when he didn't have the time; donated to the homeless and every charity that asked. I could have carried on listing his virtues for hours.

Mary reached over and pressed a red button on the wall behind the bed. 'I'll need you all to leave the room for a while, and I must remind you, only two visitors at once per bedside,' she said, preparing a syringe to administer an injection.

Richard and Sarah headed towards the visitors' room, but I'd arranged for Gill to bring Joe up that day. Not to see his daddy; under sixteens weren't allowed on the ward. Gill wanted to see Jim. I ran down the stairs, shaking to my core at Jim's first reaction to reality. At the bottom, I squatted down against the wall to catch my breath and dig out that fake smile for my son. How deep I had to dig.

It was a downcast day, the sky as grey as my mood, but we wandered over to Wormwood Scrubs Park, as Gill tried to comfort me. 'He's going to be OK, have faith.'

'I must get back to him soon.' Being too far away from him felt disloyal, a betrayal to my sick husband. I needed to be by his side as a good wife should be.

'We've only been gone for ten minutes.'

'I'm pregnant.'

She stopped pushing Joe and cuddled me. 'Oh, Eva, I had an inkling. What wonderful news. How far gone are you?'

'About seven weeks. Jim doesn't know.' I smiled genuinely for the first time in weeks. 'A wedding night baby, methinks.'

'Then that will be the best news for him to wake up to.'

'I wanted to do the genetic counselling first.'

'Too late. You can't worry about that now.'

'Something's happened.'

'What do you mean?'

'With Richard and Sarah. I feel like I'm going crazy. Things don't add up, and I can't work out why.'

'Like what?'

'I wish they hadn't been there,' I said, trying to contain the bitterness in my voice. 'I bet he wouldn't have reacted like that.'

Gill hooked her arm through mine.

'They're the reason he's here. I just know it. But I can't work out what that reason is.'

'That's a tad unfair, perhaps?'

I shrugged. I didn't know anything anymore. Joe was babbling away, smiling up at me from his pushchair, but not even his gorgeousness could raise my mood.

'He is their son, Eva. Imagine if that was Joe lying in that bed.'

Reaching the hospital, Gill prepared to take Joe home. 'I'll visit another day when things are calmer,' she said. 'I'll have a good meal ready for you later. You look like you need it.'

'I'll be busy tonight. I must go through the contents that the police found in Jim's car. I've been putting it off for days.'

'Still time for a meal,' she said, waving goodbye.

Back on the ward, to my immense relief, Richard and Sarah had gone. I resumed my normal position beside Jim, talking to him about everything, hoping he would open his eyes, squeeze my hands, anything to indicate he could hear me. But he remained as still as death until the end of visiting hours.

I caught the Tube home, more depressed than ever, aware of the job I had to face. I'd tried to do it the day the police had brought round the stuff from the wreckage: bits and pieces from the glove compartment – sunglasses, wallet, passport – and Jim's suitcase they'd had to cut out of the boot. They'd asked me if I wanted to attend the crash scene, but I'd chosen to see the photos instead. A choice I regretted. Pictures of a mangled mound of metal – where my husband's life as we knew it ended – wrapped around a large oak tree on the Hammersmith stretch of the A4. Sickening images which haunted me day and night.

I'd placed Jim's suitcase on the bed earlier that morning and prepared myself all day for the familiar waves of sadness I knew would rip through me when I unzipped it. I removed a bag of dirty washing and tossed it over to a mound of laundry by the linen basket. Gathering the remaining few clean clothes in a heap, I hugged them to my belly housing our growing child. He didn't know our love had made another baby. He needed to. If not for me, he had to wake up to hold our next child when it was born. What if it had a heart problem too? I couldn't brave that alone. He had to be with me. I scrunched the clothes up to my face and inhaled his smell still entwined in the fabric: Dior and a hint of salt. Overcome with the surprising, but strange, sense of comfort this gave me, I arranged them alongside his suits and shirts, jeans and jumpers hanging in the wardrobe above a rack of his shoes. I took a deep breath, brushing aside the sweeping thoughts that I might have to clear them all away sometime soon.

Next, I removed his black Hugo Boss toiletry bag. A present I'd wrapped from Joe to his daddy for Jim's birthday, only two months earlier. The shower gel had leaked, leaving a gooey mess coating everything else. I trudged to our en suite, where, taking deep breaths, each one accompanied by a fractious sob, I tipped everything into the sink. I rinsed each item – shampoo, conditioner, deodorant, shaving gel, razor – and then I picked up a bottle of pills. Diazepam? What were they doing in there? I sifted through all the reasons I could think of, but none of them filtered through to a sensible conclusion other than that Jim had been secretly taking anti-depressants. *That's what diazepam is for, isn't it?*

Swiping a towel from the rail, I carefully dried each item. He was depressed but hadn't told me. Why not? How could that have slipped my notice? Thinking I'd finished, I turned on the tap, washing away the remaining suds, when I noticed a black object clogging the plughole. The USB stick Jim used for all our private documents and photos. What was that doing in his washbag? I'd have expected to find it in his briefcase or wallet. I chucked the USB on the side to finish the job I'd started, because my nerves wouldn't have stood another day with it clouding my list of things to do.

Around midnight, I found myself flicking through TV channels, watching so many programmes, but listening to none. So tired, yet so awake. Everywhere I looked reminded me of him more than usual: folded copies of *The Telegraph* on the bottom of the bookcase, the walnut box containing

274

his prized, hand-crafted poker set, the crystal ballerina sculpture he'd bought me for no reason at all.

What did he have to be depressed about?

I was in limbo, pining. Neither with nor without him. I was unable to move on. The accident had disabled me as much as it had him. Knowing I had to do something to wipe away the depressing visions of my husband's fight to live, I went to find the USB so I could browse through our photos of happier times. I checked on Joe, sleeping soundly, then plugged the memory stick into my laptop. And there I found it. A file labelled, *New York, October 2011*. It looked misplaced amongst copies of our passports, birth certificates and driving licences, finance files and photos in albums dated by month since we'd met. *Is it a work file?* Curious, I double-clicked the yellow icon.

The Manhattan Plaza Hotel, New York
October 2011
I can't recall exactly where this hotel is that I checked into four nights ago...

I read until the birds began their dawn chorus, stopping only to retch my way to the bathroom as my world tilted beneath me.

Chapter 39

EVA

Questions I needed answering swam frantically around in my head. I felt like I was drowning. Why had Tammy let us get married? Why had Richard? And Sarah? Sarah! The confusion was dragging me under, sinking me to depths I'd never fallen to. And what did this mean for Joe – for his illness and for his future?

Had Jim's grief consciously or subconsciously driven him into that oak tree? I hated to use the word suicide. That wasn't Jim. The Jim I knew was made of much tougher stuff. Besides, I knew he would never leave Joe and me; but the lurking doubt continued tormenting me. What had he been doing with a bottle of diazepam?

The investigation into the accident had unearthed nothing untoward, only the tragedy that it was. They'd found no mechanical faults with the car and no involvement of any other individuals. Several people had witnessed the black Porsche travelling at speed and losing control before skidding off the carriageway and meeting the old oak head-on. I knew what he could be like behind the wheel. How many times had I told him to slow down, that he drove way too fast? But I also couldn't stop the nagging doubt. Had he driven into that tree on purpose? To hide the truth that he had married his half-sister or worse, his sister? Had Tammy and Richard's affair carried on? Was Richard my father, too?

Who was I?

I tried to get up, but the dull nausea that had been testing me since the accident wouldn't allow me. I lay back down, waiting for it to pass as questions whirled around my head. How had Tammy allowed this to happen? That was the question I couldn't answer because any response was illogical.

Always so many unanswered questions.

Anger propelled me up in the end. My hormones all out of sync, a rage was charging through my body. I was going to kill her.

I grabbed a hoodie from the dressing table chair, spending the few minutes while getting dressed in debating whether to drive north or south. Who was more likely to tell me the truth? I scribbled a note to Gill, tiptoed across the landing and slipped it under her door. I crept down the stairs. All I needed was for Joe to wake up.

How could Tammy have not told me? After everything we'd been through to fix our brokenness, how could she have done this to me? And to Jim? It was as if the past five months or so had been for nothing. She had truckloads of explaining to do.

How could she have kept this hidden from us?

I jumped into the car. My stomach contracted, my nerves stretched like a rubber band at snapping point. I blindly drove at a speed I'd berated Jim for so many times. Numerous thoughts raced through my mind competing for first place like an adrenaline-fuelled day at Silverstone. I couldn't think straight. God help me. I was going to murder her.

I phoned the hospital. The phone rang forever. Maybe he had woken up, and they were dealing with him. Would I see him today? I carried on hoping with each buzz, only to be disheartened when I heard those two wretched words, 'No change.' Next, I called Tammy. It took her a while to pick up too, but it was only six in the morning. She answered on the seventh or eighth ring. 'I'm driving up to see you,' I said, my voice filled with contempt.

'Whatever for, at this time of day?'

'You owe me an explanation.'

'What're you talking about?'

'You already know the answer to that question.' I cut her off.

Up until the accident, I'd begun to take comfort in my trips with Joe up to Dollis Hill. Three generations sitting around her dining table sharing whatever I'd managed to rummage from the fridge before I'd left home. Or what we'd picked up from the deli when pushing Joe in his pram up to the High Street. Sometimes Ben joined us too. It was the closest to family normality we'd ever known, and I had found it comforting. So comforting.

And now it was all gone. The deceit had sunk too deep. We'd never get it back.

Hail started to fall, pelting down the windscreen like bullets. I turned on the wipers as I sped along, keeping a lookout for any signs of police. All I needed was points on my licence to add to my never-ending list of worries. Skidding up to an amber traffic light, I slammed my hand on the steering wheel. 'This is perverse, so fucking perverse,' I screamed, scrunching my eyes closed. *How much more fucked up than this can you get?* Richard and Sarah's conversation echoed in my mind.

"What if he dies? Then no one need know", those were Richard's words. Now I knew what he meant. If Jim died, no one would ever find out that we were brother and sister.

Unless Tammy decided to tell me. Why had she kept it quiet?

Waiting for the lights to turn green, I felt *him*. Octopus hands, touching me, prodding and poking, trying to provoke a response. He couldn't be back? I froze rigid. *He* was back. Oh, please, no, no, no. I had to escape. Breathe, Eva. I stamped my foot on the accelerator and roared away from the lights which were still on red, swerving around a couple crossing the road. They shook their fists at me. 'My mind is strong. I can cope with this,' I repeated. Hailstones hammered on the windscreen, and I started counting all the shops, cafés, and bars the remainder of the way to Dollis Hill.

He would never beat me again.

Tammy was still in her nightie, her hair dishevelled. 'What are you doing here?' she asked as I stood on her doorstep waiting for an invite in.

Confusion had stolen her manners. Her face darkened, her expression guarded. I pushed past her. 'You've some talking to do, Tammy.'

When she closed the door, I shook the USB in her face. 'And, for once, only the truth will do.' I stormed into her brown lounge. Grabbing a cushion from the sofa, I clenched it in my hands and stood facing the window, my back to her. My body was rigid, my stomach clenched with anger. I took deep breaths as I counted the dots on her patterned net curtains.

'Eva, whatever's happened?'

I spun around to face her. 'No lies.'

'What're you talking about? I don't understand.'

'Why didn't you tell us? You knew Jim and I were committed when Ben got in contact with you. You should've told us the truth then.'

Her jaw dropped, her head trembling. 'You know, don't you? How did you find out?'

'I need to hear it from you.'

'I thought we all had a chance of reconnecting. If the truth had come out, it would've broken up the Barnes family. I thought I'd never see any of you ever again.'

'Are you sick? How could you have let me marry my half-brother? Or my brother? Is Dave Pilgrim actually my father? Or is Richard?'

She jerked her head back, startled. As if my words had smashed her in the face. 'What're you talking about?'

I held the cushion up to her face, my heart pounding. 'No more lies, Tammy. I know Jim's not really Jim, is he? He's the other baby you abandoned. He is Christopher Peter Mitchell, isn't he? He's my brother.'

Her jaw dropped further, if that was possible. 'Oh, no. No, Eva, you've got it all wrong.'

Still holding the cushion, I tugged her shoulders. I would shake the truth out of her if I had to. 'Don't lie to me.'

'I'm not. Eva, I promise you, I'm not.'

'I've got proof.' I shook her harder. Her eyes flashed with fear. She could feel my intention to harm. 'Jim wrote it all down before he tried to commit suicide. You and Richard and Sarah, you're all as bad as each other with your lies. You all put Jim in that coma. If he dies, I will hold each of you accountable for his death.'

'No, Eva. You've got it all confused. Jim's not Christopher. Dan is.'

Chapter 40

EVA

'I'm sorry you had to find out this way, but Dan is my son. Dan is Christopher, not Jim. Whatever made you think Jim was?'

I stepped back. She'd unnerved me. Of all the things I thought she might say, this hadn't figured on the list. The cushion dropped to the floor, as did my jaw. 'Tammy, you're confusing me here.'

'The one taken away from me at birth by my mother.' She dropped her head. 'After a one-night stand I had with Richard when I was fifteen.'

My mind spun as I tried to understand the complex family dynamics. I wanted to ask, 'Does this mean what I think it means?' but the words stuck in my throat like a lump of glue. I stared at her in disbelief. This couldn't be true. Richard and her? Dan? My stomach lurched. 'What're you saying?'

Her shoulders stooped to such an extent she looked like a hunchback. 'I regret it every day.' She sat down heavily on her brown sofa, her arms open-handed above her head. A sign of acceptance that her day of reckoning had arrived.

I glided over to her like a ghost, feeling like I was in some surreal dream where I'd lost everything, but the hope of gaining it back hovered in reach. I stood in front of her, trying to unravel the implications of her revelation. If Dan was her son, and Richard was his father, then he was also my brother. Dan was my half-brother. And Jim's too. And Ben's. This couldn't be happening.

'I never meant to hurt anyone.'

'Tell me, Tammy. Tell me what happened. How did we get here?'

She looked up at me. 'Do you really want to know all this?'

I didn't need to speak. My incredulous stare answered her question.

It took her a while to get going. If a packet of cigarettes had been lying around, she would have reached for one. 'It was one night. Just one brainless, stupid night. My parents were throwing a party for a group of my father's colleagues. They'd attended a conference all week at the hospital my father worked at. My mother was so excited about it because one of them was also a top dog councillor she'd been trying to butter up for ages. Some of them were staying the night because they lived all over the country.' She screwed her eyes up as if preparing herself for the disgust her next words were going to cause. 'Richard Barnes was one of those colleagues, and when everyone went to bed, he came into mine.'

I closed my eyes, unable to look at her. Bile stung my throat. *How could she?*

'When I started showing, my mother sent me to Devon to stay with friends of hers in this small seaside town. I can't even remember its name. I planned to run away, you know. I took everything with me. I was going to stay there until Christopher was born then get a plane somewhere they would never find me.' She scoffed. 'Oh, the naivety of a fifteen-year-old. I stayed there until Christopher was born. I even registered the birth. Then my mother showed up and took him away.' She stopped to take a deep breath. 'She and Richard arranged for Dan's parents to adopt him, so Richard could watch his son grow up next door. They stole my son from me, and at fifteen there was nothing I could do about it because, by the time I found out the truth three years later, it was far too late.'

'Is this some sick joke?' I asked, but the stricken look on her face told me there was nothing to laugh at.

'You remember me telling you about when I ran away from home? I ended up in Soho for about three years, and every single day I thought about my Christopher, wondering what he was up to, what he looked like, was he crawling, walking, talking. Then one night, I decided, enough was enough. I had to see my little boy.'

'I discussed my dilemma with my friend Katie. She was the only person I could talk to. I didn't have anyone else in the whole world. "You need a plan. Come on, Tam, scheme something up. The bastard can't get away with what he did to you," Katie said.'

She paused and reached for a tissue from the box on the coffee table and dabbed her eyes. 'I often dreamed about murdering that man. Visiting him in the middle of the night and sticking a knife in his heart. Katie said that was unsatisfactory. She said that bastards like him needed to pay on earth before they fell to hell.' She gave a brief laugh. 'She had a real way with words, that girl.'

'It was she who persuaded me to blackmail him. "Tell him he needs to find out where your mother took your son. And if he doesn't, you'll telephone his wife, and your father, and tell them all about his sleazy conduct. The dirty fucking pervert," she told me.'

She looked lost, as if she'd removed herself from the situation to curb further pain. I wanted to slap her back to reality, but then reminded myself that this was all as fucked up for her as it was for me. She was a victim in all this too. Not beyond reproach, but still a casualty of Richard's sordid behaviour.

She continued. 'So, I hunted Richard down. It didn't take me long. I knew which hospital he worked at, St Bartholomew's. He'd mentioned the name the night we'd had sex.' Her body recoiled. 'So, I waited for him after work one day. I was shocked when I saw him. He barely resembled the man I'd met that night in my parents' house. I remember thinking, What on earth had I seen in him? His eyes were all dark and baggy, making him look as though he hadn't had a full night's sleep in three years.'

'And do you know what he did?' she said, laughing sarcastically. 'He pretended he didn't know me. Like I was a piece of dog shit on the ground. So, I started following him and yelling at him. He soon realised he couldn't silence me. We went to a nearby pub, and then he told me the truth that only he and my mother knew. He'd wanted to see his son grow up and thought I was too young to take that responsibility and, of course, my mother would never have let me keep the baby and tar the Mitchell name. Richard and Sarah's next door neighbours, Barbara and Bob, had just lost their second child. Stillbirth. Barbara was so distraught she couldn't tell anyone, so she pretended she was still pregnant. She and Bob went away to France on a long holiday for her to come to terms with the loss of their child, and that's when Richard and my mother arranged for them to adopt Christopher and raise him as their own.'

She looked up at me as tears started to fall. 'I still think of him as Christopher, you know. In my mind he's still my Christopher, not Richard's Daniel.'

'What did your father think of all of this?'

'He never knew. He was too wrapped up in his work to notice the real world around him.' She shifted in her seat, coughing heavily as if the cancer was reminding her never to pick up another cigarette. 'Richard told Barbara and Bob that the baby was from a teenage mother, which was the truth to a certain extent. He and my mother had connections. They knew officials in all kinds of places. They obtained a forged birth certificate, falsified birth records as well, I suppose. Facilitated an illegal adoption – changed the name from Christopher Peter Mitchell to Daniel Sullers, changed the date of birth, and voilà, a ready-made son.'

It was all becoming too much to comprehend. 'Did Sarah know?'

She shook her head. 'As far as I'm aware she knew nothing.'

She did know. I was sure of it. That's why she'd acted so strangely lately, had lost all that weight. She'd found out. How? 'But Jim found the original birth certificate when he was a kid.'

'Richard must have kept it.'

'Why did you let him get away with it?'

Her voice was barely a whisper. 'Because by the time I found out where he'd taken my baby, Christopher was no longer a baby. He was three years old and had a mum and a dad and three brothers and lived in a massive house with a massive garden and had holidays and toys and bikes and friends. A life I knew I could never give him. That's when I blackmailed Richard. It wasn't my intention, initially. It just came to me as we sat in that pub. I told him to make plans.'

'Plans?'

'I told him I was coming to live in his family home as the new family nanny to his three children and to make formal arrangements to such effect. Either he had to make it work, or I'd tell Sarah everything and have him struck off the medical council and down the divorce courts before he had time to register his next patient.'

'So that's how you ended up being Jim's nanny?'

She nodded.

'And you just watched Dan grow up from over a fence?'

'It was more than that. For the first few years, anyway. Dan and Jim were best friends.'

'They were half-brothers.'

She nodded. 'Dan was always over playing with Jim. I saw him every day. Barbara went on to have another two boys. She suffered dreadful postnatal depression and so was more than happy for Dan to be with me, Jim and the girls.'

I stared at her, perplexed. 'And Sarah just bought that? Richard turned up with you one day, and she just accepted you into her fold?'

'He told her funds were too short if she wanted the extension for her new utility room and his office, what with the cost of the kids in private school, and so she had to go back to work. He faked a CV for me. Detailing that I had worked on the children's ward at St Bartholomew's. Told her all the kids and parents loved me. He was scared of me, you know. Really scared. Still is.' She smirked, acknowledging the control she had had over the situation. 'I impressed Sarah at the interview, and, as Richard had said he already knew me and wanted me to have the job, she went with it. Like she went with everything he said.'

Nothing had changed there. Sarah had always been Richard's marionette with strings he controlled so tightly, it was a surprise she'd never died from strangulation.

'And Ben and me? Who is our dad? Is it Dave Pilgrim? Be honest with me.' I gritted my teeth, waiting for her to tell me it was Richard too.

'Oh, Eva, yes. There is no doubt about that. I loved Dave. I met him while I worked as their nanny. I had Ben, and then when I got pregnant with you, everything fell apart. Sarah told me she was giving up work and didn't need me anymore. I'd been drinking heavily since my days in Soho, but it got worse. Your dad left me.'

'Why?'

'He found out about Dan.'

'How?'

'I got really drunk one night. Really drunk. So drunk, I couldn't even remember doing it, but I ended up confessing to him about Dan. He walked out, and I never heard from him again. I had no money, so I started blackmailing Richard for my silence, which he agreed to as long as I moved away. So, I moved back to London. And, well, the rest you know.'

'Do you not have any shame?'

'Shame for what?'

'Blackmailing him!'

She snorted with contempt. 'That man ruined my life. He needed to pay. I will never be able to punish him enough. Just before you and Ben were taken into care, I took the two of you to visit Sarah and the girls. That was the last time I saw Christopher. He'd had a sleepover with Jim, and I thought I'd get to spend some time with him. I was so excited, but when he and Jim came downstairs, they went straight out. All I got from my son was a quick hello and goodbye. Typical teenagers, I suppose. It was exactly twelve o'clock. I know because the midday news came on the kitchen radio. John McCarthy, a British hostage held in Lebanon for over five years, was free at last. And I thought to myself, I've been in prison for the past thirteen years and will remain trapped in it for the rest of my life.'

I gulped. 'Jim. Is he Richard and Sarah's son?'

She nodded. 'Yes.'

On the drive over, I would never have thought it possible to hate someone with such a ruthless vengeance yet simultaneously feel genuine compassion for the far-reaching consequences of one mistake. However, seeing her pain reminded me that this woman had really, really lived. On both sides of morality.

'Where do we go from here? You've got to tell Dan.'

'No, Eva. Some things are best left well alone.'

'You are kidding me? He's my half-brother. I can't keep that from him. Even if I did, one day he'll find out, and then he'll hate me for not telling him. And Jim needs to know the truth. Oh, God. He had that accident thinking he was your son. That I was his half-sister.'

Two tears bounced out of her eyes.

'Richard said after the accident, "If he dies, then no one needs to know the truth." *He wouldn't kill him, though, would he?* I shot up from the sofa. *Am I being too dramatic?* 'Oh, God. I have to get to Jim before Richard does.'

She called out as I ran up the garden path to my car. 'Eva, please, tell me. Can we find a way to get through this?'

Turning around, I allowed her one last look but no further words. Not for now, anyway. I fell apart as the engine started.

288

Tears of relief that things weren't as bad as I thought, of regret for what could have been, and for the final realisation that I would never have someone I could properly call Mum.

Chapter 41

EVA

He had the know-how, but did he have the bottle? He wanted that MBE so badly; he'd do anything to silence everyone. Was I paranoid? Is that what everyone had done to me? Everyone I was meant to trust. Getting to the hospital was my priority. I had to protect my husband. 'Stay strong, little one,' I mumbled to my unborn baby as I ran to the car.

I was half an hour early for visiting time, so I waited in the visitors' room, gulping bitter coffee I'd bought from the vending machine in the corridor. I hated it in there. Too much sadness stifled the air. An unshaven man in crumpled clothes, about my age, sat on a chair in the corner, gazing into a plastic cup and taking heavy, drawn-out breaths. We exchanged nods of mutual understanding, downturned lips and furrowed brows. He started talking to me. 'My girlfriend's got sepsis,' he said. 'Came in last night.'

'I'm sorry to hear that,' I said, 'I wish her well.' I couldn't find further words for his emotional heartache. I had enough of my own. So I pretended to make a call.

When he left the room, I phoned Gill to check on Joe, trying to act normal, but I had never been able to fool her.

'I can tell by your voice that something's up,' she said.

'I don't know where to begin. I promise to tell you it all later.'

'Any news on Jim?'

'I can't go in until ten, but there was nothing when I called earlier this morning. Keep Joe safe.' Nothing could happen to Joe now. I found Dan's number. I had to talk to him. He needed to know. Impatiently, I waited until the rings died into his voicemail.

A call came in. It was Sarah. 'We're not coming to the hospital today. I'm feeling under the weather again. Hopefully we'll see you tomorrow.'

Damn. I had to see them.

Just before ten, I made my way to Jim's bedside. 'There's been no change,' Mary told me before I even asked. No change. No change. No fucking change. 'The night staff said he had a calm night. No repeat of yesterday's reactions. Are you OK?'

'Family issues.'

'You want to talk about it?' she asked, smiling in that reassuring manner of hers.

'Thank you, but I wouldn't know where to start. And if I did, by the time I got to the end you wouldn't believe me anyway.'

'That bad?'

'Worse.'

'Take it easy on yourself, Eva.' She nodded over at Jim. 'The road to recovery will be long and hard.'

'Do you think he'll make it?' I asked. My voice cracked. 'Please be honest with me.'

She walked over and put a hand on my shoulder. It took all the strength of my being not to break down. I couldn't.

Not now. 'Believe me, I've seen people worse than him make it,' she said.

When she left the room, I pulled my chair as close to Jim as I could and took his hand. 'You got it all wrong.' I squeezed his fingers tightly, willing him to open his eyes. 'Jim, listen to me. I read all your writing on the USB. You are not Tammy's son.' I jumped up. Did he just blink? 'Jim, open your eyes. Look at me.'

An hour later, I was still fruitlessly repeating the same words.

I picked up a teddy that I'd brought to the hospital on the second day of this nightmare. It smelled of Joe. That creamy, comforting scent of snuggling a baby against your chest. Jim had to wake up. The thought of our children growing up without him was intolerable. Birthdays, school plays, scary stories without a father, my children could not suffer as I had. I rested my head on the bed, still holding his hand with earnest hope, and closed my eyes. Sleep deprivation and pregnancy hormones were catching up with me, but today didn't allow for a nap. I had to have it out with Richard and Sarah. I couldn't wait until tomorrow. I needed to hear it from them because I didn't know if I could totally believe Tammy's words anymore.

I drove haphazardly down to Surrey, no plan in hand, only a head full of verbal abuse to hurl in their deceitful faces.

When Sarah answered the door, she didn't have to ask why I was there.

'The only thing that matters now is that I get the truth. My husband is lying in a coma, and I don't know if he'll ever come out because I'm not sure he wants to.'

'Why ever would you say that?'

'He hit that oak tree believing I was his half-sister.'

'What?'

'Don't play dumb, Sarah.'

'You've got this wrong.' She flapped her hands at me, flustered. Her face reddened. 'Richard is in the garden. I'll go and fetch him.'

'No, I want to hear this from you.'

She opened the door wider. 'You'd better come in.'

I followed her to the kitchen. 'Jim thinks Tammy is his mother. He fled to New York thinking that. But that's not the case, is it?'

She was shaking her head, her hands clung to her flushed cheeks.

'I need the truth, Sarah. I've heard Tammy's version; now I want yours.'

'You have to believe me. I've only recently found out about Tammy's involvement in it all.' She reached for the kettle. 'Let me make some tea, and I'll call Richard in.' She started to fill the kettle with water. 'I've thought no end about telling James and you, really I have.'

'Tell us what?'

She spooned tea leaves into a teapot as she confirmed Tammy's story, filling in the missing pieces of the jigsaw for the full picture to take shape.

'But you're an intelligent woman. It's not straightforward to adopt a child. How did Richard and Tammy's mother get away with it?'

'They wouldn't have today.' She rolled her eyes. 'Then again, you never know with Richard. But in the seventies, things were different – processes not so stringent, paperwork less thorough. Child protection wasn't taken as seriously as it is today.'

'Why did you allow her into your home? Her son was growing up next door. How could you let that happen?'

She shook her head repeatedly. 'He had sex with a girl of fifteen who turned out to be Tammy Mitchell. I don't know what was worse, that scandal or the fact that he gave in to her blackmail and allowed her to return here to be our family nanny when he forced me back to work.'

'And you never guessed? Didn't even have any suspicions?'

She leaned against the kitchen worktop. 'I promise you, not even with hindsight. These last few months, I've gone over the past thirty-odd years, time and time again. I was never even remotely suspicious. Dan looks nothing like Tammy or Richard, does he? And Richard is so persuasive. I wanted the extension built. A utility room for me, a playroom for the kids, and an office to rid the lounge of his mess. He told me money was too tight for such a project with three mouths to feed, so I had to return to work.' Her voice thickened. 'I know he's nothing but a tyrant who I should've divorced years ago. I have thought about leaving him. Honestly, I have, but we're in our seventies now. What would I do? Where would I go'

Is this what happens when you grow old? You accept second best because you can't face life alone. 'How did you come to find out about it all?'

'Richard had become dreadfully difficult since he took on that part-time job at the university, what with all the voluntary work up at the surgery, and the medical negligence reports he was preparing for the lawyer. He was meant to be taking it easy, enjoying life. I know we live in this big house and there are bills to pay, and I wanted the cruise, but he has his pension – me too, from my nursing days. People survive on far less. So, for the first time in our married life, I decided to look at our finances. He's always taken care of that side of things, and I was happy for him to. All that paperwork stuff bores me. But I had an inkling something untoward was going on. I guess I didn't want to face reality. To cut a long story short, I found bank statements. And a monthly direct debit to a T Mitchell.'

The truth was slotting each piece of the puzzle into place, and the resulting picture was a grotesque landscape shaped by deceit.

'When did you find out about all of this?'

'Just before Joe left hospital.'

I gasped. 'And you knew nothing about it until then?'

She shook her head. 'I've thought of nothing else since I found out, though.'

'And, what, you just brushed it under the carpet with the rest of your husband's crap?'

'I decided that it would be better if the truth stayed buried.'

'Better for who? What about Dan? Doesn't he deserve to know the truth about his parents?' I sighed heavily. 'So, let's get this straight. Richard and Tammy are Dan's parents. That makes Dan my half-brother. And Ben's. And what about your own children? Jim, Christina and Vic have a half-brother they've never known about.' I jabbed my index finger at her. 'And you thought it OK to keep this from us all?'

'What good will it do, Eva? Think about it. I thought that if the truth came out, it would rip my family apart. Some things are best left well alone.'

I glared at her, unable to believe what I was hearing. 'But it goes deeper than that. Richard has committed a crime. Several crimes. A man of his standing shouldn't be allowed to get away with that, let alone be awarded an MBE.'

'I've been so scared; I haven't known what to do.'

A brief smirk pricked my face, disbelief mixed with dismay. 'Emmy would have a field day analysing us dysfunctional lot.'

She started sobbing. 'Eva, please.'

'That's why Richard hates me. Why he never wanted Jim and me to get married. He knew Ben had found Tammy, and he was scared his sordid secret was going to come out.' A sickening rush of adrenaline shot up my throat. 'It's all making sense.'

'Eva, what are you doing here?'

I swung round to see Richard walking towards us, a calculating look in his evil eyes as if he was figuring out his next move.

'You would've done anything for us not to get married, wouldn't you? You're capable of anything.' Unable to control my sudden outrage, I drew back a hand and took a swipe at him as Sarah stepped between us.

Chapter 42

EVA

It only took a single blow. Fury powered me beyond my perceived competence. I struck her face. She stumbled and tripped, smacking her forehead on the worktop.

Bone smashing onto stone.

A sound that would stay with me forever.

Nothing registered at first. Paralysed, I glared at the motionless body.

He thrust his fist at me. 'What have you done?'

*

'Me?' I cried out as Sarah startled us both by trying to haul herself up.

I held out my arms. 'Sarah, stay there. You've had a nasty fall.'

But she wasn't listening. Frantically, she seized the nearest object which could deliver the most damage. The ruby-red bowl that Jim had bought for their anniversary. As if it had been waiting on the side to be used as a weapon.

'No,' I screamed, but I was too late. She hurled it at him. It struck his face then smashed to the floor, scattering shards of glass across the floor. He lashed out at her, striking her across the head. She crumpled to the floor like a building in an earthquake.

'This is all your fault. All your fault,' Richard roared at me, his face flaming with blood and anger.

I crouched and turned Sarah's head. Blood oozed from a gash at her temple, pooling onto the tiled floor. Curling my fingertips around her wrist, I waited for a beat. Nothing.

My knees cracked as I stood.

I turned to the door.

'You come back here at once.'

I spun around to see Richard glaring down at his wife.

'Help her, then,' I screamed at him, but he stood stock-still as if the shock had immobilised him. I ran back to her and knelt down. 'We need to raise her head. Get me a towel. Anything. We must stop this bleeding. Richard, quick.'

He made no movement to assist.

I ran over to the radiator and snatched a tea towel. Scrunching it up, I squatted beside her and pressed it on the wound. The discolouration of her face horrified me, as did all the bleeding. It was as if all the blood in her veins was leaking out through the gash in her head. Sarah couldn't die. She was as innocent as Jim and me and Dan and Ben in all of this. Wasn't she? Or did she have a part to play? Like Tammy, Sarah wasn't beyond reproach. She should have wised up to him long ago. But, like Tammy, there is no helping some people.

Still applying firm pressure to her head with one hand, I removed my jacket with the other. Rolling it up, I formed a pillow and edged it under the base of her neck. Blood, warm and stark red against my cold white skin, smeared my hands as I pressed harder and harder to stop the life bleeding out of her.

What if I couldn't stop her dying? I was studying to be

on the right side of the law, not the wrong side of it. 'Come on, Sarah. Stay with us.'

'We need to get an ambulance,' I screamed at Richard. 'Go and call one.'

He made no attempt to move.

'And the police.'

He finally spoke. 'Not the police. No need to involve them. We can say this was an accident.'

'What, because the truth is all going to come out now?'

'You keep that mouth of yours shut. We'll just say she fell.'

I reached for my bag to find my phone. 'No, Richard Barnes. I'm not your puppet. You won't tangle me up in your shameless lies. This is all your doing.'

'It was all OK until you came along.'

'What, because you thought you'd got away with your crimes? MBE? I know everything about what you did. About my mother. About Dan. You're nothing but a vile criminal.'

'From the first time I saw you again, I knew you'd turn out to be as much trouble as that mother of yours.'

'Rephrase, Richard. You got away with all your corruption until I came along.'

'It isn't all my fault, you know. Your mother is as guilty.'

'No, Richard. She was fifteen years old. You stole her son.'

I dialled 999 and relayed details of the emergency. Then I panicked. Like the night I gave birth to Joe. Excruciating wave-like movements travelled through my belly as if my growing baby could feel all the angst. My baby. My baby. I dashed out into the hall with his roars of, 'Get back here!' echoing in my ears. I ran to the car. My head spun with thoughts of what to do next. I turned the ignition, looking out of the window to Jim's childhood home. Elm House. I'd been in such awe when I'd first seen it last Christmas. A magical castle embellished in a circle of icicle lights. Now all I could see was a house of horrors.

I had to see Jim. He had to know the truth. And Dan. And Ben. I needed to award Ben the treasure he had spent so long hunting for – a family. I pressed my foot down on the clutch, rammed the gear stick into first, then stopped. I wasn't thinking straight. I couldn't leave her with him.

I had to get her blood off my hands.

Otherwise, that monster would blame all this on me.

I staggered back in, my stomach churning, Clutching the dado rail like a lifeline, I returned to the kitchen to find Richard slumped against the kitchen cupboards, staring at his dying wife who lay at his feet. He was vacant like a drug addict, overdosed on years of his own gross misconduct.

I knelt and placed my index and middle fingers on her wrist. 'There's no pulse. She's not breathing. You need to give her CPR.' He didn't acknowledge me. He was going to let her die. 'Richard, help me.'

Shuffling closer to her, I leaned over and started pumping her chest. I didn't know exactly what I was doing, but it was better than the nothing he was doing. Twenty compressions, or was it thirty? I was too spaced out to think clearly. 'Richard, how many do I do? Twenty?' Still silence. 'Richard?' I couldn't remember. I'd done some basic first aid training during sixth form, but this was no Rescue Annie.

Ambulance and police sirens wailed in the near distance. 'Hurry, please hurry,' I cried as I reached twenty pumps, and a pair of more competent hands took over.

Richard remained slumped against the cupboards. His deadly game was up, and he was by far the biggest loser.

Sarah took precedence, but it didn't take long before I found myself enfolded in a blanket of foil with a Velcro band strapped around my upper arm. 'We need to get your blood pressure down,' a heavyset man dressed in dark green said. He smiled and handed me a plastic cup of water. I looked around. I was sitting on the bottom step of Elm House, the wind gently blowing strands of sweaty hair into my face.

'Have I lost my baby?'

'You're pregnant?'

I nodded. 'I hope I still am.'

He shouted out to his colleague busy in the rear of the ambulance, 'Call for backup can you, Reg. We need to get this one to hospital too. Pronto.'

'Is she going to be OK?' I asked, nodding towards the ambulance.

'I can't say.'

A police officer came bouncing down the steps. 'Mrs Barnes, we need to ask you a few questions, please.'

'She's pregnant; we're taking her straight up to A&E,' the paramedic said. He snatched up his jacket from the stones and, lowering it over the foil, swaddled me with comfort. 'Come with me, love. Best we get you checked out.' Then with a, 'One, two, three,' he helped me up.

*

Jim opened his eyes that evening. Ever since I'd first seen him in that coma, I'd planned so intricately how I'd react when the moment came. When I would know for sure that he would live on to walk by my side, whatever form that walk might take. But plans rarely evolve as we so carefully make them, no matter how much attention we pay to their details.

Too many external forces are flittering about affecting their outcome. I thought I'd sing and dance and cry, but all I could do was kiss his lips and quietly tell him that everything was going to be OK.

When Ben and Dan arrived, I made us all link hands – each hand holding the wrist of the next like Karen Fleming's family ring of unity – as I calmly announced, 'Brothers, I have something to tell you. Make of it what you will, but, as Gill always reminds me, flourish or fail. Victory or victim. It's up to you.'

BOOK CLUB QUESTIONS FOR
LEAVE WELL ALONE

1. Mental health issues are woven throughout the story with regard to the main characters. Discuss each one and how their issues affected each character's daily life.
2. Which key moments in Eva, Jim, Ben and Tammy's stories made you feel the most compassion for them?
3. Eva, Jim, Ben and Dan were all affected by their childhoods. Which one do you think was affected the most?
4. Who was your favourite character, and why?
5. What impact do you think Emmy had on Ben?
6. Jim first came across 'Christopher's' birth certificate when he was eight years old. Why do you think he blanked out the memory for so many years?
7. Do you think Jim tried to commit suicide, or do you think that his car ending up 'wrapped around a large oak tree' was a pure accident?
8. Even when she found bank statements and a monthly direct debit to a T Mitchell', Sarah stayed with Richard. Why?
9. Which character did your feelings change the most towards as the story progressed?

10. Do you think Eva can ever truly forgive Tammy and forget the past? Is it possible to forgive and forget, or does the old adage 'You can forgive but you can never forget', always prevail?

11. Were you surprised when you found out the true identity of 'Christopher'?

12. Which scene stuck with you the most?

13. How did you feel about the ending?

14. Where do you think this story goes next? Write a one-liner for Eva, Jim, Ben, Dan, Richard and Sarah.

15. Did this book remind you of any other books you've read? Describe the connection.

A NOTE FROM AJ

Mental health problems affect around one in four people in any given year (MIND). Someone you know is suffering. Do look out for them and show your support. Always be kind.

I hope that you enjoyed reading my debut novel *Leave Well Alone* as much as I adored writing it. Eva and Jim's story continues in my next novel *Don't Come Looking*. To hear about this and future releases, please visit my website:

www.ajcampbellauthor.com

For me, building a relationship with my readers is one of the joys of writing. I set up the AJ Campbell Readers Club so that I could keep in contact with you all. New members receive:

1. *Choices* by AJ Campbell, A FREE short story, exclusive to club members.
2. A copy of the social services report on Eva as a teenager before she went to live with Gill, and Eva's story of her life with Gill.
3. Access to AJ's Reading Corner, my online book club. We're a friendly group, sharing reading inspiration and chatting about our latest book club title. There are quizzes and competitions and monthly book giveaways.

Follow the link below to join me. I look forward to welcoming you personally.

www.ajcampbellauthor.com/download

As for all authors, reviews are the key to raising awareness of my work. If you have enjoyed this book, I would be very grateful if you could spend a couple of minutes leaving a review on Amazon and Goodreads. Honestly, it will make me dance with joy.

ABOUT THE AUTHOR

AJ Campbell was born in Hertfordshire, England. She spent the first half of her career working as an accountant, until the birth of her twins in 2005 radically changed her life. One of them was born with severe disabilities, as a result of which, she had to give up work to care for him. It was during this incredibly challenging, but rewarding, time that AJ began to draw on her love of the written word, partly for day-to-day inspiration and partly for her mental health, and she started writing *Leave Well Alone*.

AJ now lives on the Essex / Hertfordshire border with her husband, three sons and fur friend, Max. She devotes her time to caring for her son and family, and writing.

Connect with AJ online
Web: www.ajcampbellauthor.com
Facebook: @AJCampbellauthor
Instagram: @AJCampbellauthor
Twitter: @AuthorAJC

ACKNOWLEDGEMENTS

It's not until I contemplated writing this section that I realised how many individuals it takes to publish a novel. I owe a debt of gratitude to so many people. Firstly, to those who generously gave me their valuable time to read my story when it was still a work in progress: Julieanne Steel, Ellie Ferguson and Roy Taliotis. To Karen Sheairs, Caroline Wilman and Nikki Sammons for reading the second draft and cheering me on to publication. And a special thank you to Christine Henderson and Claire Cook for your tremendous support throughout the final stages and for rereading it before I pushed the button.

A huge thank you to my editor, Louise Walters, whose invaluable contribution and skills helped me develop this story into what I wanted it to be.

Thank you to my tutor, Julia Crouch, from the Faber Academy who helped me piece together the first draft of this novel and who introduced me to my trusted writing buddies, Charlotte Valentine and Bridget Guzek. Thank you, Charlotte and Bridget, for your support and advice, and for providing much humour along the way.

Thank you to the wonderful team of carers who support me in looking after my son and giving me the breathing space to write. To my husband Andy, for taking on the role of head chef so that I could get this book to publication and still eat delicious meals, and to Edward, my number one fan. Thank you to Billy for being you, and to Max who never leaves my side.

And finally, to Josh – you have taught me so much. Your smile is the light on darker days.